BEFORE THE QUEEN
FALLS ASLEEP

HUZAMA HABAYEB

BEFORE THE QUEEN
FALLS ASLEEP

Translated from the Arabic by
Kay Heikkinen

MACLEHOSE PRESS
QUERCUS · LONDON

First published in the Arabic language as قبل أن تنام الملكة
by The Arab Institute for Research and Publishing, in 2011
First published in Great Britain in 2024 by

MacLehose Press
an imprint of Quercus
Carmelite House
50, Victoria Embankment
London EC4Y 0DZ

A CIP catalogue record for this book is available
from the British Library.

ISBN (PB) 978 1 52941 565 0
ISBN (eBook) 978 1 52941 566 7

10 9 8 7 6 5 4 3 2 1

Designed and typeset in Minion by Libanus Press Ltd
Printed and bound in Great Britain by Clays Ltd, Elcograf S.p.A.

Papers used by MacLehose Press are from well-managed forests
and other responsible sources.

CHAPTER ONE

Concerning the Second Departure

"Your sandwich! Run and rescue your sandwich, Your Majesty, it's burning!"

I had not thought that your second departure would be very hard on me, intolerably harder than the first. I had not anticipated that it would bring me so much sadness, that it would sicken my body and trample my insecure existence with a heavy, negligent tread, that it would cut so deeply into my spirit. After all, I had prepared myself for your departure, that self that incites to harshness and ostensible callousness, by inventing quarrels and bickering during the last few days before you left – quarrels of the kind that harbour mounting intensity arising from nothing, absurd, painful rudeness, and unjustified flares of rage. Quarrels that are a rebuke to the self, to my own self, a deepening evocation of pain in the heart, in my heart, loaded already with many times more than its capacity to comprehend absence. As usual before a difficult departure, I unloaded my accumulated wrath with the world on you, pouring out my resentment of the intransigent arrangements of life onto your own arrangements, which you wanted to keep far from my own. I struggled to love you less, but all I could do was to love you more.

"I hate you." You said that to me in a voice that tattled anger, your eyes shooting out burning rage.

"I love you." I whispered it in my heart, covering my face with both trembling hands so I would not see you while you hated me.

Then you said, "I hate you, I hate you, I hate you!" grinding your feelings and gnashing your teeth – those very teeth that had made me drag you to the dentist two days before you left, so he could clean the plaque from their roots, after I had scolded you for not taking good enough care of them. Then I closed my ears so that my troubled spirit would not be able to hear "I hate you" repeated three times, emphasised by the eruption of your young body, still childishly disdaining all rules of adult nutrition.

At your first departure, I shed burning tears for an absence I had not yet experienced or prepared for, one likely to bring yearning yet unknown. "It's only a few months and I'll be back with you," you said, struggling with a tear stuck at the edge of your eye. When my sobs became audible, mixing with airport announcements asking travellers to make their way to their flights, you hugged me, becoming a youthful mother. You borrowed my clinging arms and impressed your body on mine, your body bored and hurrying to slip away from my embrace, mine worn out from weeks of preparation for your departure. You spoke with a smile that held some disapproval of my weeping, which embarrassed you amid all the people in the airport, who enjoyed the dramatic scene of the touching farewell: "I'm going to study, I'm not going to war!" Then, when you succeeded in freeing yourself from me and passed through passport control, you half turned and from afar gave me a look that crushed my spirit for days to come. You were afraid, really afraid. But the childish pride dormant within you, so gentle secretly but outwardly rebellious, kept you from saying, "I'm scared."

At your second departure, I wept hotly for absence I had experienced, absence that delighted in its deed as it distanced itself, not looking back, striking to the depths of life, of bodies, of souls yearning to meet, absence rooted in the routine. It was not yet routine for me. Its obdurate and probable unrequited yearning seemed improbable to me and unbearable, utterly improbable and un-bearable. I swallowed the sobs rising urgently from the heap of bitterness accumulated in the valley of my soul. I strangled them before they reached my throat, which I constricted violently. But I could not strangle my tears. They flowed densely and slowly, thick and freighted with sadness unrelieved by any hint of joy, sadness of the kind that turns into a permanent condition of daily life. We were in the same airport; perhaps we met the same faces as before, though neither they nor we remained in the other's memory. For airports are repositories of absences and passing lives; meetings and embraces in them are only temporary victories or the reflections of recorded defeats, since there is no true, stable victory other than departure. What grieved me was that your face turned less towards me and more towards passport control. When my tears would not stop flowing you shot me the reproach-ful look of a child who has grown up a little, saying with a touch of toughness, "It's only a year and I'll be back with you." How can the trip stretch out longer, and yet the thought of it still seem reasonable and less painful? It's not because the first departure was less anguished, but because the second, with its proposed absence of a year, could be expected to be the norm. Does one trip pave the way for another? Do we practise on a shorter trip so we can bear a longer one? Or do we become professionals at leaving and travelling, as we have become professionals at living in cities that are not ours, in homelands that belong to others and that spit us out when they tire of us? Have I ever told you how much it angers me to come across the phrase "The time has come to leave" in wretched, meaningless writings? As if leaving is assumed to have a time. Leaving, little one, for people like us, for people who are hereditary refugees like us, spans our lifetime, and it may even overflow our lives and go beyond them.

I wanted to keep you as long as possible in the ambiguous space for leave-takings in the airport, while you wanted to disappear quickly into the distance. You were listening more to the announcements urging travellers to head for their flights than you were to my advice, repeated for the millionth time. You weren't listening to my disjointed, breathless, disorganised phrases, which fell from me and scattered in every direction on the floor while I futilely tried to gather them and put them in order. My words during the very last moment before your departure were not intended for their content so much as they were to cover an imminent collapse that was stealing into my joints and gnawing at them with increasing speed. I did not collapse, however. I believe the reason was related to my broad experience in enticing sadness and having compassion for it, related to being accustomed to living in its frustrating, demoralising climate. My feet carried me to the scene of the expected parting at passport control. "Don't cry!" you said to me; "I won't," I replied, nodding, but the tears did not listen to you. "I love you," you said, embracing me quickly. "I love you more," I said, trying to prolong the embrace. You moved away. I waited for a look from you, by which you would sign the painting of your second departure as you had the first. But you did not turn around, you did not send me so much as a glance I could lean on during days at odds with each other, as sunrises with sunsets. To console myself for the fact that you did not look back (unintentionally, as I hoped), I tried to convince myself that like Majnun's beloved Laila, "your tears flowed only from afar".

When I got home I closed the door and turned the key twice in the lock. Then I leaned my back on the door and gave my soul over to collapse.

I collide with your smell, playfully present in the house. I listen to your talk that does not want to end, then suddenly you disappear, just as you used to alternate between appearing and disappearing when we talked in the kitchen while you made me a cup of tea with mint. I would be looking for something in a kitchen cabinet, and when I raised my eyes I would not find you; only the tail-end of your endless talk would be clinging to the tea bag plunged in hot water, coloured by the radiant green of the mint leaves. Then I would hear a voice or what seemed like a group of emotional, entangled voices. I would imagine that you were conversing intimately with your leaping imagination. You don't know that I observed you at times during the manifestations of your sudden disappearance in the middle of our talk. Once it was as if you were speaking to someone in the empty space before you, then your eyes darted and your head lifted as if you heard a story you had yearned for, or had stumbled on a great discovery. You turned in a circle, trying to embrace the surprise that had struck you, so that it would not strike any being other than your own. Once you stood at the window of your room, inclining your head to one side, humming a song whose echoes slumbered within you, like an old woman cautiously, selectively spooning out her secret memories.

I put my hand on my cheek. "You forgot your favourite cork sandals," I say to myself. The remains of a drink stagnate in a glass

11

standing on the edge of your desk; you've become addicted to iced peach tea. Your little silver earring lies abandoned on the computer table. You've hated earrings ever since you were little, and now that you're older (though not very old), you still resist adding any adjustments or embellishments to your clean look. Your fresh, girlish form refrains from any artificial luxury, refuses the cosmetic lies of adults. Even now there is a struggle when Evie, the Indian woman skilled in hair removal, places you in the beauty salon chair to shape your eyebrows, left in their natural state. You used to kick and rebel, unleashing a torrent of Arabic invective, drawn from the dictionary of childish anger, at poor Evie: "Damn her father, *inshallah* she'll die!" Evie would laugh, sensing your rebellion, then put her hands around your lovely face, reddened from fury and the pain of plucking the small, sensitive hairs. I bought you pink lipsticks and others that were transparent and shiny, just to protect your lips that cracked quickly in the dry air, or to add a touch of colour and shine to them; but you did not use them, leaving them to dry out. I bought you a hairdryer and two styling brushes, but you let your hair dry in the open air after washing it. If your hair rebelled and raged, you tied it all uncombed in a wild ponytail, or twisted it quickly into a braid that was neither in the middle nor on the side. I bought you hair clasps, slides, coloured ribbons, and small combs studded with beads and crystal stones; you filled your drawers with them and made do with black metal hairpins, pinning your hair back any which way, for you would never allow a single stray lock to impede your eyes as they advanced slowly over a painting by Frida Kahlo, from a volume of her work that you refused to lend even to me, or while you savoured the flavour of a work by Andy

12

Warhol in the huge, daring volume I had given you for your eighteenth birthday.

You had not hidden your desire to own the book, that enormous volume bearing the title *The Giant*, gaily acknowledging that it was nearly half as tall as you were and half as heavy. I had sneaked back to the bookshop in the market one evening without your knowledge; I was frightened both by the size of *The Giant* and by its price. I returned home weighed down by it, and put it on your bed while you were in the bathroom. I expected you to be surprised by it. I expected that you would shout, as you usually did when something unusual in life, in your view, surprised you with joy. You entered your room; I stood outside. There was a moment of silence, and then a cry flew from you that pierced the very ears of the sky. You ran towards me, leaping, spreading your happy being all around me. You were joyful in a way I had never before read in your eyes or your body. You picked up the huge volume and clasped it to you. It was too heavy and you fell over on your back, with the giant weighing down your chest and covering you. You laughed, you laughed a lot, and long, and loudly; you laughed until you choked. At that moment I hated my life less. And only at that moment, I loved my life more.

I enter the kitchen, smelling something scorched in the heavy, enclosed air. You had eaten your last grilled cheese sandwich before you left. I scrape off the remains of the burnt bread and the melted cheese from the toaster. How many times have you forgotten your sandwich, leaving me to rush towards the odour of burning bread and melting cheese, while you were absorbed in some beautiful or exotic scene on YouTube, or in a pirated version of Vittorio De Sica's film *Bicycle Thieves* on some Internet site, or in the translation of lyrics by Jean Ferrat, at the request of Friends of Poetry on Facebook. I pick up the remains of your "crime", which you've left in the toaster, and spread them in front of you. "Look at that!" I say to you. "Look at that!" you say to me, pointing to a web page showing a black-and-white picture of Bobby Sands. With the ardour of a believer who has just found the superior qualities of a new religion, you talk about the Irish resistance fighter and leader of the hunger strike movement in 1981. After the strike had gone on for sixty-six days, Sands died of grief, injustice, and emaciation, at twenty-seven years of age. You open your eyes wide, as wide as the horizon, as you describe the popular anger aroused by Sands's death, as if you had been part of that anger. I ask you about the burnt sandwich, and you join the thousands of Chilean activists who were taken early on the morning of the military coup against the elected president, Salvador Allende, and brought to the Stadium of Chile in Santiago in 1973. The Chilean singer and poet Victor Jara was among them. In tones of mourning unaffected by the passage of time, you say, "They beat him, tortured him, and crushed his hands, which had played the most beautiful songs on his guitar." From the heart of the events, which your spirit has lived through moment by moment, you tell me how his torturers mocked him, asking him to play his guitar when he was stretched out on the ground, and how Jara challenged them by singing part of "We Shall Overcome". In the end, they fired all the rounds of their machine guns into his body and threw the corpse into the street. You read me part of a poem Jara wrote just before his execution, writing it on a scrap of paper he hid in the shoe of a friend who had been with him in the humiliating march to the stadium. Hope retreats from your voice as you enter the seasons of black sadness. Then you claim that something has got into your eye, as you rub it and keep the tear you've hidden from falling.

"And the scorched sandwich?" I ask, irritably.

"So what? Is it the end of the world?"

I talk to you about the mistakes of revolutions; you talk to me about the crimes of regimes. I warn you about embracing puritanical ideas that cannot be shaded, and you warn me about wearing shades that don't suit me. "Fine! What do you think of this shirt on me? Is it pretty?" You shake your head, unconcerned. Here I must admit that you lead me more than I lead you. You pull me out of the dictates of my reality, to which I've submitted, and return me to the age of dazzling dreams, if only for a time. For days and weeks I surfed the net to find the song "El Aparecido", in all the versions available. The one I liked best is the one sung by Victor Jara; I downloaded it from YouTube, accompanied by an album of pictures of Che Guevara from the era of his quixotic rebellion, from the dream to the nightmare, ending as the song finished with a picture of him shrouded on a stretcher after his execution, giving his torturers the exact same look as had Christ from the cross. I wept for him with a broken heart, as if he had died yesterday.

You don't like crying, at least not in front of me. If tears should overcome you, you take refuge in the nearest shadows to conceal them. But you don't know that I see you. I can make out the water in your eyes about to spill onto your face, I sense your tears wanting to speak while you silence them. You mock me, the weeper, with my appetite for tears at any and all times. I weep over a song with an anguished melody, without understanding the lyrics. I weep over a film, even if it has a happy ending. I weep for a worker washing cars, his face burnt from the embrace of God's own dispassionate sun, eyes yellowed from successive hardships in an extremely rich emirate. I weep over an old man in his sixties with one leg and a worn crutch, dressed in camouflage pants left over from bygone military service, selling lighters and cheap packets of tissues and balloons in the shape of rabbits that don't hop and birds that don't fly, at a traffic light in a kingdom that houses all the contradictions on earth. I weep for a little boy who has spread a display in front of him on the pavement, offering keyrings and cheap leather wallets and fake Ray-Ban sunglasses, while he leans his shoulders against the wall of a mosque and lets his head hang down like a heavy fruit on a thin branch, in a city that has deviated from any rational historical context, where a handful of cursed people are crammed into a cramped life. I imagine this little one dreaming that he's sleeping in a bed, covered by a blanket with pictures of cartoon characters, in a room over-flowing with stuffed animals. I cry over him and over the dream I have imagined for him. I weep over a woman standing in line at some bakery in Cairo, who calls to witness the correspondent of one of the droning satellite news stations, in a rush to move on to someone else, showing him the few loaves of bread she has bought at last, after waiting for six hours – loaves from which the embezzling baker has stolen the subsidised flour, the water, and the flavour. "Who can put up with that, O Lord!" The woman's face indicates that she's from one of the dingy quarters of Cairo. She knocks the loaves of bread together like dry firewood, then she asks pardon of her Lord, in spite of herself, fearing that her ingratitude for the blessing will lead to some harm for the heap of hungry kids waiting at home. Lifting her face to the sky, she says, "There is no power or strength save in God alone! May God repay the cheater!" I weep over the remains of cheap sandals tossed heedlessly in a market in Baghdad, after their owners have been blown to smithereens in a daily explosion. I weep over images from the serialised drama of our massacres, with multiple episodes and seasons. I gather them in private collections that I return to more than to the family albums. Perhaps I'm unconsciously waiting for a massacre reinforced by accompanying images that are models of disfigurement and repugnance, a massacre I'm anticipating and rushing, so I can add it to my accumulated archives of weeping.

When the massacre of "Operation Cast Lead" fell on terrified bodies in Gaza, I was beset especially by the images of the children who were killed. It was one of the campaigns of liquidating the Palestinian body during which the ceiling of life was lowered in unprecedented fashion. I was besieged most by images of those who had died with their eyes open, eyes filled with heedlessness. I collected the pictures of children who had passed away with their eyes open, like someone who collected rare stamps or someone who picked up shells with strange, unusual shapes from the seashore. These pictures alone establish the fact that God, if He wills, is capable of not existing. One picture in particular, of a girl in Gaza, brought me an era of weeping. She was ten, a little younger or a little older, wearing a cumin-coloured blouse that was split open at the waist where the shrapnel had stolen from her all time to come. She was stretched out on a metal table in one of the hospitals in the Gaza Strip. She leaned her head towards me, looking at me, scrutinising me with brown eyes that retained their glow even after her tender life had faded from her body, which had not yet blossomed. Perhaps the little one foresaw that the picture would fall into my hands; she aimed at me a look of censure and blame for a sin I was certain I had committed, as certain as she was.

You also wept, in your student room thousands of kilometres from my bedroom where I sought shelter, exhausted from sobbing alone, after seeing the pictures of our dead of all shapes and sizes. You wept without letting me or anyone see you weep. I knew that from your Facebook page, where you posted a picture of the Gazan child who went to school at the end of the season of harvesting youthful Palestinian bodies; he was sitting at his seat in the first row and sitting beside him was a piece of cardboard bearing the name of his classmate who had died. Behind him were classmates next to other pieces of cardboard with full, three-part names that had disappeared forever. The child was hanging his head and covering it with his hands, crying for the companion with whom he had shared sandwiches of zaatar and olive oil, or on prosperous days, sandwiches of labneh and cucumbers. He did not want anyone to see his tears.

I was at work, stealing a little precious time to visit your page, when your head appeared to me, bent over, in class, covered by your hands. You were avoiding looking at me or at your classmate, of whom nothing remained but his full, three-part name on a piece of cardboard. I feigned a sudden attack of sneezes, covering my nose and half my face with a tissue. In front of the computer screen my tears flowed behind my glasses. I bowed my head and covered it with my hands. I did not want anyone to see me cry.

Who knows, you may discover that you are a weeper like me, even though you resist crying. Just as you have inherited my stubbornness and foolishness, perhaps you have inherited my easy tears – easy, but not light or to be taken lightly. You saw me one day crying in front of the film *A. I. Artificial Intelligence*, the only film I ever liked by Steven Spielberg. (As a director he was untouchable, even when he approached controversial topics like *Munich* in a way that did not completely condemn the Palestinian, though without incriminating the avenger, who flagellates himself after every justified operation to kill a Palestinian. He had the grace to give the Palestinian a palpable, lifelike portrait that makes him more than a mere name on a list of those to be liquidated.) You were astonished, not just because I was crying, but because it was the third or fourth time that I had cried over the same film. I became burdened with feelings previously unfamiliar to me as I watched the desire of the mechanical child, David, for the love of his human mother, who had adopted him from the factory of mechanical children with advanced feelings. Then she abandoned him to his tragic fate in the forest, to be crushed by humans with true feelings, as he was mechanical. The eyes of the little boy yearning for love wrung my heart. Humans become extinct after two thousand years, while David, the child seeking a human mother's love, remains. He obtains that love for one day only, but it is a day that's worth eternity. I choked on my tears as I watched David receive the love of his mother, who had been created for his sake for a single day. She tells him before passing into the depths of death, "I loved you, I always loved you."

You asked me, laughing, "Haven't you cried over that film before? What's different about this time?"

I believe things were different with you. Do you remember that night when we sat watching the film *Billy Elliot*? I had seen it in the theatre and had talked to you in glowing terms about the boy who had abandoned boxing gloves to try out ballet slippers, in secret. By chance my eyes fell on the film for sale in Carrefour, among the displays of home videos. I flew home with it joyfully, promising myself an unforgettable night of tears you and I would share. At first you preferred to watch the film alone, then you permitted me to watch it with you, so that I could not accuse you of weeping in secret, provided that I not catch your eyes or observe them too closely as we watched. In the darkness of the television room, relieved only by the timid light of the screen, I caught sight of the reflection of your weeping in your glasses. Your tears flowed hot and pure over reddened cheeks; your wide eyes were clouded and your thick eyelashes were moist behind the lenses. You wept when Billy's father was forced to destroy his late mother's piano so they could burn the keys to keep warm during the miners' strike in the 1980s. You wept when Billy recited for the ballet teacher, by heart, the letter his mother left him just before she died; then you wept when the angry father, defeated by poverty, caught his son dancing. When the film ended, our spirits were exhausted from crying. We did not speak; we hid our faces from each other. You watched the film many times behind my back, and every time you cried behind my back. You sobbed, choked, gasped, and trembled behind my back but before my spirit, watching over you.

On the days when we were not involved in weeping, stubbornness, and picking quarrels between your noble, misguided opinions and my ideas, ravaged, tossed, and overturned by time, we would fight. Our quarrel might be malicious, stirring up all the violent feelings in the world, which we would cram into the narrow space between us, into the freighted air between our opposed faces, openly agitated, ambiguously rebellious.

"I hate you." You shout it to my face.

"I hate myself." I shout it to your face.

Then when night came and griefs had retired to their chambers, you came to me barefoot, half your hair hanging down over your face, smelling of fresh sweat from your reckless waking dreams, of chocolate that you're licking without much guilt for breaking your fragile diet, of bread toasted to the point of burning, the crumbs all over your pyjama top. You slip into bed next to me, sniffing my bare arm, saying you love the smell of my body. You tell me that you search for it, or something like it, in your distant city, without finding it. You bury your nose in my neck and say,

"Tell me your story!"

CHAPTER TWO

Concerning Where the Money Went

It has reached me, O auspicious queen, whose views with wisdom don't align, and whose dreams are utterly unbenign . . .

You grimaced in annoyance all the way to the airport, because of all my useless talk about money – tools for saving it, respecting it, and holding it tightly rather than spending it wastefully, ways to protect it, to avoid flaunting it or squandering it, according to the wisdom that results from meagre earnings.

Know then, my queen, that I come from a family who knew more scarcity than plenty, though there we always had plenty of worries and concerns, in addition to bad judgment and bad management. Still, the good life did not turn its back on us completely. We lived as refugees in Kuwait, and money flowed away from us immeasurably faster than the current brought it to us. But we thanked God because we spent more than our income without being exposed, without our backsides being uncovered for the world to see, as my mother always said. If anyone asked us how we were doing, we replied automatically, "We're fine," and when we rebelled at "fine", as it was submission to a fate we had never wanted, my mother repeated in our hearing all the same resigned expressions: *Thank God for the blessings you have; others don't have a bite to eat; the food you throw in the rubbish would feed fifty-six families!* We didn't know why my mother chose the number fifty-six specifically, instead of a simpler round number, such as fifty or sixty. One of my many sisters would ask her, to tease her, how she could divide our rubbish among fifty-six families, and how she could calculate it exactly. My mother always detected the underlying mockery in the question and would target my sister with the empty laundry basin she was carrying, after hanging out a load of washing on the balcony, or maybe throw a slipper or a shoe at her, or any household object within reach. But usually, my sister would avoid the expected projectile.

We might even go further on the path of rebellion, pride, and ingratitude for God's blessings to us, which included our unending appetite for life and for food. My mother would give us an elbow in the ribs if we made our bites too large, or if we hurriedly chewed one mouthful after another so we would be able to grab the greatest possible amount of food in the least possible time, or if we singled out the dish of eggs and minced meat at dinner, and turned away from the other, ordinary, "fine" dishes – olive oil and zaatar, tomatoes cut into half-moons, wilted slices of cucumber that had not made it into a salad in time and were discovered by chance in one of the drawers in the fridge.

Also among the Creator's blessings to us were the itinerant pedlars of cheap clothing, who knocked on our door before going to our neighbours'. My mother bought from them in boring instalments our socks, our underwear, and our pyjamas, which we consumed like bread. Among our blessings was good health, generally, so we stuck to the government clinics and hospitals for our check-ups, going to a private doctor very rarely and only if absolutely necessary. If a tooth was loose it fell out by itself, and if it took too long my father tied a string around it, attached it to the doorknob, and pulled open the door, as we gazed in amazement at his creative ideas. The operations we underwent in the free clinics did not go beyond removing the appendix for three of us, the tonsils for two, the adenoids for four, treating a hernia for my father and haemorrhoids also for him, aside from the eight times my mother gave birth, and two miscarriages, which spared us two additional mouths. We went to Kuwait's public schools. That was before the decision was taken to deprive the large majority of expatriate children of the right to a free education, a move aimed at eroding people's livelihoods when there was already little left to erode. At that point, in the face of our shameless demands (like the insistence of one of my brothers on a pair of authentic Adidas, black with red stripes), my father would issue his final judgment: "If you can't afford it, you don't need it." When we took our despair to our mother, since she was the one in charge of the household expenses, she would strike one helpless hand with the other and say, "Where will it come from, for pity's sake?" Then if we went on insisting, she would put her hands on her waist, turning to show the curves of her motherly body, and assure us that there was no way open to her other than "that work", meaning work as a prostitute. But we knew that my mother could never do "that work", given her dreadful lack of any physical or psychological qualifications.

We, O most splendid of queens, are among those beings who are raised on the idea that a penny is minted, or divinely imprinted, to shrink. Thus we put our hands on our hearts and examine our pockets, driven by the superstitious belief that the money has fled without our consent (though that does not mean that it flees with our consent, most of the time). We developed the theory of "secret hiding places" in numerous varieties and for innumerable purposes. Some of these hiding places accompanied our thinking from our very earliest consciousness, so we invented them without seeking any authority or relying on any previous experience. Others we seemed to inherit, so they took over our behaviour and conduct and directed our ways of thinking, even when scarcity was not the apparent or dominant state of affairs; for character, innate or learned, constrains that other life that we desire.

I think my mother's sister Rahma, who resembled all the maternal and paternal aunts and large women of the family in having tender and overflowing breasts, was the most practical in her choice of a secret hiding place. (My aunt was a refreshing presence in life, individual and original; perhaps my tale will turn aside, if the nights to come permit, to tell some of her story.) My aunt hid money in her bosom, and we little ones were amazed at the inexhaustible spring of shiny silver coins that fell into our hands like broad, warm drops of rain. My aunt seemed delighted as she ladled some of her wealth from her chest and distributed it to us. In the primitive time of wonder, I believed that when I grew up my breasts would rain money, though I was confident that I would not squander it the way my aunt did. I would save it to buy all the packets of coloured marshmallows in the world, and the gum that came with transfers for me to stick on my arms with saliva, even though my mother bit my arm later, as punishment for what she called filth.

In the summertime, we would descend as guests on many houses in Jordan, as refugees from Kuwait who were better off than refugees in Jordan; that's how the others treated us, exaggerating in their expectations of us. One of the houses my eager spirit loved the most, in that ancient time, was my aunt Rahma's spacious house, in Jabal al-Taj, in Amman. There was a small garden beside it, which she had embellished with a grape arbour, trees of figs, lemons, and apples, and beds of mint, tomatoes, and native flowers of the kind that grow with no effort. One day I asked Aunt Rahma for a ten-piastre coin. She was in the middle of a flurry of preparing stuffed mahshi with my mother, who yelled at me to get out of their way. But my aunt swore an unbreakable oath that I would not leave the kitchen until I had taken the coin from her. She was sitting next to my mother on the floor, hollowing out small marrows and aubergines; each of them had hitched up her clothes to the top of her thighs, revealing a lot of loose unbound flesh. Since my aunt did not stop hollowing the marrow, continuing to turn it and dig out the insides with the corer, the seeds scattered on her hands, she asked me to open the front buttons of her house dress. I hesitated so she scolded me to hurry, and I opened the first button; but she said it wasn't enough, I had to undo the two others as well, so I did. Her warm chest peeped out at me, shining with drops of sweat and whiter than her face, which was sheathed in a light tan with an evening glow. She asked me to put my hand under her sky-blue bra, which firmly compressed her breasts. I froze, so she cried, "Go on!" I stuck my soft, frightened hand under one of the wide cups of her bra, feeling stickiness and paper money. I swallowed hard, while Aunt Rahma laughed and pulled back, saying I was tickling her. Then with a glance from her eyes she pointed to the other breast, where she deposited the metal coins. "Go for the other boob!" I slipped my hand into the fearful darkness and extracted my coin, hot from where it lay atop the moist flesh. But Aunt Rahma pretended to be angry. "Look at that!" she said, showing me the marrow, which was now pierced at the bottom. Then she let loose one of her musical, lilting

29

laughs, leaning back and spreading her long legs, as she gathered the dress she had lifted between her soft thighs.

Aunt Rahma was beautiful and remained so even as she aged, for she had a kind of preserved, radiant beauty that does not get old with the passage of time. Her beauty was more like a stable thought, an irrefutable truth. For her husband Mundhir, Aunt Rahma was as beautiful as the moon, the very symbol of beauty: "O Moon!" he would call, "What is it, Moon?" "Look at me, Moon!" He harassed her with his talk the way he would harass some unknown woman, or the way he did with their neighbour, whose husband had taken off and left her with a flock of exhausting children. He would do that within earshot and under the eyes of Aunt Rahma, whose feelings for him had died. Both she and her neighbour ignored his harassment. The only thing that bothered Rahma about his attempts to flirt with her neighbour was that she felt sorry for her; the neighbour complained to her one day, and Rahma suggested to her, in all seriousness, "Kill him, and relieve me of him!"

"Come on, Moon! I've been patient with you for a long time."

Aunt Rahma would give him that look that he well understood, saying, "I don't have a penny."

"Liar!"

At that point Aunt Rahma would let loose on him and not stop, reminding him of what he did not want to remember: his share in his father's house which he had wasted on gambling; the fridge that one of his companions in an evening of cards had taken away when he bet money he didn't have; the television that he had given to one of his many creditors. Then she taunted him for living on the pennies that came into the house thanks to her toil and the sweat of her brow. Then he would pounce on her like a madman, throwing her to the ground and trying to open her dress, while she struggled to get out from under his heavy, sluggish body, amid the shrieks of her four daughters, who were trying to defend their mother and free her from him. But my aunt's resistance would quickly collapse. Her husband would split open her dress and stretch her bra; her breasts would spill over and he would gather up the money that poured out and be on his way. She would stand up, bracing herself after her defeat, and ask one of her daughters to put the kettle on the fire and the others to help her get dinner.

My fine-boned paternal grandmother Fatima, who lived in the Wehdat Camp in Amman, could not depend on her breasts very long, as they sagged and flattened early in her relatively long life. But she nonetheless developed a technique of concealment that allowed her to stay close to her wealth and feel secure, materially, during her days and nights. Grandmother Fatima wore white flowered knickers that were long and wide, with a waistband, like a man's *sarwal* pants; they were narrow at the bottom and enclosed her ankles. Some ended in gathers and lace and showed under her long *thaub* when she sat or when she raised it off the ground, so the dust of the roads would not cling to it. Grandmother Fatima sewed these undergarments herself, and unlike standard feminine underwear, even the very modest kind, hers had many pockets – pockets behind, pockets in front, and pockets on the sides, all of them hidden, like an interlining. Some of the pockets intended for large sums had zippers. Grandmother Fatima resorted to her hidden vaults only in emergencies; for daily use she had her small purse of burnt brown leather, with its many hollows and openings. She slipped it into her bosom, in something like an open, internal sock, which she had sewn in the lining of her *thaub* for this purpose. When we grandchildren crowded around her, asking for shillings and ten-piastre pieces to buy rings of egg bread with sesame, or cakes, or Eskimo ice cream, or to pay for a few turns on Abu Saeed's swing in the camp – the most we could hope for from her – Grandmother Fatima would seem delighted, examining our wheedling expressions. She would slowly reach into her bosom and bring out her leather purse, opening its metal clasp with a popping sound that foretold good things. Then she glared at the internal folds and pockets with her small eyes, before opening the zipper of the middle pocket, with its piles of red pennies, shillings, and silver ten-piastre pieces. There would be five or six of us, our circle around her narrowing as the moment came for her to distribute some of her wealth. "Who held out his hand first?" she asks, a laugh ruffling her face and erasing some of the misery detailed there. We unfold our little hands before her, pushing and shoving, nearly coming to blows, so she threatens to put the money back in her purse if we aren't good, obedient children. We remember our manners, temporarily assuming a humble stance in her presence. Grandmother distributes the shillings to the hands, carefully, one at a time, then she closes each small hand on the shilling and pats it; it's as if she wants to keep the money for herself, or for looming days of want, or as if she were imploring us to be sensible and not waste it on cakes or Eskimos or swings or other pleasures.

Grandmother Fatima felt secure in her long underwear as a hiding place that never left her, except for the day she went to the baths, when she exchanged "the safe" for another garment. But one summer evening she stretched out on the ledge in front of her house, after the evening prayer, and dozed off. She dreamed that she became light, flat, and softened, and then hovered at a low elevation before coming down on the fresh earth, which moistened her dry bones and tickled her. She became still softer, and her narrow mouth opened in a wide smile. Then Grandmother Fatima, who had risen in the air, became more aware of the cold creeping over her body and pinching her flesh under her long dress, so a tremor ran through her. She opened her eyes and saw dark night around her; her dress was raised above her ankles. At first, she thought that she had imagined that she saw her bare ankles, but then she lifted the dress a little and yelled – her knickers had disappeared. My aunt Najah, who was her only daughter and who lived with her, hurried out at the sound of Grandmother's voice. She told her, trembling with fear and cold, that she had been robbed. "The knickers? Where did they go?" cried Najah, in a panic. But Grandmother, who seemed less concerned about her nudity than about the money, told her someone had stripped off her knickers as she slept without her feeling it. Aunt Najah beat her breast and Grandmother Fatima was about to rend her garment and loose her lamentations to the heavens when Aunt Najah hugged her close, placing her hand over her mouth and looking around in terror lest human eyes or ears might see or hear. Then she pulled her into the house and shut the door, saying to her, "We killed it here, and here we'll bury it!"

"And the money? The money, the money, *the money*?"

Grandmother was not asking a question or looking for an answer. She was beating her head with her hands, repeatedly. What Aunt Najah cared about was to bury the story, so Grandmother

Fatima would not become a scandal. But the camp learned about the affair of the knickers the next day. Neighbour women thronged to Grandmother's house, inquisitive, some gloating, asking about the underwear thief. Aunt Najah quarrelled with some of them, who openly exchanged knowing winks, not believing that anyone could pull off a sleeping woman's knickers without her feeling it. But what amazed people more than the incident itself was that my grandmother's knickers concealed a thousand dinars, distributed in the hidden pockets. My grandmother swore on the noble Qur'an that the money was no more than forty-seven dinars, but no-one believed her. Even my uncle Abu Taisir, whose blood boiled at the beginning over the theft of his mother's knickers, blamed her later, once the story had died down. How had she kept a thousand dinars in her knickers when he could barely feed his family, he wondered bitterly. Wasn't he more deserving of the money?

As for my maternal grandmother Radiyya, who considered herself clever in matters of both life and money, she was the most patient and inventive in contriving secure means of deposit. She distributed her wealth among dozens of little pouches, which she sewed from white linen for this purpose. Then she would put the pouch in a plastic bag closed tightly with a rubber band, feeling the belly of the pouch that was swollen with money: coloured bills and heavy metal coins. She would approach her hiding places with great excitement and secrecy (except, God knows, from us children, who were always underfoot and everywhere in her life). Her hiding places were the jars of rice, lentils, bulgur wheat, chickpeas, white beans – all the jars of dry seeds and grains in the old kitchen cabinet in her house in the city of Zarqa, near Amman.

She would bury the pouches, protected by plastic, inside the jars, taking care that they were completely covered. Often her caution and care would lead her to put a mark on the bag or to affix a stamp to it to distinguish the amount of money confided to each pouch, for the one with five dinars was different from the one with ten or twenty – though to be honest, Grandmother Radiyya did not need to mark or differentiate the pouches, since she could tell what was in them from a close look at how rounded they were. In fact she knew that the pouch in the rice jar had ten dinars while the one buried in the jar of beans had five. When she finished shrouding the money and burying it, she would look at the jars lined up next to each other in order, like elegant tombstones, and examine them with a smile of victory.

One day Umm Subhi, Grandmother Radiyya's neighbour, sent her son Subhi over for a handful of lentils. My mother and grandmother were at the market, so I took care of it. I did not understand why Grandmother Radiyya pounced on me when she found out about it. She grabbed me by the shoulder and planted her eyes in my face like two sharp knives, shouting, "How could you give him the jar with twenty dinars?" I was oozing fear. She pinned me to the wall and shook me violently, this weak woman whose hardness was immense. My mother's reaction was to soothe her from a distance, telling her to remember God and calm down. My tongue stumbled as I tried to explain to my angry grandmother that I didn't know how much Umm Subhi wanted, so I gave the jar of lentils to Subhi so they could take what they needed and return it to us. But Grandmother Radiyya, who had reluctantly let me go after a sharp exchange with my mother, began slapping her face, time after time, constantly repeating in tones of disapproval and disbelief that showed the gravity of the blow:

"The jar with *twenty* dinars? The one with twenty, the one with twenty, the one with *twenty*?"

When Subhi brought back the lentil jar with a bit less inside, Grandmother Radiyya submitted him to an interrogation, with questions like, *Who opened the jar? Did your mother take the lentils or one of your sisters? Was anyone in the house with you when your mother opened the jar?* Then she grasped it intently, spread out a paper bag on the floor, and emptied the lentils onto it. They formed a small orange mound. She hollowed out the mound with her fingers, looking for her hidden pouch, but it did not appear. She turned the mound into a flat plain, then she scattered it nervously, then she flung the lentils about in a rage. When she was sure that the pouch had disappeared, she rushed out of the house in slippers and a sleeveless house dress, with bits of tomato paste on her chest. On her way out she grabbed a towel from the clothes line in the courtyard and threw it over her shoulders.

"Where're you going?" my mother asked.

Without looking around she replied, "To that bitch." We caught up with her and tried to prevent her from quarrelling with "that bitch", but Grandmother Radiyya heard only the voice of the anger that enveloped her all the way to Umm Subhi's house, two houses over from her own.

As usual, the whole neighbourhood gathered around the two women. Umm Subhi swore on the mercy given to all her dearly departed that she had not taken any money from the lentil jar, while Grandmother Radiyya went on calling her a despicable thief with low morals, a low-down daughter of a lower mother. Umm Subhi was inhibited for a time by my grandmother's old age, but then she bared her verbal fangs and repaid the insults many times over, calling my grandmother a wicked, quarrelsome old woman. Then as the quarrel grew, they waded into matters of honour.

My grandmother: "You traipse around all over the place and don't even care what people think!"

Umm Subhi: "You invite taxi drivers to come in and have tea from morning till night."

Grandmother Radiyya: "Don't give me shit, my shoes are more honourable than you! Those guys are helping me."

Umm Subhi: "You old hag! You dye your hair red! Go find a man to take you in hand!"

Grandmother: "That's henna, you tramp! Anyway, do you think your husband is a man? He's worse than useless."

For as long as Grandmother Radiyya lived she continued her feud with Umm Subhi, neither one rejoicing with the other in times of joy nor grieving with her in times of grief. Grandmother continued to explain to the neighbours that the taxi drivers brought her home and then helped her to carry all the bags she brought back from the market, out of respect for her stature. She might ask one of them to come into the house with her to attach the gas canister in the kitchen, or to pick up the washing machine and move it from its place. "Is it forbidden for me to repay them with a cup of tea?" she would ask, seeking the seal of approval from her neighbours, as they drank tea and ate cake with coconut. Then she would show them her hair, tinged with an orange red, looking for more support: "Since when is henna forbidden, I ask you?"

What my grandmother Radiyya and possibly even Umm Subhi did not know was that Subhi, whose eyes followed me for years whenever we visited my grandmother's house, bought cold juices and expensive chocolate and bottles of Pepsi (not minding having to pay the deposit) and falafel sandwiches with tahini, for himself and me and for many friends from the neighbourhood, for days after the event. He bought me a double mirror in a metal case with the picture of a beautiful girl on it who he said looked like me, and I loved this unfounded belief. He also gave me a gold chain that rusted after I had worn it for less than a week, and three bottles of shiny nail polish. The kids in the neighbourhood liked Subhi. For many indolent, light-hearted days that seemed as if they would never end, Subhi was a happy king.

Distant days, which are all stuck fast together in my heart's memory, O my queen, have taught me that secret hiding places are life. Forgive me my helplessness and wasted imagination, compared with the exuberant imagination of others and the resourcefulness of real people, who have embraced life and hidden it in the hollows of days, fearing sudden, terrifying loss. Forgive me my ignorance, nurtured by stiff readings and words crammed into byways of speech that are hard to explore, if I exaggerate, and exaggerate, and exaggerate still more, and tell you that secret hiding places whose virginal secrecy is forced open are life, with its measured delights and enduring pains, with its timid joy and settled sadness. They are life, passing as does . . . life.

My mother always seemed judicious and precise with respect to her hiding places, even when the action appeared to be improvised on the spur of the moment. For there were details related to specific characteristics of the hiding place, details that reflected a certain sensibility we had acquired, by habit at times, by familiarity at other times, and by compulsion most of the time. The goal was to keep the money for a while, not out of stinginess but rather to extend a temporary sense of security and prolong a false feeling of confidence; thus the money would remain sleeping in its hiding place for as long as possible before the hand of necessity reached for it, hesitantly, with great caution, with a touch of guilt, and with a measure of fear that our "fine" state, held together by our stratagems, would tumble down.

My mother would put a sum of money that was supposed to be reserved for coming eras of want in the fourth drawer of the chest of drawers, under a pile of bedsheets set aside for later use. There was a sum that was supposed to be reserved but not for a very distant era among all the ages of need, and that was in my father's underwear drawer in the third section on the right of the wardrobe. Another sum, designated for the monthly *jam'iyya* savings club, went under the thick vinyl tablecloth on the second shelf of the buffet holding the gilded teacups. Another sum, for the weekly savings club, went in the ladle drawer, under a layer of yellowed newspaper that my mother used to line the drawers of the kitchen cabinets. Naturally, there was a sum designated for emergencies and instances of urgent expense, which could be taken from under one of the sofa cushions in the "salon", our formal living room.

Although these hiding places were secret, or such was the description they were given, nonetheless many people knew about them. Once when our neighbour Umm Muaadh was sitting with her full weight on one of the sofas (she was the neighbour closest to my mother's heart, with her gossip that didn't lack a touch of the bizarre), my mother put her hand under her rear, saying in commanding tones, "Move your arse!" So Umm Muaadh lifted one side of her rear, suspending it in the air as she continued her gossip, taking full advantage of her body language in all its eloquence, while my mother shoved her hand under the cushion and brought out five dinars, folded, after which Umm Muaadh resumed her original position. Then when the couch cushions were sinking under the weight of four or five neighbours, gathered at my mother's for an afternoon of tea and pastries as they dug into people's conduct and spoke of indecent marital secrets, my mother might be forced to shove her hand under all their rear ends, rummaging in the warm, cramped darkness for two dinars, since she couldn't remember under which cushion she had hidden them. The women turned about in their seats, their lazy flesh shaking according to the rhythm of my mother's seeking hand. They would lean to the left and to the right and might spring up at the strong thrust of my mother's hand when at last she found what she was after.

My mother did not spare any effort, carving long and slowly on the hard, blank stone of our life in order to extract a penny, just as she hoped one might rain down from the dry skies of Kuwait. However difficult and rugged it was, her path did not always come to a dead end, helped as she was by singular techniques such as "passing on the hat" (a form of Ponzi scheme): she took from this one to give to that, or subtracted from that to give to this, or withdrew from the other for the sake of this. Certainly the *jam'iyya* savings clubs with the neighbours were a useful strategy, at least for a time, until she reached the point of being forced to start a third or fourth savings club to pay off the second, since she had spent that money, either by necessity or in a temporary absence of wisdom and sound reason. There were savings clubs with a few dinars as the weekly contribution, and monthly ones with more. My mother was usually the one responsible for gathering the contributions, overseeing the drawing of lots and then distributing all of the week's or month's money to each woman in her assigned turn. The neighbours might have recourse to her to mediate between them, to change or exchange the turns assigned to them

41

by lot. She would cajole Umm Muaadh to give up her turn for Umm Husam, or she might get Umm Muhammad to pass up her turn for Umm Luayy, after becoming certain that Umm Luayy's need was greater and more urgent than Umm Muhammad's; and Umm Muhammad would agree out of embarrassment, so her neighbours would not shun her, after my mother promised her that she would be the first one to be paid in the next savings club. That's because the savings clubs followed one after the other in the women's lives as long as their lives reproduced the need, promising them scarcity that was relieved only rarely. In any case, my mother would voluntarily give up her turn for Umm Hana', who was always complaining of how much more she lacked than we did.

Naturally there was also theft, more as an inevitable, despairing option than as a strategy. When all ways of managing were blocked before her, my mother would extend her hand, a hand she had trained in marshalling proofs and seeking justifications, to the point that it no longer trembled or shied away, just as she no longer brought to mind the fear of God, who saw her from above all His seven layered heavens. She would reach for the back pocket of my father's trousers and slip out of his wallet a handful of dinars whose absence would arouse no suspicions, with the lightness of a believer rightly confident that compelling necessity has its own law, and without entertaining any ideas concerning unanticipated consequences or evil outcomes. In fact, alongside my mother's inventions, necessary to ease our life, she developed an audacious system for stealing from my father before his very eyes and ears, exploiting a valuable trait of his for which she was envied by the women who knew our situation, which was no more secret from them than their conditions were veiled from us. This trait was that my father was inclined to forgetfulness, not remembering the fate of the dinar that had just left his pocket. In the morning my mother would remind him of the electricity bill she would have to pay the collector while he was out, so he would count the sum into her hand, eight and a half dinars, one by one. The evening of the next day, she would warn him of the threat of the electricity being cut off because he had not paid the bill – the collector had come, and she had asked him to wait one more day. He would raise his eyes to hers in a searching look, but my mother's bold gaze would not swerve nor waver in its claim of truth, never falling to the floor but continuing to meet his troubled, confused eyes. His gaze would collapse at last. My father would lower his eyes then put his hand in his pocket, bring out his wallet, and give her ten dinars. He gave them unwillingly, retaining them in his despairing hand in an attempt to catch one last revealing look from her that would coincide with his internal disturbance, hoping that her gaze would fall and shatter, and reveal what was behind that thick glass – for he knew, but he could not be certain. But my mother's eyes never fell, nor were they stripped of their fearsome certainty. Then three days later, my mother would ask him for ten dinars! My father would rise up in anger, taking out a paper from a fold of his wallet where he had recorded the date three days earlier, along with a detailed explanation of the incident of her receiving ten dinars from his hand to pay the electricity bill. This time he would declare his certainty openly: "I gave you money for the electricity bill three days ago. Look here, I wrote it down so I wouldn't forget! Do you think I'm senile?" My mother would laugh and wink at him: "Of course I paid the electric bill. I know you're not senile yet!" Then she would explain, without giving much consideration to his

43

outburst or to the evidence that was supposed to prove her bare-faced theft: the ten dinars were for the plumber, who was coming tomorrow to fix the pipe that had broken in the bathroom wall.

Nonetheless a feeling of guilt pierced my mother deep down and came to the surface when my father would stand lost before her, directing his wandering eyes to hers as he tried to dig out a truth he could never capture by sight or by insight. The feeling would come to her when he withdrew from the confrontation, defeated. The twinges came and went, like a pin she had forgotten in the bodice of her dress; but one day the feeling intensified, and she confided to Umm Muaadh what was bothering her. Umm Muaadh gave her the look you would expect from a wife whose husband knew what happened to every penny that came out of his pocket, when it came out, and how, and where it went. "I wish I could make off with something from Abu Muaadh without him noticing it!" she said, her voice tinged with a bit of resentment, sorrow, and envy, none of which affected their friendship or loosened the bonds of long camaraderie, reinforced by shared shameful secrets. But my mother seemed really disturbed and fearful, confessing to Umm Muaadh that on some nights she no sooner stretched out in bed than she felt a weight pressing down on her, keeping her from breathing.

"What should I do, Umm Muaadh? Should I confess to Abu Jihad and leave it in God's hands?"

My mother had always convinced herself, the self that scolded her at distant intervals, that she was right, or at the very least that she was forced to do what she did. For the life that she understood was not the one my father understood, or imagined he understood (acknowledging that not all his suspicions were the sinful ones).

44

He remained immersed in simplicity, or according to another version, in simple-mindedness, in easy, obvious explanations that did not bear deep contemplation or wearying research. My mother knew what my father did not and must not know: it was better for him to strut in blissful ignorance, so that additional knowledge, which he had not sought, would not cause him pain in his heart or in his pocket.

My father never dreamed, not even in his most wildly extravagant dreams, that the electricity bill he had paid three times (or even more), along with the bills for water and other necessities, was what my mother used to buy trainers for my brother, and a school backpack for my other brother (replacing the one my father had bought him two months earlier which had come apart, without her daring to inform him of its shameful state). She might also buy elegant shoes with heels that my sister coveted; my sister was younger than I was, but she had summoned the woman lurking within her body before me. My mother might buy a red shirt with many ruffles framing its collar for my other sister, and a pair of stonewashed blue jeans for me, which she would exchange many times over before I was satisfied; she might buy dozens of socks for my father, cheap underwear of all sizes from the garment pedlars, and white unisex vests for the smallest girls and boys. She might buy creams for removing excess hair from our girlish bodies, which vied with each other in growing fast, until we eventually discovered the virtues of lemon and sugar paste, more effective in pulling out hair by the roots. She might buy styling gel for the boys' hair, as they competed with the girls for the most time at the mirror, as she would buy us headbands, earrings, necklaces, and cheap wristwatches, those small pleasures that complete a girl's life.

My father could never imagine, even under the most extra-ordinary circumstances, that the few dinars distributed without abundance on our irrepressible lives could grow wings when he was unconscious in sleep, or plunged into his wandering, distraction, and forgetting, which became absent-mindedness with the coming of difficult days, as a substitute for thinking thoughts he did not want to entertain. Money flew from him: individual dinars, fives, and tens, even if these last did cower and shrink in upon themselves in his wallet, for fear that their light, hidden wings could not bear their weight. But none of them hovered in open space for very long, for however little she pilfered, my mother contrived to buy a lot cheaply. Some of it was necessary and most of it was not, yet it was needed for the ample life that proliferated around her. She acquired plastic sets of drawers, which she distributed in the kitchen, the bathroom, the corridor, and our room, to contain the scattered evidence of our existence – books, toys, combs, hair ornaments, jars of creams missing their tops, extension cords, three hairdryers (of which two did not work), bars of perfumed soap, Nabulsi soap (we were well stocked with that after returning, broke and exhausted, from summer holidays with our relatives in the cities and camps of Jordan), toothpaste, dish sponges, bath loofahs, boxes of Tide, and family-sized bottles of shampoo. Nor did my mother hesitate to buy curtains of beads to separate the narrow passageway between the kitchen and the bathroom from the lone, formal salon, open to the outside, even though the curtains went to pieces periodically: they could not stand up to our hurried, rash hands, or our arms that seemed to move independently of us, or our bodies that collided violently with everything in our way as we crowded through the narrow openings of our house.

Nonetheless my mother's intentions were not altogether pure in her interpretation of the concept of needs and requirements that legitimised her thefts, as she had a special passion for acquiring figurines, and she satisfied it at least partially by what her light fingers extracted from my father's pocket. She was especially enamoured of statuettes of elegant, beautiful people: little girls in embellished glass dresses; attractive women, half undressed, carved in stone as they swayed or bent over in moments of loveliness, seduction, and beauty that my mother had never known, though she might timidly imagine living them, hiding from her own realistic thoughts; and fascinating men, harbouring mischief, who followed us with their eyes wherever we turned or twisted, confidently aware of the impact of their captivating features on us, with all our clear, crude flaws.

Among her many idols, extravagantly placed in the few empty spaces in the house, my mother was particularly attached to one ceramic figure of a thin ballet dancer wearing a pink dress. The upper half of the dancer's body hung down as she adjusted the ribbon of her satin shoe without bending her thin legs, the pose an imitation of a world-famous painting. Alone among all the figurines, this diminutive dancer, with her elegant legs fixed to a square wooden base, was given a small table all to herself. My mother was always looking at that dancer, and it was always as if she were seeing her for the first time. She would touch her smooth ivory cheek, moving over her bare arms and stroking her ceramic skirt as if she were feeling actual fabric, chiffon over stiff tulle, and her eyes would suddenly widen, as if touched by a life awakening unexpectedly from the slumbering ceramic. She was hopping mad whenever she saw that my father, who prayed in the front room most of the time, had taken her dancer from her special place on the side table and turned her over on the sofa, or had veiled her with any covering that came to hand, arguing that she hindered his prayers: every time he lifted his head from a prostration his eyes fell on her rear, barely covered by her very short skirt, so that his concentration was shattered and his mind strayed to inappropriate matters.

Then the dancer broke in two. My father's prayers were not the reason. My mother was dusting her elegant dancer when she slipped from her hand, falling on the floor and breaking at the waist. My mother cried, bit her lips, and sobbed bitter tears. My mother's weeping was mixed with the guffaws of one of my sisters, who was watching a scene from the play *The Kids Have Grown Up* on television. The laughter entwined with the crying, and then the blithe laughter overcame the bitter tears. My mother ran into the family room. My sister was stretched out on the floor, chuckling still, when my mother's face turned into one we had never seen, and she stepped on my sister's belly with her bare foot. She went on crushing her and then kicked her, still clutching the upper half of her dancer in one hand and the lower half, still planted on its wooden base, in the other. We managed to save my sister from her attack with difficulty, while my sister was trying to understand what had happened or what she had done wrong, protesting loudly, "What did I do? What did I do?" When we saw the broken dancer in my mother's hands, we understood.

So it was that my mother sought Umm Muaadh's opinion, then decided to go to the imam of the nearby mosque after the evening prayer, to ascertain from him the ruling of the religious law with respect to her thefts (which were completely warranted, she would explain, laying out before him her argument and her need). On the way she reviewed in her mind the points of her defence, which she had lined up with care, recalling the reasons she had contrived to oppose the likely decision that the thefts were forbidden, supported by examples that would soften the heart of the imam. All of his harsh logic might collapse, given the perspective that the permitted is clear and the forbidden is clear, but there is always a middle ground, where this might slide into that, or intersect with the necessities of life.

But my mother never reached the mosque, nor did she seek the opinion of its imam. An unusually attractive man winked at her and captured her heart in one glance. He was a handsome young man in his thirties, wearing a black ceramic suit and leaning provocatively against a light pole of ivory, confident that his woman would pass before him soon. He had his hand on the brim of his disturbing hat, and he was smiling from behind the glass window of the boutique where she bought her figurines. She read the price tag on the wooden base: nine and a half dinars.

Over our ample dinner, with our many hands crossing and vying with each other, my mother reminded my father to give her ten dinars for the plumber who was coming to fix the pipe that had broken in the bathroom wall. He scratched his head, trying to remember if he had given her ten dinars the day before yesterday for that purpose or something similar; he groped blindly in an ocean of confusion and wandering, but he could not remember.

Meanwhile my mother went on eating, relaxed, as if she were a happy queen, in fact as if she were the happiest of all God's creatures on earth.

Hold on, O queen of my days, days past and days yet to come – don't rush.

Don't let your tender soul beguile you into believing what must not be believed. Don't let your feelings, newly formed, or your opinions, still in that hardening stage where the truth and the true are clear and irrefutable – don't let them show you my father as someone inclined to hateful frugality, close to stinginess and bordering on the miserly, or tight-fisted for no good reason. For plenty (apart from plentiful children and all that entailed of plentiful need) was not among the characteristics of his existence, just as comfort was not among the good things of his life, not that the good things in his life were completely good.

Perhaps I should explain, so your thoughts don't go to something other than what I wanted to make clear. I wouldn't want the lesson to be lost on you just at the point where I stopped, during these last nights of talking. No, never! My father was not tight-fisted, though the hand of God, stretched above us, was. The little money that did fall to him in sporadic raindrops did not water our thirsty earth; in fact it evaporated before it touched the surface of our life, often going where it shouldn't go, for expenses that were not urgent, into channels that were not altogether pressing. This violated my father's essential principle that "if you can't afford it, you don't need it", and in our recurring times of hardship it contradicted his rigorous explanation of necessity. Our money was lacking to begin with, and it diminished even before it got to us; for our life was not ours alone, and the lives of many others were linked to ours, by an unfair fate. In fact my father's untimely generosity nearly shook the foundations of our house, held together with such difficulty, countless times.

Have I told you about that night when my mother attacked my father? She bit him on the cheek and grabbed his neck in her hands, hands which had absorbed all the wrath and duress in the world. My father would have died of strangulation and asphyxiation, crushed under the weight of her body (burdened by frequent childbearing and all her expedients in life), had we not intervened and pulled them apart, with difficulty. Listen, then.

My father worked as an electrical technician in the maintenance division of the Kuwaiti Health Ministry. His salary did not increase with the same regularity as our increase in numbers, in height and breadth, in requests and requirements, in dreams and developing bodies, and in resentments. When we reached half our eventual number and half of what our life turned out to be, my mother sold her gold jewellery and gave the money to my father. It allowed him to join a co-worker from the maintenance division in opening a small shop in Hawalli, to repair electrical appliances, televisions, refrigerators, tape recorders, and then video recorders.

Then came a night not at all romantic, sweeping into the streets over a sediment of daylight miseries, to the loud throbbing of air conditioners protruding from the walls of human boxes (boxes euphemistically called "apartments"), when my father saw someone collapsed in a heap on the pavement. He was coming back from the shop; his car broke down, as usual, so he parked it, as usual, in the first empty space he came across, covering the remaining distance to the house on foot. In the silence crowned by faint light from the street lamps, there was a sound like stifled weeping. He went towards the person; it was an old woman wearing a *thaub* that looked very much like his mother's, and black shoes with worn heels like the shoes in which his mother moved gracefully through the crooked streets of the camp, despite the heavy woes that had stiffened her body. It was as if the old woman, who looked like his mother with her triangular face and her features that spoke of living on borrowed time, was waiting for him to ask if she was alright. She talked to him, though he had not asked, about many things: the lands they left in "the country"; the white mare she rode as a bride; the new, gleaming gold liras lined up across her broad forehead, so shiny that when she swayed on the horse it was as if the sun was going down. She also told him about the rifles the dearly departed (my father supposed this was her husband) had taught her to clean and load; about the carpet of olive trees spread as far as the eye could see; about the mounds of sacks containing flour and grains; about the abundance of blessings in the big clay storage jars; about the aromatic olive oil; about the winds sweeping over broad open spaces. Then her cracked voice caught in her throat.

My father stopped to gather the pieces of the evening incident. He fought off a few tears, keeping them shut away in his eyes. My mother maintained the stance of someone likely to pounce, while we were divided into two teams: the first, which included me, to restrain my mother, and the second, composed mostly of the younger ones, to protect my father from the effects of her still raging anger. What we understood from my father, his voice plunged in his watery throat, was that the woman who looked like his mother told him that she was a widow staying with her son, his wife, and their six children, and that her son had been sacked from his job in one of the sea freight companies a few months earlier. They were living on meagre charity in an annexe to an apartment building consisting of two rooms, and the owner of the building knocked on their door every day at any time, threatening to throw them into the street if they didn't pay the rent they owed for the last three months. The woman who looked like his mother covered her triangular face with her hands, hiding her shame over a time that had brought her to sit on the pavement in a night soaked with humidity and the dregs of a miserable day in a country that wasn't like "the country". Then she began to pull on her face with her dry fingers, so my father sat at her feet, put his hand in his pocket, and pulled out ninety dinars, all he had with him. He put it in the lap of the woman who looked like his mother and went on his way.

My father wiped away the tears about to spill from his eyes with the palms of his hands, then he lifted his face to my mother and said, "But if only you had seen her! God, how much she looks like my mother!"

My mother relaxed. We felt that from her body, where the beat of the anger had receded and the tension had diminished. Her eyes were glassy, expressing no meaning, holding no spark, not even a smothered one, not harbouring any feeling of any kind. She looked at my father and said, emphasising every letter, "Fuck your mother!"

The little money my father did collect was supposed to be divided among the necessities of our large existence, abundant

53

and overflowing, to cover us, without excluding the possibility of our being left uncovered. His income from the electrical repair shop did not make any essential difference in our life; in fact, often the shop only covered its own expenses, and that only barely. My mother would stroke her bare arms and move them in the air, half shaking them and half dancing, bringing back a distant, precious flash and metallic noise that shone in her memory, reminding my father, who did not want to remember, that he had not yet replaced a single bracelet she had given him with ten others, as he had promised her.

In addition to meeting the requirements of our exuberant existence, a part of my father's money went to my grandmother Fatima and my aunt Najah. The matter wasn't limited to the expenses of the two women, one awaiting a good end (with the lightest of any remaining losses in life and the fewest possible illnesses), and the other seeking a quick end to her compulsory spinsterhood. From time to time, my father would suddenly send Grandmother Fatima a sum she was supposed to invest in clinching some possible marriage for Najah. My grandmother would set out for the post office in the camp to make a reverse charge call to my father, asking him to send her two hundred dinars. Her voice would be flushed with joy, giving hope that the anticipated happy ending for Najah was near. Once she asked for three hundred dinars! The hoped-for groom was Rizq, who worked as an engineer in Saudi Arabia. Grandmother plucked Aunt Najah's moustache and her downy sideburns; she had her spread out her brown hair, wavy because it was always braided; she bought her an Aleppan necklace, two bracelets, and gold chandelier earrings, as well as two new dresses, so that Rizq's mother would not think that

Najah was living on God's mercy and just waiting for clothing and jewels from the groom. In fact, Grandmother hinted that it was worthwhile to "buy" this groom of good family, who was pious, content, and God-fearing personally and in his family, by investing money. Umm Rizq repeated my grandmother's words and patted Aunt Najah's hair when they visited her; my aunt looked fresh and happy, gleaming with precious metal that had not been consumed even in sudden times of relief. At the end of all the coming and going, Umm Rizq offered Grandmother and Aunt Najah nougat candy with nuts, in celebration of the engagement of her son Rizq to his maternal cousin.

Likewise during our difficult days, my father was forced to send money, at irregular intervals, to my uncle Abu Taisir. He moved around among all the vegetable stands in the Wehdat Refugee Camp, as a salesman known for his attacks of blazing fury, especially if a customer argued with him too much, that is, more than he thought was necessary. His head would spark like a Primus stove before it's lit, and the matter would usually end with him hitting the customer on the head with the sack of potatoes he was weighing for him when the customer protested that the scale did not show three full kilograms. "What do you think now? Ith your head feeling like three kiloth of potatoth hit it?" (My uncle lisped, pronouncing the letters *siin* and *saad* as if they were *thaa'*.) He might not even hold back from insulting women, the toxic ones who drove him crazy with their wrangling, bargaining, and picking out each individual vegetable. Soon he would lose patience with them, he who was not patient to start with, and after much irritation on their part and irritability on his, he would suggest to one of them that she stick to her house and get

55

out of his face, before he . . . (leaving the rest of the threat to his eyes, blazing with spite in their sockets). In fact, many instances were recorded in which my uncle Abu Taisir intentionally attacked the shop owner himself, if the owner lost his temper with him when my uncle thought that was unwarranted, or asked something of him that seemed out of place, according to his narrow understanding, or in a tone that seemed to him too demanding or disrespectful. For being the owner of the shop did not give him the right to demand, let alone to be disrespectful! Often the matter required the intervention of the salesmen from neighbouring shops to separate them, pulling my uncle – with his thick body that struck terror into the souls of those who did not know him, before they discovered his goodness (or his imbecility, as Grandmother Fatima labelled it) – away from the cowering shop owner. Once the men had got Uncle Abu Taisir out of the shop, something that might require two or three men to carry him, the owner would bristle all over again. Now that the danger had passed, he would assume a size bigger than his natural one, catch up with the men carrying Abu Taisir, and shout loudly,

"I don't want to see your face in the shop ever again!"

My uncle, borne by three men like a stake planted in space, above the heads of the men, as if he were leading a street demonstration, would answer in a ringing voice,

"My arth!"

For my father, the world had not changed from yesterday to today, even if yesterday was twenty years or more in the past. Did it make any sense that he would go to sleep and wake up to find that the dinar no longer bought today what it bought yesterday? In his clear understanding, empty of any complications and reclining in a pleasant past that reached the present slowly and with no changes worth mentioning, my mother's harlotry was barefaced, when she demanded of him what went beyond the necessities of life. *By our Lord, what are these shoes that cost ten dinars?* "How brazen can you be, by God?" He would say that to my mother when she laid out before him the needs and urgent requirements of our life. He could have sworn – lost in his doubts, his thoughts confused, the scenes and the incidents running together in his head – that he had given her the money for the water bill. But my mother would swear by still more solemn oaths that she had not taken a penny from him. My father would go back to his pockets, nearly empty, to make sure of what he could not know for sure. He would go back to his knock-off Samsonite briefcase that he liked to carry when he went to the repair shop in the afternoon. It contained old receipts and shopping lists in my mother's childish handwriting; unimportant papers that gave the impression of the importance and seriousness of his work when he first opened the briefcase; catalogues of electrical equipment; leather sandals stuffed into one of the inner pockets (he would put them on in the shop when the heat and humidity began to prey on his toes, already beset by fungus); and a little money that he hid there on the very scarce days of plenty, keeping it for darker days that brought the unforeseen – and guaranteeing, as long as the briefcase was with him, that it was beyond the reach of my mother's grasping hand. For my mother, for those who don't know, did not restrict herself to preying on my father's sieve-like memory and to plundering his pockets. She also presumed upon his Samsonite briefcase the few times he left it in the house, cracking its passcode. The code was usually made up of three numbers, which my father deliberately made easy to remember, knowing that his memory was full of holes. They might be three zeroes, for example, or successive numbers, such as 1, 2, 3; my mother would find the correct code after a few attempts and without any effort to speak of.

My father did not know how fast we grew; that our shirts, trousers, dresses, and shoes, even our underwear, all of which we passed down to each other, became too small for the smallest just as they did for the largest. When the hole in the jacket became large or the rip in the trousers lengthened, that was because our chemistry and our temperaments were also changing – so how could my father appreciate or grasp the fact that our greedy bodies devoured our clothes? They bit them, tore them, ripped them, so the garments' actual life ended before the expected term, and they could no longer be handed down or made to fit. And then, how could he understand that our feet, which broadened in the space of a few evenings, could not stay crammed into the same shoes for ever and ever? No, my father was neither miserly nor stingy. It was just that his reading of the meter of life did not change, for we, his children, were still his beautiful people, his beings who did not grow up no matter how big we got, and no matter what fearsome quantities of food we consumed.

Perhaps my father did squander his skimpy substance in his own way, especially when he raided the large vegetable markets, dragging half of us behind him to help with carrying the crates of tomatoes, aubergines, marrows, squash, green peppers, cucumbers, and lemons, the sacks of onions and potatoes, the boxes of Chiquita bananas and American apples, with skins that shone the deepest red. There were tangerines and grapefruits and kiwis and persimmons (my mother's favourite fruit), and quinces, from which she made the jam for which she was famous. There were Iraqi watermelons, Syrian melons, grapes with graduated colours from green to red, prickly pears, small fresh Barhi dates, and coconuts with their milky juice. If we craved fruit that was out of season, my father would tour the shops that imported highly esteemed fruit, the product of precise natural engineering, where individual pieces were displayed seductively on trays, covered with plastic. As for the cooperative grocers, those were the scene of our weekly raids: we would load two shopping carts with frozen foods, canned goods, cheeses, dairy products, chilled meats, and everything that came by the dozen or in family packs or on offer, like buying two trays of eggs for the price of one, or six tubs of Kraft cheese spread for the price of four. Since our 22-square-foot refrigerator was never empty and could not hold all our food, which barely satisfied our constantly hungry tribe, we bought a freezer and put it in the corridor leading to the kitchen, which was open to all three rooms in the apartment. It held piles of bags of vegetables and chicken, and bags of cut-up meat in equal packages which all together formed a lamb, our monthly allotment.

Food, and more precisely feeding us, was a pleasure for my father. The greatest joy for him was that we spread a cloth on the floor after his return from the shop, to have dinner. He would call us by name. His existence, which began and ended with us, would not seem sweet to him until we flooded it with our exuberant existence, on evenings free of any suggestion of the stars setting, drunk on the possibilities of life, with all its flaws. He followed us with benevolent eyes as we stretched our ravenous hands to the many dishes. He would peel a boiled egg for the youngest among us, so we would not waste our time doing anything but eating, or so the largest would not take the share of the smallest. He would push the dishes that were luxuries, like Bulgarian white cheese, corned beef fried with onions, mortadella, and black Greek Kalamata olives, closer to the shortest arms. My father would hold back at dinner, beginning a round or two after us, and when he did stretch out his hand he would choose the less agreeable dishes, or those our picky appetites refused. My father was happy that we were eating, that we were eating a lot and getting fat under his roof, in his domain that was shrunken spatially but vast emotionally. According to his deep-rooted convictions, we could go to sleep naked, but we could not go to sleep hungry.

My father's eyes would follow our attack on the food with love and tenderness. He was a king, O my queen, delighting in his people, wishing this moment would never end.

As for me, O queen of queens, I am who I am: the daughter of my bewildered father, who lacked any true intention to discern the path to a well-guided existence, and the daughter of my mother, who abused my father's bewilderment, sustained herself on his straying, and struggled to outsmart life – as much as she could, given her native intelligence, her limited education, and her contrivances born of need. I grew up amid ample human flesh spreading out in a narrow home, the collision of demands and the entanglement of wishes, with much food that did not fatten me very much or satisfy my greedy desires. There were even more cautions about money going where it should not, as losing it was likely, even when it was trussed, bundled into small bags, and enclosed in the contours of the secret hiding places.

I stopped hiding small banknotes in books after the books became reference works (not necessarily read) for my sisters, who by a chance I had not foreseen came across five dinars inside *Chronicle of a Death Foretold*; the book had fallen from my hand when I dozed off as I read it. I had put the note in the pages where Santiago Nasar still had a chance of escaping, despite the unequivo-cal title. From that time on I dispensed with the pages of books as hiding places, since my mother and sisters rifled through them line by line, and contented myself with my handbag, which carried all my wealth wherever I went. It helped that even in the best of circumstances, that wealth never exceeded several dinars and a few coins. In the beginning I was happy with large women's satchels with many interior pockets. I would distribute the money in every pocket, leaving only a little in the pocket close to hand and hiding most of it (which was still not much) deep inside, and using a coin purse for the change. This was not to hide some of the money but rather to delay spending it, so I could push the feeling of need deeper into my unconscious. It was to protect it from being lost, adding to an overall sense of loss – of everything and anything – that had made its home in my thoughts and remained with me wherever I went in life. I was someone who didn't try to find a thing so much as I feared losing it.

Then I came to prefer university-style shoulder bags that had a casual, youthful look, with endless internal and external flaps and folds. They could harbour hard-to-digest plays by Williams (like Shakespeare's *Hamlet* or Congreve's *Love for Love*), part of the required reading for English Drama, as well as literary articles cut from the newspaper's cultural supplement, some passages marked in red pen. They could hold the literary magazine *Al-Adab*, folded so that its distinguished title protruded from one of the external pockets of the bag, and scraps of coloured paper that contained writing with new ideas, newly minted ideas of the newly educated, not of the newly modern. There were many pencils missing their erasers or with chewed ends, the result of ideas rattling around my head without producing anything worthwhile. This was owing to a strange delusion on my part, in those distant days, with no basis whatsoever, that great words might descend on me from the realms of inspiration at any moment; consequently, I had to maintain a high degree of readiness, so the vessel of my writing would be ready to catch them. That does not mean that I have been cured of my delusions today, nor that I have caught much of value from the words that did descend. What came down to me gave me neither happiness nor understanding nor illumination. Instead my words themselves often increased my darkness, loss, and straying.

My father, based on his extensive experience of being lost and losing things, taught me to take necessary precautions, such as having a shoulder bag with a long strap. That way it could be suspended on one side and hang down on the other, so it would not be easy for some hand to snatch it, in a strange country that we did not know and where we could be robbed at any time. I likewise learned to distribute money in the few spaces that accompanied my peripatetic existence, so my handbag was not the only mobile treasury. I avoided putting money in the outside pockets of my clothes, where it could be seen and where light fingers could reach it easily. I shoved some of my wealth in the dark hollows of my shoes, after wrapping it in a tissue so that it would not soak up the yeasty odour of sweat from my feet, just as a few dinars slumbered on torpid days on the bed of my breasts. These last had attained their feminine form at their natural time, but even at a later stage, they were never as wise a hiding place as my aunt Rahma's breasts, which were extremely sturdy and expressive, amazingly outspread and ample, ample both in compassion and in money. It was certain that my experience in this area could never match that of my aunt. At times my consciousness of the money sleeping on my youthful breast might be dulled, as I was taken by enthusiastic, quasi-revolutionary talk about life; about school or university, as an official, organised institution; about God, whom I was trying to decipher; and about fathers, the other face of God, both potent and impotent. I would talk a lot, and so would my body; I would reflect a bit, and my body would settle, reluctantly, as I tried to understand what others were saying, or seem to understand. I would laugh loudly at a dirty joke. Meanwhile, the small amount of flesh stuffed into my bra would strain and the edge of a folded banknote would pop up from the opening of my blouse, restlessly escaping the bra and the heat of my breast, in the unbridled intensity of my emotions. It would meet the eyes of my classmates and partners in the discussion, who would be surprised by the sight and reminded of stories of aunties keeping locked safes in their breasts. As for me, I was a failure as an auntie, they said, laughing.

On those nights that did not allow for much roaming or any secret acts of the sort needed for emotional growth or bodily release, because of the many people competing for a cramped space, I would bury the money under my mattress. On winter evenings when rain buffeted our thin windows, the youngest of my sisters would fly from her bed to land on mine, curling her body next to me and taking over my space with her little limbs. The rain would slap against our walls from the outside, on the verge of coming right through them, and I would dream that I was tossing on sheets made of the sea itself, still wetter because of rain from above. When I woke I examined my money; it was soaked by my sister's pee, which had not stopped flowing all night long. I stood at the kitchen window, seeking the morning, while the sun stood at its borders. The symptoms of winter had lightened and the sky had pulled off its clouds by their dark woolly collars. I spread the notes on the window ledge, waiting for them to dry, while I drank hot coffee. Its appetising aroma mixed with the overwhelming morning stench of pee coming from my pyjamas, and from the money brushed by an innocent breeze announcing the beginning of the day.

Then when the money increased, though it never increased very much, and the likelihood of losing it also increased, I developed a secure hiding place that seemed sensible to me, which I depended on for years of my life (a life that weighed me down more than it lifted me up). I contrived the idea of a mobile, secret safe by turning a small sock into a pouch for money that I pinned on the inside of my pants. The credit for inventing it does not belong to me; rather Maryam showed it to me, the teacher of Arabic language and my colleague in the school where I worked for six years in al-Rusaifa in Jordan. Maryam's company appealed to me from the first day. Like all the teachers, she was presumably a believer, and conformed to wearing a full hijab in company. But unlike others, she did not act as if God or anyone else owed her anything because of her faith; she did not pray aloud for me to be set on the right path, nor did she see in my status as a young divorcee any reason for feminine wariness of me. She was less certain than others and more questioning concerning the nature of her relationship to God on the one hand, and her relationship to the many imposed religious rituals on the other; for what need did God have – God the rational, who managed His affairs without us – for all these formalities in worship? But when the sound of Qur'an recitation rose into the air from somewhere nearby, announcing a death, Maryam would become concerned, repeatedly ask forgiveness of her Lord, and set about all the prescribed rites, the supererogatory before the obligatory ones. Then, when the fear faded and talk of the torments of the tomb and the horrors of hell receded, along with the gatherings exhorting to faith and warning of inattention, Maryam would return to her old habit of questioning and avoiding certainty. She was charming, merry, and perceptive, with a laugh that never left her face, white like a peasant's and tinged with a natural red that was not muted by any modern beauty products. She confessed to me that she stopped at the pavement displays of used books in the market to buy novels, taking them into the house behind her husband's back, and that she liked to buy the newspaper from the shops in the morning, excited by the smell of the paper. I sneaked other books to her, beyond novels. She would read them voraciously and then come to me to discuss what she had understood or tried to understand, confiding her observations to a small notebook slipped inside her book of lesson plans.

When our relationship became firmly anchored, even as our colleagues found it strange that a believer and a bare-headed woman would spend time together, Maryam opened up to me about old secrets left to rust – men she had loved, words she had written, ideas still suspended from the clothes lines of her imagination, which had been cut. She mocked herself as much as other people. She showed no enthusiasm for her work, which she accepted as the one choice open to a woman expected to work in an intellectually degenerate, exclusively female environment, to marry, and to bear children. She timed her childbearing for the months of the school year, avoiding marital encounters that might lead to an untimely pregnancy and a useless delivery during the long summer holidays. She despairingly counted the days and even the minutes, using her fingers, until her hoped-for early retirement, when she would be free to raise her three girls and the one boy who had come to her recently, silencing her mother-in-law's nagging. Perhaps she would have a second longed-for boy, and a third for good measure. Maryam contented herself with delivering the bare minimum of the curriculum, relying on the adage, "Sit at your desk or shit on the pot, you'll end up in the very same spot." Like most of the teachers, she only gave what she was forced to offer at one or two grade levels, emerging victorious, if with difficulty, from the battle over the teachers' schedules at the beginning of the year. Maryam had held on to the seventh and eighth grades without any changes since she first became a teacher, amid a saga of shouts, quarrels, battles, and insults that ended with teachers in tears when they had been saddled with higher-level classes, demanding preparation, studying curricula new to them, and maybe even reviewing knowledge they had forgotten, if they ever had it to start with. I was more interested in my profession than Maryam was, having recently discovered (though it was hardly a pioneering discovery) that teaching was a government job in Jordan that was very accessible to a "Palestinian" like me.

I became reconciled to my profession as a teacher in Kuwait and then in Jordan. I tried to be proud of it. Among other things, I played the role of differing just for the sake of difference. I wished for change, while inside I wanted revolution. In fact it pleased me to convince my ego, slightly swollen because the classes for the final, *taujihi* exam year had been assigned to me, that I could fashion a generation. My ego stayed swollen even once it became clear to me that the final-year classes were a pain in the arse, avoided by all but the deluded. In one of the zones of despair in

67

Jordan, I was trying to shake the moths out of the students' heads while they were shaking out the moths, naphtha flakes, and the smell of mothballs attached to their cheap winter coats. I urged them to get rid of everything inherited from fathers and siblings, and to tear up the commands of the women in their environment. Those women had embarked on education with difficulty, and minimally, only so long as it led to a degree that would open the door to government work, to any work, and might perhaps widen the choice of grooms. No longer would the likeliest groom be the mechanic's boy with grease on his arms and neck, or the conductor of worn-out buses with dirt and dried dung under his nails, the ones who followed them with their eyes and words on the way to school. For the girls I taught, I discovered that school constituted a coercive upbringing that was an extension of their upbringing in the home. The few times I summoned the mothers of students who had not shown any improvement to a parent–teacher conference to discuss the matter, they simply left me to deal with it. "Break her head," or "Trample her belly," they told me. They accompanied the open invitation with a demonstration, such as the mother raising her foot a little and then lowering it resolutely to the ground, to show trampling; for greater spite she moved her foot left and right on the floor to indicate crushing, and emphasised the word "belly". One might give me an open licence to kill: "Shoot her, ma'am!" Another mother was not ashamed to mention the way to kill her daughter: "Put a bullet in the middle of 'er forehead, sitt!" I asked Maryam about the meaning of killing in this way, especially since the mother mimed the action with disgust disfiguring her features. Maryam laughed and explained to me that in some village traditions, killing by aiming a bullet at the middle of the forehead was a method of execution chosen for prostitutes.

I did not resort to trampling or shooting, however. I believed that deviating from the school curriculum within forgivable limits might open heads, without the need to break them. I explained to them that the assigned novel *Animal Farm* did not condemn communism as such, as the official curriculum planners wanted educators to suggest. George Orwell believed in democratic socialism, and he was opposed to Stalinism as a totalitarian form of government. The novel builds an imaginative dystopia in order to condemn totalitarian regimes wherever they are found, even if they are found here . . . yes, here or in any other place, under deceptive names such as a monarchy or a republic, the other face of monarchy in our Arab world. Names and descriptions do not reflect reality; in fact, the intention might be to use them to conceal it. The legacy of Stalinism was more than distress for our hearts, which have started to collapse in the middle of beating, due to strokes coming from subjugation. "Miss Abla's husband, Miss Abla the history teacher – he died of a stroke last year at the age of thirty-eight. The government put him in prison and when he came out he never found work. He was four years without work, smoking cigarettes for breakfast, lunch, and dinner." The student spoke in tones of sorrow and comprehension, as if she had at last found the secret of the death of Miss Abla's husband. I knew I had gained their attention, and that the hardened shell of their heads had cracked a little under their thick hijabs, when they trained their eyes on me and asked for explanations: *What's communism, miss? What does "democratic socialism" mean? Miss, what's dystopia, and what's Stalinism?*

"Are you with the monarchy, miss?" asked a student, with an ambiguous smile. It could be understood as curiosity, or it could very well conceal a hidden purpose.

I answered, staring straight into her eyes:

"Of course! I'm with the constitutional monarchy."

"What does that mean?" The students' voices were intertwined, and the bell sounded for the end of the period. "How are we going to find the answer?"

I wrote three English words on the board, ordering them vertically so that each one led to the next: *Question, Research, Answer*. They looked at me, lost – some frightened, others motivated, many resentful of the English language teacher who stood in front of them, bare-headed, in trousers of a masculine cut and a silk blouse beneath which the outline of her bra appeared. She was not seen in the school prayer room with the other teachers, who spread rumours about her. I was speaking to the resentful ones in particular, reminding them of the first word recorded in the text of the Qur'an. They looked at me still more resentfully. I set the chalk on the edge of the board and looked at them as I left the classroom:

"Read!"

The next day, I was summoned by Sitt Aisha, director of the school. She gave me a crooked smile, much like the smile of the "monarchy" student. A silence twisted between us, broken by a cautious psychological battle carried out in our eyes. Then she explained to me that the *taujihi* curriculum in any subject was long and exhausting for both students and teachers; therefore teachers should not waste time in talk that had no relation to the curriculum, and that could cause harm. "Harm for whom?" I asked, watching her expression as it changed from patience to temper. She took a last sip from her cup of coffee, then overturned the cup onto the saucer and rested her cheek on her hand. She said, forming her statement as a question: "Why are you absent from the morning line-up every day?"

The distance from the family house in al-Jabal al-Abyad in the heart of Zarqa, to the school on al-Jabal al-Shamali at the far end of Rusaifa, took three connections and often more than an hour, including the wait time. I had agreed with Sitt Aisha that I would take the *taujihi* classes, after the other teachers had firmly declined them, in exchange for being excused from first period. "But your being excused from first period does not mean always being absent from the morning line-up." She relaxed on her old leather chair, then put on her glasses and assumed an air of serious concentration on administrative procedures, muttering without raising her eyes:

"I could write a report to the Directorate of Education, explaining that you intentionally miss the morning line-up in order to avoid saluting the flag."

I don't understand this insistence on love of country, I said to Maryam. *Why isn't it enough for the country just to love us, unrequitedly? Isn't this the wise, intelligent, understanding father, who comprehends the straying of his children and even their insolence and unbelief at times?* When I was appointed by the Ministry of Education, I was required to complete several formal procedures, including giving the oath of loyalty, which I had never heard of before. In the Directorate building, I was brought into the office of someone addressed as "Your Excellency". He was absorbed in an angry telephone conversation, but motioned towards two books, large volumes bound in dark-blue leather and placed on the edge

71

of his desk. I did not understand what he wanted, or what I had to do with the books; for a moment I thought they were the school curriculum. He held the telephone receiver away from his ear, not caring that the other party would hear our conversation, and asked if I were Muslim or Christian. Then he gave me one of the books; it was the Qur'an, and I realised that the other was the Bible. He asked me to repeat after him the oath he recited hastily, still holding the receiver: "I swear by Almighty God that I will be loyal to the King and the country . . ." I repeated the lilt of the words without pronouncing them, as if mumbling them, while His Excellency ended his conversation swearing by God that he would not accept a penny less than the price of the land! He replaced the receiver irritably and then looked at me, examining my wicked heart. He asked me to recite the oath again because he did not hear it clearly, perhaps because I seemed to him to be mumbling and not really speaking, as he put it smugly, pulling on one of his dyed sideburns. He added that these tricks, such as mumbling, would not work with him. I refused. He threatened me:

"I could write a report to the minister, miss, saying that you refused to take the loyalty oath."

I raised my head, pushing a stray lock of hair off my forehead, and said: "And I could write a report to the minister, Your Excellency, saying that you allowed me to swear the loyalty oath without listening because you were busy with a telephone conversation about selling some land in Jubeiha."

Maryam warned me not to take "Ayush" lightly, using her diminutive nickname for Sitt Aisha, for her power to harm had been proven. She had a long record of slandering teachers, resulting in disciplinary penalties for them or in their being exiled to distant schools. She might write a report that would put a premature end to my career. But Ayush might find herself obliged to put up with me, concluded Maryam, because of the difficulty of finding teachers for the final year – especially since I had managed to please the students and their families in less than two months, and the reputation of the "clever" English teacher had grown, the one who looked like a foreigner with her mannish trousers and tight shirts, and who spoke English like a native, *mashalla!*

Then the teachers' money began to disappear. A teacher would go to the staffroom after the end of class, dusty with chalk, the routine of the lesson, and waning enthusiasm, and find the handbag she had left on the table open. She would rummage through the compartments hysterically, then slap her face or pull on her jilbab and cry, swearing that the missing five or ten dinars were all there was in the house until the end of the month, still ten days away. If she was graced by a strong faith in destiny, believing that we are afflicted only by what God has ordained for us, then she would confine herself to saying, "There is no power or might save in God," crying faintly and modestly as befitted someone who was patient and pious. Then if she couldn't control her crying, she would throw off her piety temporarily and weep and wail, following the example of her colleagues who were less firmly attached to blind fate, slapping her face hysterically and wailing. The most alarming display of all was the day that Sitt Manal, the vocational education teacher, lost her gold bracelet with its pear-shaped tips. She had brought it with her in her bag and was going to take it to the goldsmith at the end of the school day to sell it, so she could pay to renew the licence for her husband's bus, which he used to take children to the nursery school next to his work

73

in the municipality, earning something extra on the side. Sitt Manal did not shout or cry. Her eyes rolled up, she gasped, and then she fainted.

Within a month, more than half of the teachers had experienced a theft. Panic spread through the school, and Sitt Aisha mounted a relentless campaign of inspection that included the teachers' lockers, bags, and pockets. She said openly that the thief was one of us, virtuous educators that we were, and that she, the thief, was well informed about our circumstances, our handbags, and our schedules, so she could choose the appropriate time to strike. The inspection campaign also included the students' bags, school smocks, and desks, twice a day, at the beginning of the first period and before the end of the last period. Sitt Aisha issued emergency decisions as part of her martial law: the students were forbidden to come into the staffroom for any reason, and the teachers who sat in the staffroom (the main scene of the thefts) during their free periods were to report any suspicious movement made by any colleague, something they described as "legitimised snitching". The decision was made to require us to carry our handbags to our classes – something that hardly seemed appropriate if we accepted that the students were under suspicion, since we would then be bringing the spoils to them.

I read fury on Maryam's face when she threw her lesson-planning notebook on the table where we sat in the staffroom, scattering chalk dust in the air and making the muddy tea tremble in our cups. A peasant flush blazed in her face, and a few copper-coloured locks of hair escaped from under her grey hijab. Her blue eyes (emphasised by her contact lenses) were spitting fire. She began clapping her hands as if she were shouting insults at a neighbour. I was correcting exam papers and lifted my head in enquiry.

"That piece of shit Ayush has doubts about us!"

I did not understand what she meant and widened my eyes seeking more clarity. She explained quickly, studding her words with every possible insult to the honour of Sitt Aisha and her family, that the director and some of her tail-wagging operatives (as Maryam termed them) among the teachers were spreading it around that they believed that we, Maryam and I, were behind the thefts from the teachers' bags. It seemed illogical to me. I wondered:

"Because we haven't been robbed?"

A number of teachers had not been robbed, so why would she accuse us? Maryam gave me a half-insinuating look, as if to say, *Are you that stupid, or just pretending?* She didn't wait for me to arrive at the one logical explanation, in her view, but gave it in words that reflected her underlying spite:

"Because you and I are Palestinians."

"But nearly half the teachers are Palestinians."

She shook her head, unconvinced. "*They* have turned themselves into Jordanians!"

I wasn't convinced that Sitt Aisha would accuse me or Maryam of the theft just because we were open about being Palestinian, even if that openness was considered indictable. Inside I knew that she was motivated by a personal dislike for me and Maryam, by mixed feelings of jealousy and rejection. Maryam was confrontational, her intentions public, her feelings neither in agreement with the administration nor reconciled to it or to anything representing it. All the teachers, together with the director, feared her sharp tongue and avoided antagonising her, staying away at any cost from the evil shot out of her blue eyes. As for me, Sitt Aisha did not care for my stepping out of line inside class or outside it. She did not like my appearance, distinct from the others, who flocked together in their jilbabs, especially since I blocked her in her first attempt to show me the right path. Then when she found out that I was divorced and unconcerned about the adjective, openly joking that I pronounced the word as "liberated", she became more irritated by me. She most certainly did not like my inflammatory ideas. She might not object if I kept them to myself, and she was somewhat resigned if the sedition remained within the class. But if it was a matter of inciting the teachers of the good ship *Bounty*, which she was steering, she was not going to tolerate it. She bellowed into the confined space of the school if she discovered that I had inspired a teacher to deviate from the script she had set for her.

We have to catch the thief – that was the conclusion I came to with Maryam. Even though I didn't take Sitt Aisha's doubts seriously, nonetheless privately I couldn't shake a lack of confidence, not trusting my ability to dissipate these doubts by a strategy of indifference. I was also worried that the doubts would turn into a standing accusation, perhaps into an established crime. And then the looks we got from the teachers, since the doubts had begun to circulate more widely, put me on the defensive and reinforced Maryam's aggressive behaviour. If she thought, even mistakenly, that the conduct of a teacher diverged however slightly from its actual intended goal, she would quarrel with her verbally and stab her with her sharp tongue. Inside I was at odds with myself, fearing that my insistence on catching the thief was related in some way to Maryam's conclusion that the director's accusation was tied to our being outspoken about our Palestinian identity. The thefts did not stop, and one after another the teachers withdrew from the table where Maryam and I sat. They stopped drinking muddy tea with us during our common free periods, and whenever they saw us coming into the staffroom or leaving it they deliberately picked up their handbags and held them close to their chests.

I was visiting my grandmother Radiyya to take her the hair dye she had asked me for when she noticed the worried expression on my face. I explained the problem to her, and she nearly died laughing, beating on her belly. She was remembering a similar incident in her neighbourhood years before, when almost all the houses had been robbed before the thief was caught. As expected, it was one of the neighbour women, who knew the houses and their owners. I asked Grandmother Radiyya how they caught her, so she got up from the sofa in the front room, where she had been sitting cross-legged, and disappeared into the kitchen for a few minutes. She rummaged in the large wooden cabinet filled with jars, then returned with a small paper bag of red powder.

"What do I do with it?" I asked her, eyeing the blood-red powder.

Grandmother Radiyya enfolded me in a look that revealed a magic solution. "It's turnip dye. Its secret shows in water!"

Maryam was delighted with the solution, despite her initial resistance, believing that we should not be forced to disprove the accusation that Ayush had levelled against us. We had to persuade Sitt Nabila, the assistant director, to help us carry out the plan; she agreed under the pressure of my insistence, and to avoid Maryam's sharp tongue. She invited the teachers to a meeting in her office during the last period, making an exception for those who were teaching then. When the bell for the period rang, those teachers went to their classes and the others went to the assistant director's office, carrying their handbags. I left my own bag in the staffroom after putting five dinars, dipped in the powdered turnip dye, into the inner pocket. After ten minutes, we noticed the school caretaker, Umm Bakr, hurrying across the hall to the kitchen. I called her, and she stopped without turning around. She was folding her arms across her chest, her hands closed and tucked under her arms. I met Maryam's eyes, and we walked towards her. Umm Bakr walked away quickly, then began to run. Maryam and I ran after her, while the teachers watched us in amazement. Maryam jumped on Umm Bakr and threw her to the floor. Maryam tried to lift her by her shoulders, but Umm Bakr planted her heavy body, burying her arms beneath her. I helped Maryam to turn her over on her back and I sat on her. The teachers gathered around us watching the scene, as did the students and teachers from the classrooms that overlooked the open-air passage where Umm Bakr, Maryam, and I were engaged in a three-way physical struggle. Sitt Aisha came towards us, agitated and calling on us to let go of Umm Bakr, but we paid no attention. She tried to pull me off Umm Bakr but I shoved her away with my hand, then I bit one of Umm Bakr's hands, amid continuous screams from her, until she opened it. I found that the turnip dye was imprinted on her palm, but I did not find the five dinars. Maryam bit her other hand and she opened it, in pain, but we did not find the money. Maryam called for Sitt Nabila to bring a glass of water. Our shouts were mixed with the roars of Sitt Aisha, who was threatening to turn us, Maryam and me, over to the Directorate for investigation. Shouts rose from the girls who were watching the three-way struggle: "Yes, miss! Yes, miss!" Then traces of the red powder appeared on Umm Bakr's chest, so Maryam could only rip open her jilbab. Sitt Nabila was standing stupidly in front of us, asking Maryam if she wanted to drink the water. Maryam took the glass of water and poured it over Umm Bakr's chest, and a red stream ran from her chest to her neck. Umm Bakr relaxed, submitting, so I opened the rest of the buttons of her jilbab, still holding her down. From beneath her white bra with the dissolved red on it, I pulled out the five dinars. They had not slept long on the bed of her breasts, completely dyed in red.

What was unknown to Sitt Aisha and the teachers, whatever their allegiances and origins, was that ever since the dramatic increase in the series of thefts, Maryam and I carried our handbags to school only for show, or for keys, sandwiches, or other inconsequential things. Maryam had recommended to me the sock for money (an idea she took from an aunt of hers), which we fastened to our knickers with a safety pin. Maryam would lean over me, patting her pants and whispering in hushed gaiety,

"This is the one thing we will never take off unless we want to!"

I carried the secret money sock in my pants even when I left the school, when I left the city and the country foreign to me, when I left its lives behind me. I travelled through many places of absence with it, and thanks to it I created a sense of temporary security, feeling its quiet bulge at the edge of my pants, whenever the feeling of loss loomed from my own diaspora. Until the time for the renewed diaspora came, Maryam and I sat at our usual table in the staffroom, resting our feet on the table, eating zaatar mana'ish pastries and calling Umm Laila, the recently hired school caretaker, to hurry with our tea. Maryam told her that Umm Bakr, may God ease her path and remember her good deeds, was cleverer than she was and moved more lightly. Then we cracked up, our loud laughter splitting the sky in the room, while the other teachers gathered the shame that clung to their jilbabs, and avoided looking at us.

We were two happy Palestinian queens, Maryam and I, sipping seasonal pleasures along with our muddy tea.

CHAPTER THREE

Concerning Our Names

(Not Ninety-Nine, and Not Beautifully Divine)

It has reached me, O auspicious queen, whose desires teem and whose ideas contravene common sense . . .

You don't like your name. You don't sense yourself, so magnificent without any magnification, in its magnificence and glory. The impression of grandeur that it gives does not please you, and you confide to others, present with you when I am absent, that your name intimidates you, especially if someone calls you by it, and you look up fearfully. You hide it away, as if it feels too much for you.

Know then, Your Majesty, that names, like religions, are not something we choose. If we are able to shed the tribe's religion, by later, rational thought and by great conscious effort, nonetheless we are not able to shed a name. It becomes our own thing, a part of our innate character. You might be surprised at how much we derive our meaning, and even its opposite, from our names, which are bound to our flesh to some extent as we are formed, to a greater extent amidst the dilemmas that form our lives, and to a still greater extent in the final form to which we come. It's not only, my sovereign, that we have something of our name, as the saying has it. No, the name is our allotted share in life, even if it disappoints us – and it may be all the more fitting as its meaning may come from its opposite. For it is destiny, even if it's different from our desired destiny. Our names are our other face; they are what is behind the face with which we confront the world.

If the name transgresses a power greater than ours, however, it turns into a burden for us, becoming an abiding concern that might make our life miserable. Just ask my mother about what happened to her paternal aunt Qadira! My mother told the story of her aunt Qadira ("Powerful") to us, just as she told it to the neighbour women, as she told it to strangers with whom she shared the six-bed ward in the maternity hospital during her eight deliveries, as she told it to strangers with whom she waited in infant vaccination clinics, and just as she told it to everyone she came across in life. Qadira was fifteen when she married, and five years passed without a pregnancy. They made the rounds of midwives and doctors, including a famous German doctor with a clinic in central Amman, without learning any clear reason for her belly's refusal to harbour the seed. Qadira's mother was afraid that her son-in-law would turn against her daughter, so she searched and enquired, and respectable people told her about a shaykh called "the Arab Shaykh", in whose hands the shackles of secrets were broken, even those buried in the deepest depth of a raging sea. When Qadira's mother went to him, calling to her daughter, "Come in, Qadira!" the Arab Shaykh jumped up immediately, asking God's forgiveness, and shaking himself and his aura of goodness to chase away any devils of accursed names that might be hovering over him. Thus he solved the secret of the curse without any deep thought or complicated manoeuvres; for the name Qadira had brought barrenness on her and sterility had stricken her womb. That was because it trespassed on the power of God, who alone is the Powerful over everything, who alone is the Potent and the Omnipotent, who alone is the Lord of Power. Qadira wrote her name on a piece of paper five times horizontally and five times vertically, as the Arab Shaykh asked of her. Then she burned the paper, gathered the ashes, and dissolved them in a bowl of water; she carried it herself to a land she traversed on a journey, and poured the water containing her burnt name onto a desert with neither crop nor cattle. Then the Arab Shaykh bestowed upon her Khadra ("Green") as a new name. Khadra conceived, and her womb neither dried up nor found any rest, for she bore so many girls and boys she couldn't nurse them enough. In the end her husband took a second wife, because he discovered that he had disliked her for some time as a woman, not because of the sterility of her womb. Nonetheless the intended moral of the story of my mother's aunt Qadira is that her name, or its history, stayed with her, and we went on calling her "Mother's aunt Khadra whose name used to be Qadira".

Perhaps it would have been better for our neighbour Umm Muaadh if she had changed her name, as my mother teased her. That's because her name was as close as could be to a cruel irony in her life. Umm Muaadh's mother had bestowed on her the name "Mahziyya" ("Lucky"; often, "Mistress"), changing the *z* to a *d* to make it easier to pronounce, so that it became "Mahdiyya". Most likely Mahdiyya had no idea of the meaning of her name or of its history, and never stopped to think about its lusty connotations. When she married her cousin Abu Muaadh, who was a carpenter's apprentice, the groom left the house on the wedding night and returned in a sulk to his family's home. It was no secret that Fayez ("Triumphant"), as he was before he had children and became Abu Muaadh, was passionately in love with Mahdiyya's sister Hadiyya ("Gift"), who was much more beautiful than she was. But her family wanted someone better than a carpenter's apprentice for Hadiyya, so they saddled him with Mahdiyya for a dower payment of only one dinar, and delivered her to him with a full trousseau. But Fayez's heart remained with Hadiyya, who married a veterinarian and then emigrated with him to Australia, where she had three sons and the family bought a farm. Hadiyya took off her hijab, dyed her hair blonde, and began wearing shorts. She came to be known in the new, distant country as Hadya, rather than Hadiyya, and she sent back many cheerful family pictures of herself, her husband, and their sons, with their foreign looks, playing on their farm. The farm's green colours delighted the eye, and the pictures could have been printed as postcards. It was said, on the word of the midwife, that Mahdiyya was exposed to a strong draught when she was born; it caused a downward slant on one side of her mouth, a tremor in one of her cheeks, like constant blinking, as well as the narrowing of one eye, and the lifting of one eyebrow, in a way that made her appear constantly surprised and uncomprehending. Mahdiyya can lose herself in an enormous laugh, not caring that it reveals a dark, empty space on one side of her mouth, where she lost two teeth to a punch from Abu Muaadh, who was always angry. She told my mother how poor Fayez felt his heart sink when he saw her in her make-up on the wedding night, for the lipstick emphasised her crooked mouth and the eyebrow pencil made her look as if she was making fun of him. Mahdiyya later learned that his mother slapped him with a slipper when he went back and taunted him, saying that the woman was the one who shied away from the marriage bed, not the man. He was compelled to go back to Mahdiyya's bed, but he held out for more than forty days without going near her. At last his uncle threatened to take his daughter back to his house, along with her gold jewellery and her household furnishings, so Fayez was forced to consummate the marriage. But he prepared the way by beating her with a cane until she was swollen all over, so that Mahdiyya became convinced that Abu Muaadh was aroused by beating her.

Mahdiyya did not change her name, but she did separate herself from it. Otherwise it would have been hard for her mouth to remain open in abundant guffaws and swooning laughter, despite the successive diminishing of her teeth. In fact, she derived original meanings from her name, apart from its historical allusions, telling my mother – as if gloating over Abu Muaadh – "Fayez, I fucked up *his* luck!" Then it would be hard for her or for my mother to hold on to their gales of laughter.

My maternal aunt Rahma ("Mercy"), for her part, did not separate from her name, but her name decided to separate from her, even though she continued to beg for mercy. Rahma had developed a home-based *biznis* that allowed her to push her husband Mundhir out of her life, at least materially, even though he did not stay out. She sold peas and green beans, which she shelled, processed, and packed in bags for freezing. She also bought pounds and pounds of mouloukhiya greens and then sold them either as dried leaves, or as dried and rubbed, or as ground and frozen, upon request. She was famous in her quarter for preparing the best dishes of maftoul, to which she added her own special spice mix. Then she extended her services to taking in pounds of marrows and aubergines from her neighbours, hollowing out the vegetables rapidly and precisely, without splitting the waist of a baby marrow or piercing the bottom of an aubergine. Finally, my aunt became a real caterer, cooking what the women of the quarter and of neighbouring quarters ordered. She might prepare an entire dinner *boufay* or savoury dishes for birthdays, with pastries, vine leaves, and fried kibbe meatballs, for women who came to her with the condescension of the superior quarters of West Amman. They did not leave their dark cars, merely honking the horn rapidly; Aunt Rahma and her daughters would hurry out with the dishes covered in aluminium foil. Aunt Rahma could not escape her husband Mundhir, who wrung her money out of her, and who abused her spirit and her body in front of her daughters, even though they stood as an ineffective barrier between him and their mother. Samah, the youngest, would climb on her father's back and plant the spurs of her heels in his hips; she might bite his neck, overcoming him temporarily, before he threw her on the floor with violent hands. Meanwhile, her sisters took the greatest quantity of the kicks and blows aimed at their mother.

My grandmother Radiyya says that Aunt Rahma has bought her own trouble (i.e., her husband) with money, and that it would be better for Rahma to have mercy on herself and not wait for God's mercy from on high, because God, as Grandmother Radiyya sees it, "doesn't have time to take care of every little thing for His servants". Grandmother Radiyya has not entered Aunt Rahma's house for years because of her husband Mundhir, "a pair of old shoes" as she calls him, meaning the lowest of the low. She expresses her unhappiness with Aunt Rahma by saying that she chooses to be beaten, insulted, and plundered by a pair of old shoes rather than to be called a divorcee. Aunt Rahma insists on visiting Grandmother Radiyya with her daughters, trying to soften her mother's heart by pointing to them, daughters who have grown up without anyone ever coming to knock at their door. "It's because of the girls!"

My grandmother Radiyya ("Content") was not content with many things in her own life. She had insisted on being divorced from my grandfather Amran, even though he adored her; she says that a time came when she woke up and found that she did not love him. Even when "that" illness assailed her body and shattered it cruelly, she kept on looking in the mirror, searching for a forgotten body, for abundant, lustrous hair, and for a distant face that had long enchanted the men of her neighbourhood (it had been very late to show its age, thanks to the moisturising creams she was devoted to using). Grandmother Radiyya yearned constantly for many things that played her false, that walked near her and then passed her by. She lived discontented and passed away still blaming life.

My father, however, was pleased with his life, or so it seemed to me. My father was Naeem ("Bliss"), and bliss was not his state but rather the name that was attached to him by force, for his bliss was barely enough to cover his nakedness and ours. Likewise my uncle Abu Taisir was Muwaffaq ("Blessed with Success"), a name that seemed to strut proudly but not in real life, where success shunned him. My mother was Rauaa ("Amazing Beauty"), with her square stature tending to roundness, her short fat legs, and her long broad laugh that seemed to split her face in two. The names complemented each other perfectly, however, in all their accumu-lated and assimilated meanings, in a scene where Naeem would fix his eyes like a sword (though not a sharp one) on the penetrat-ing eyes of Rauaa (very small for her round face), asking her about the monthly housekeeping money that had evaporated before the middle of the month. She would put her hands on her waist, even though it had in fact disappeared, and answer him in tones that alluded sarcastically to the bliss in which she lived with Naeem: "By God, I spent it all – one day on breakfast at the Holiday Inn, the next on lunch at the Sheraton, and another day the neighbour ladies and I had dinner at the Hilton." Then, giving free rein to her mockery, "Oh! And I also bought a diamond necklace!" – fingering a neck bare of anything except its own compact flesh. My father would lift his hands to heaven, entrusting his case to God, appealing for His wrath to descend on this creature, meaning my mother, and make her ugly. But she did not fear the consequences of his appeal. She would rapidly take the measure of her figure in front of him with her two short arms, and ask, with an annoying laugh, "Uglier than this?!" Then my father would swear that, from next month on, he would not entrust her with the responsibility of managing the household expenses. As always, Rauaa would make light of this oath, to the point of answering it with a fart, both metaphorical and actual, as she would produce a tuneful wind, its rhythm matching the rhythm of Naeem's threat. She would mourn the wealth she would miss, the bliss she would lose after Naeem confiscated the household allowance. "Gone are the days of indulgence and luxury!" she would lament, in a farcical performance. Naeem would shake his head, not dismissing her but deferring the accounting. In fact, even he knew very well, on the basis of previous, documented instances, that a few days after the noisy orgy of anger he would approach her, head bowed, seeking compassion and mercy from the well-spring of precautionary measures and shrewd management: might she help him with a little of what she kept in the secret hiding places, to pay for an inevitable repair to the car, or to settle a debt for which his payment was even more overdue than usual? This was even though she claimed that the secret hiding places did not exist, for Rauaa was a lioness, as Naeem said: "And the lioness's den is like the lion's, it always has bones!" Then on the first of the next month he would obediently put the housekeeping money into Rauaa's hand, perhaps counting on her practised skill in stretching the shrinking money to cover their existence, stretching in every direction – even if he was horrified, between one fearful moment and the next, by how money flowed out of his pocket in a series of thefts and losses for which there was no explanation.

The clash between Naeem and Rauaa is interrupted only by the ringing of the telephone. I answer, and a polite voice asks me if we will accept the reverse charge call, so I assume the caller is Grandmother Fatima or Uncle Muwaffaq. Grandmother Fatima asks Naeem to send her two hundred dinars. "This time the groom is guaranteed," she tells Naeem enthusiastically. In every phone call, Grandmother seems confident that "this time" success is the lot of Najah ("Success"), and that "this time" the groom will ask for her hand within days. One of the grooms was in a bigger hurry than all the other "guaranteed" grooms. He lived in America and had American citizenship, and he had a supermarket there; he had come to see his family in the camp, his visit was short, and he wanted to get married within a month so he could finish all the paperwork for his bride in the American embassy quickly and then take her home with him. But what made an American think of marrying Najah? Naeem could not hide his amazement, since he knew, as we all did, that the chances of grooms thronging to Najah were slight. Grandmother Fatima admits, grumbling, that the groom is "a little" older. It turns out that he's twenty-five years older than Najah, and that he was married to an American who gave him two sons before he divorced her; after he gained his citizenship and some dollars, he decided that "a girl from his own country" would safeguard his honour and his offspring better than the American. But the American groom who was "a little" older did not knock on Najah's door, though she had got her hopes up more than all the other times, on the basis of accepting the worst (which then did not accept her, as the saying goes). What Naeem later learned was that the American groom discovered that his citizenship and his dollars would get him a girl from the camp who was younger, prettier, and riper than Najah.

It might be Uncle Muwaffaq on the line, so Naeem would intuit that his rash brother was once again out of work. The owner of the vegetable stand where he worked, "the thoo, thon of a thoo" (shoe, son of a shoe) had fired him, because of a customer who was just as big a "thoo" as he was. It was for no reason except that he, that is Muwaffaq, had thrown a crate of tomatoes at the customer, who had "thpent more than an hour" turning over the tomatoes in it and examining each one "until he thplit them open", and then in the end he didn't buy a single tomato. Naeem tries to explain to Muwaffaq that he must moderate his temper, and Muwaffaq insists, as he does every time, that "thith time" he's in the right. Naeem discusses with him the possibility of mediation with the shop owner so he would take him back, if not for his sake, then at least for the sake of his children; but Muwaffaq bellows from afar that the job is lower than his "thoos", that his dignity comes first, "and that'th a matter", i.e. his dignity, that cannot be subject to bargaining or concessions. Then he asks Naeem to send him a sum of money, to "thee him through" until he finds work.

Naeem reads scenarios current and coming, none of them

encouraging for his situation or that of Muwaffaq; he sees dark clouds growing heavier and shrinking the possibilities for his life. He goes back to his pockets, the outside ones, the hidden ones, and even the secret ones, counting what he has, what might come, and what might enter the pockets of days to come: little money, precious and hesitant, imperfect blessing and grace that rushes to leak out of the wide holes in his life. What he might lose, and it is a lot, seems to him a torrent without value, like rain that falls on rocks and does not water the thirsty dirt. At that point clouds clad in the black of looming events gather in his mind, and he sits listlessly on the couch, as if he has just come from a shocking defeat; he puffs repeatedly on rough cigarettes, his face darkening and his deep-set eyes, with their lost expression, turning red. Rauaa comes to him, her face softened and her long, mocking laughter gone. Her eyes widen and spread over him a covering of compassion. She gives him her hand, smelling of the small, safeguarded home, holding many things and feelings and people, and cooking that's never left over due to the many souls with large appetites at mealtimes and all other times, too. Rauaa plants a kiss on Naeem's forehead, saying, "We'll manage, Abu Jihad."

My father yearned for a son as his first-born. He wanted the boy desperately and gave him his name before he saw him, unsheathing the desired name before he even married. "Abu Jihad", that was the title he chose for himself, in his bachelor days when he held fast to grand wishes. When I arrived as his first fruits my father did not disguise his disappointment, not because I was a girl but rather for the sake of the name. He was afraid it might be delayed, or that it might lose the impression it made on his friends, whom he had persuaded to use it for him. He admitted to himself that when they called him "Abu Jihad", he felt as if he was going to the top of the world and that loud drumbeats accompanied him on his way.

I went for five days without a name. I received money, dresses, gold *mashalla* necklaces (praising God's creation), and blue beads, gifts for the first-born daughter. Those whose arms took turns holding me competed in finding cheerful names, suited to a baby who was abundantly healthy. On the first day of my life, my mother wanted to name me Najla after the doctor who delivered me. "What do you think?" she asked my father; maybe I would grow up to become a doctor. But my father did not give his opinion. On the second day, my mother suggested "Maram" to him. "Whyever?" he asked. She told him that she had heard a woman in the street calling her daughter Maram and had liked the name, it was pretty. My father contemplated my face, looking for Maram, but he did not find it. OK . . . what do you think of Amal ("Hope"), suggested my mother on the third day. She practised calling me that all day, but when the day was over, Hope had disappeared. On the fourth day, my father was watching Farid al-Atrash in the film *Love of My Life*, and outside of any context related to my name, and without any forethought, he told my mother that he liked the dancing of Samia Gamal. My mother said that she would not name me Samia, but my father was not thinking about the name that night. On the fifth day, I was still without a proposed name.

On the sixth day, my father woke up and cried out "Jihad!"

My mother resisted the name. She tried desperately to keep me from being named Jihad. She cried, but my father's heart did not soften. She shouted at him and threatened to take me and leave the house without letting him know where in the world we were; he did not budge from the castle of his conviction. She pleaded with him to leave his Jihad for a son. "And if a son doesn't come?" he wondered, fearing the absence of the name, not the absence of the son. She suggested that he record my name as something else on the birth certificate and call me Jihad, or even Piece of Shit. He announced decisively, "Jihad! Jihad only!"

My mother gave in. She did achieve a partial victory, however, when she prised a promise out of my father that he would leave the names of the other probable daughters to her, whereas the boys' names would be up to him.

A second daughter came a year and a half later. "See? What did I tell you? The son did not come!" he said to my mother, as if he were gloating over her. Then a third daughter came two years

95

after the second, and my father revelled in his wisdom and in having held fast to it from the beginning, since "Jihad" would have come very late if at all. Then after two more years the son finally arrived, and he named him Jamal. My mother rejoiced over the long-awaited son, who shut the mouths of those in the family who feared that her belly would produce only girls. But the son was the reason for a dispute my mother did not expect to have with my father.

"Abu Jamal!" she greeted him, on the first morning after Jamal's birth. He gave her a warning look.

"Abu Jihad!"

My mother struggled to give my father the name of his son, as was the case for all fathers, but my father clung to his Jihad.

The second son came four years after the first, with one miscarriage and one daughter in the interval. My father gave him the name Nasir, as the completion of the name Jamal (after Gamal Abdel Nasir). Jamal and Nasir lived life on the sidelines, taking everything in the usual measure. Their lives passed with a smoothness so strange it was almost surreal. They embodied the complete cycle of life, based on growing, procreating, and cultivating existence with the minimum of acceptable effort in exchange for an acceptable degree of survival in the world. They did not stir up revolutions or participate in them or come under their influence. Both sons married at the expected age for males, biologically and socially, a few years after graduating and beginning work in dull government positions. Jamal studied economics at Yarmuk University in Jordan, then he was appointed to a department with limited work and no product – or nearly none – under the Ministry of Planning. He married a woman he did not know before he married her, through the good offices of one of the women of the neighbourhood, who acted as intermediary. He found what he was looking for in this bride: a woman who worked in a governmental administrative position and who shared his ambition of buying land, by means of a housing loan he would obtain through his job, and of building on it with another housing loan she would obtain from her job, as well as buying a used car on credit. Nasir, for his part, graduated from the Accounting Department of Mutah University, then was appointed to the Department of Lands and Survey. He married a girl suggested to him by respectable people, one who matched many of his requirements and aspirations. He shared her passion for travelling to Saudi Arabia every year to make the Umrah minor pilgrimage, an excursion that ended in a visit to Jeddah, the bride's family home, where they spoiled their daughter and her husband with the most delicious food, expensive abayas, eastern perfumes, and jellabiyas. Jamal had four sons and expected to add to that number, while Nasir was blessed with three and did not expect the number to increase, since all his wife's deliveries had been by Caesarean section.

Jamal and Nasir expressed their devotion to religion more than my father did. He always lived adjacent to religion and across from it, taking from it enough to keep his family and acquaintances from rejecting him. He always distinguished what belonged to the Lord from what belonged to Caesar, oscillating in the middle region of faith. He might wonder about what had become divine text and precept, not subject to question, and openly express his doubt; then a neighbour or friend or colleague would confront him with a rebuke because he was questioning what was not subject to question and doubting what was stable and established, something from which science and logic turned away. Then my father would refrain from questioning and doubting, and fulfil the required obligations minimally. When his sandals were stolen from the mosque during Friday prayers, in what was almost a weekly tradition, he would return home barefoot and bitter, his spirit in the dust, his tongue striking out left and right and cursing, internally, creation and the Creator.

When the third son and last of the desired males arrived three years later, after my mother had had a second miscarriage, my father was still harbouring delusions of freedom and independence. He chose Ahmad ben Bella as a compound name for the baby, not allowing it to be separated. My mother tried to object, but my father reminded her that he had not interfered with the names of the girls, which he had not agreed with at all. She tried to conciliate him by speaking softly. He relented a little and gave her the choice between two names: Ahmad ben Bella or Hwari Boumediene. She chose Ahmad ben Bella as the lesser of two evils, expecting logically that Bella would fall away from the name in time, and that Ahmad would endure. But what happened, as things naturally do in life, was that Ahmad never stood firm from the beginning; we and everyone else called him Bella. We enjoyed shouting for the little boy whose naughtiness drove us crazy, at home or in the street. In fact he was the reason my father was dragged to the police station more than once, including the day Bella stole the car keys, when he was ten, and crashed into the wall of an apartment building, destroying the car. The accident could well have ended tragically, with someone run over, if not for the grace of God the All-Knowing.

"Bella . . . Bella . . . Hey Bella!"

When he did not respond to the call, my mother would helplessly lift her hands to heaven and say,

"Bella, *balaa'* take you!" calling down a calamity on him.

Bella was the closest to me of my siblings despite the thirteen-year difference in our ages. If I had been created as a boy, as I wished in some periods of my life, I would have been Bella. I loved him, and for a long time I gave him my back as a barrier and curtain to hide behind when he fled from my mother or my father after one of his many sins. From his earliest childhood in Kuwait he loved to raise pigeons, using the kitchen balcony in the apartment for a few, after I interceded for him with my mother. I persuaded her that raising pigeons would pull him in from the street and keep him under her eyes most of the time, and she liked that idea, even if she regretted it later when the pigeon droppings began to bedevil us. When we were displaced to Jordan, after Iraq's Mother of All Battles in Kuwait, Bella found that the roof of our house in al-Zarqa was an ideal space to build a pigeon house, an obsession from which he could not easily be separated. He acquired dozens of pigeons, together with a deep knowledge of their species, the varieties of their behaviour, and how to shoo them away or attract them to his kingdom. Within a short time and by pure natural talent, he became a formidable pigeon keeper. He did not shrink from feeding his pigeons bread soaked in water the evening before he sold them, so they would seem fat and attract buyers, before becoming thin again the day after the sale. The people of the neighbourhood constantly complained about Bella and his pigeons, and about the stones he threw on the roof, shattering neighbours' windows on more than one occasion. One day, a pigeon keeper knocked on our door and accused Bella of stealing two pigeons from him. My mother destroyed the pigeon coop on the roof with a huge steel hammer, then she poured kerosene on it and burned it, shooing away the pigeons and throwing angry stones at any who tried to return. "All I needed was a pigeon thief!" she shouted furiously, as she brought the hammer down with determination on the wooden shelves. Bella cried for a long time, lamenting his creatures. He grew feverish from his sadness over the birds and was sick for a week. My mother went to him with kind words, trying to make the obstinate boy understand that the testimony of a pigeon keeper wasn't acceptable in court and that no-one would agree to marry their daughter to a "pigeon man" like him. From his ocean of tears, Bella cried,

"I want my pigeons! I don't want to get married!"

The pigeons and their era were gone. It took Bella a long time to recover from the loss of his creatures, but at last he did recover. For years, I concealed from him the events of that distant dawn, a month after the destruction of the coop and after my mother sprinkled poison on the surface of the roof to kill any pigeon that was tempted to return. That day, I was awakened by indistinct sounds that drew me from my bed to the roof. Dozens of pigeons stood on the metal frame of the television antenna erected in one corner. They were cooing in grief, lamenting someone dear.

For the girls my mother followed the fashion of delicate names, their letters few and their rhythm smooth, easy on the ear, soft in their effect on the soul; after me came Rania and Rima, with Rula between Jamal and Nasir, and last of all we greeted Rasha, our youngest, about five years after the birth of Bella. (My mother claimed that the pregnancy was accidental until we discovered that she had intentionally neglected the strip of pills to prevent pregnancy, in the hope that the number of males would balance the number of females, though we ended up outnumbering them even more.) My father did not like his daughters' names, finding them ugly and foolish, but he kept his promise not to interfere or object to them after he pulled me out of shallowness and gave me Jihad. Nor did my father understand my mother's insistence on the same initial for the daughters' names; he called it a stupid fashion, convinced that it was a feminine fad, along with the fad of names ending in a weak vowel, amputated of their final consonants, lacking any flavour, since they don't leave any taste to speak of on the tongue when they're pronounced.

My mother had one married cousin, who was her only relative in Kuwait. They visited each other regularly, on holidays and for congratulations on births. They were engaged in a contest of births, as no sooner would one come out of the hospital after a birth than the other would enter it; in fact, once they shared the same delivery room. But my mother's cousin had seven males, earning her more quality points than my mother. She also, like the other idiotic women, chose a single initial for them, the letter *ṭaa'*; she named her first-born Tayil, then followed him with Tariq, then Talal, Tahir, and Tamih. We visited them to fulfil our obligation to congratulate them on the day the sixth was born. My father came only under duress, since he didn't like my mother's cousin or her "jerk" of a husband, as he described him, who always acted high and mighty because of his position as a financial director in an insurance company. The mother, proud of what she had produced, complained to my mother that they still had not named the boy, since they had not found an appropriate male name beginning with *ṭaa'*. She was not raising the matter as a problem or a worry but rather to taunt my mother still more, since she claimed they never dreamed when they chose *ṭaa'* that they would have all these boys, who could not be accommodated by the letter. Since she was a believer, she was ceaselessly extending her hand in front of her as she spoke about her boys, imprinting her five fingers on the air as a precautionary charm to ward off the expected envy of my mother, who bore girls.

As a matter of fact, the cousin's boys were no cause for envy or delight, either for us or anyone else, for they were dull, slow, and listless, with a collective weight that was the other face of bad nutrition. They were raised and replete with milk-enriched bread, packs of high-fat cheese, rice cooked with clarified butter, and the meat fat that rose to the surface of the dish; all of that was reflected in their oily, fat bodies, engineered with a solid trunk that could not be melted away. In addition to their frightening stoutness, their faces exuded foolishness, as if stupidity had chosen to express its form through them. They were its symbol and its ignoble emblem, with their lifeless glances that faltered under sagging eyelids when they struggled to follow any talk or conversation, without seeming to understand or even to make any effort. When my father picked up the new baby born to the noble letter *ṭaa'*, he examined his puffy face, ready to acquire more fat and stupidity, and he was horrified that the infant was another edition, only a little smaller, of his dull brothers. My father, who was known for his tendency to make heavy, tasteless jokes rather than appropriate ones, and for having a sense of humour that was usually insensitive, said that he had found the most appropriate name for the baby. All eyes looked at him enquiringly, even the stupid ones, and he announced happily,

"Tabl!" ("Drum!")

I loved my sisters' names, and often, when my own name disappointed me, I wished for one of theirs. I was not enchanted with the initial *raa'* or with the meanings; rather I was taken with the lengthening at the end of the names, just waiting to escape, going on as long as it was possible for the voice to go. When my mother shouted for them to do something and they held back, the last syllable would continue to fly, in great yearning, clinging to the wings of space as if it never wanted to alight on the letters of their names again, as if the lengthening thought itself too grand to remain under the care of their dwarfed spirits. When the lengthening returned to them at last, or the scattered fragments of its echo, it fell back broken.

My sisters were not up to their names. They disappointed the lengthened syllables, and they folded and locked away their other letters, cutting them short consciously and unjustly. They resembled each other a lot, exchanging the same well-worn skills and pat convictions, uncompromising in dismissing their muddled fantasies, sharing feelings that remained immature for a long time, confused about how to explain love if they found it or about how to find it in the first place, since they did not understand that it is unconditional. Eventually this all turned into an emotional disability and physical listlessness. When their bodies awakened, and with them desires that must be expressed, they loved fleetingly, rationing what they gave of their bodies so as not to lose the chance of divine forgiveness. Then, as established wisdom would have it for girls with pre-packaged desires, they married the first one who knocked on their door, without bargaining or haggling. They watched their bellies swell, as they were given the fruit of motherhood. They were round-hipped, coddled, and completely convinced that they had attained the goal of life and represented its fulfilment. In the end they weren't bothered if their names dissolved, together with their lengthened syllables, and if their soft letters were concealed behind the form of their bodies, which became very round, as was suitable for their precious motherly titles. Life was secure and peaceful, with no deviation expected in their desires.

I remained myself . . . Jihad, the last letter "silenced" by stripping it of any following vowel to mark a case, after a lengthening that tried to be longer. There was no security and no peace in the silencing of my last letter. Silencing the final letter might keep me from making a grammatical error, but it could not guarantee that I would not make mistakes.

I did not argue over my name, at least not with myself, when I was first being formed. Along with all the fabrications of life, my name dominated me. It cast a long shadow beside me, then it swallowed me. I tried in vain to get out from inside it.

I am Jihad, O queen of my past and my present. I am the struggle I did not choose, the jihad I did not ask for.

My name did not seem strange or forced, to me or to others, despite its tyrannical masculinity, its proud tone, and its fighting spirit. There were many other girls named Jihad in my generation. Our fathers, who were from the first generation following the Nakba in 1948, poured out on us their expectations for jihad, their dreaming predictions of a noble, pure, genuine, and ethical revolution, trimmed of all intrigue, protected from being infiltrated, preserved from turning against itself – expectations exaggerated under the influence of exile and the countries of the diaspora. The name acquired a special momentum in Kuwait, perhaps because the Palestinian revolutionary movement embraced its first leading personalities there, so we believed that we were very near to Palestine. In school, during the years of idle play, a unified curriculum, simple education, and going along with others' perceptions, I knew more than one Jihad. The classes overflowed with revolutionary names, such as Nidal, Kifah, Fida', and Intisar ("Struggle", "Battle", "Sacrifice", "Victory"). There was one decisive name with

105

respect to the certain results of the revolution, which I encountered at least once: Tahrir ("Liberation"). This Tahrir liberated herself from school after her middle-school diploma and got married. I was a classmate of Jaffa and Beisan, neither of whom could place their cities on the map. All of that was before the ebb tide took away our jihad, our struggle, and our sacrifice, before purity pulled away from our revolution. Then, after our era that had been nourished by illusions, names stripped of illusion came to our school classes and our life, names cleansed of irrational expectations, inciting revolution less and counting more on unseen forces, such as Duaa', Isra', Ala', Aya, and Ayat ("Prayer", "Ascension", "Blessings", "Sign", "Miracles"). Like their names they turned themselves over to God, the only one capable of returning Palestine to us from the river to the sea, a promise referred to in God's precious word.

In the second, third, and fourth years of middle school, Palestine was always with me. She wore a hijab, she was ugly, and she was academically delayed, so "all flaws met in her", as my mother whispered to me when she saw her. But my father, with his humour that lacked any sense of propriety, did not conceal his alarm when he met Palestine for the first time, saying to her face, "If Palestine looked like you, they would have thought twice before seizing it!" I faked a laugh to keep Palestine from understanding the disgusting joke, but she did not notice the unamusing implications, or chose not to understand.

Palestine stuck to me despite all my despairing efforts to avoid her company. She seemed happy and at ease when she visited me, even temporarily liberated. She would talk a lot, in contrast with her continuous silence at school that irritated the teachers, who would test it by directing verbal insults at her, such as, "Hey, Dummy!" or "You, Stupid!" or "Retard!" But she did not answer, nor did she quench their rancorous thirst by any reaction. She would come to us once or twice a week and usually at the weekend, so she could spend more time with us. She loved our house, she said, she loved my mother, and she loved my father, despite his comments that would make us all look for a hole to bury ourselves in, cringing from embarrassment and chagrin. He would ask her every time about the reason for the burns spread over her face, and she would explain to him that they weren't burns but how God created her. Then he would continue, asking her about why she walked as if she were dancing, and she would continue to answer him, without showing any irritation over the repetition of the question and the answer, that she suffered from a slight lameness in one of her legs. Then he would look at her face for a long time, ending with a comment that didn't so much require an answer as it called for a bullet to his mouth, such as, "Whoever said that God is beautiful and loves beauty?" Once I asked her why she wore a hijab even though her sisters did not, so she took it off and wide areas appeared on her head that were bald, except for a few patches of downy fuzz. Then Palestine stopped wearing her hijab in our house, not embarrassed to reveal her bald spots, marked by a red glow that shone under the trembling lights.

Palestine lived in our neighbourhood of al-Nuqra, four buildings away from us. She would tell her family that she had to study as an excuse to come to me. She would drag her little brother Aamer with her, and he would shout "I'm hungry!" as soon as he came into our house. My mother would make a sandwich for him and one for his sister, and he would devour them both. I asked her why she insisted on coming with her brother since she squabbled with him the whole time, and she told me frankly that her family sent him to keep an eye on her. Aamer would leave us to hover in the kitchen and get under my mother's feet, asking her about something to eat and giving himself the right to open the door of the refrigerator and to examine what the pots on the stove held for lunch. My mother would give him something, to rein in the curiosity coming from his belly; she called his mouth a drain that would refuse nothing, despite its small size. He might pick up one of my mother's figurines and turn it around on every side; then my mother would run to him, terrified that the figurine would fall and shatter, shattering her heart as well, a heart that had been shattered many times. On one of his visits, imposed on us and on Palestine, he looked at the ballet dancer (before she met her end), saying to my mother, "Auntie! Her shameful parts are showing!" My mother scolded him: "The shame is that you're looking at them!" After Palestine's family was reassured about us, especially after I visited her without bringing any of my brothers with me, she was liberated from Aamer's surveillance and started coming alone. During those hours, dear to her heart, she would talk a lot and laugh even more. She would sit with us at dinner, waiting her turn for my father to strike her forehead with a hard-boiled egg and then peel it for her, and my mother would pass her the falafel and slices of mortadella which her short, timid arms could not reach. When the time came for her to leave, her face would close up, her talk would be turned off, and curtains of melancholy would fall over her eyes.

I became used to having Palestine in my life. Perhaps I loved her, inside myself, without there being even one thing in common between us, as the theory of human love would require. It was a love that did not approach pity or become sympathy for inferiority. It was a love of a special kind, sufficient unto itself. I would look forward to her visits, and if she was late I would be afraid I had lost her. The likelihood of losing her was clear in my mind after she herself had sketched it for me, confidently, telling me secretly that when she grew up the hair would grow on her head and her walk would become normal. She assured me that she was going to leave the house, closing the door on her mother, who was withdrawn from them, and on her father, whose presence increased her limping and whose hand, falling on her and on everyone in the house on the many days when he was "down", made her own hand creep nervously under her scarf and pull out more hair from the places on her head that were not completely bald. She promised me that it was only a matter of time, even if the time was a little long, until she knew many things and saw and understood. She said that she did not understand now because she did not want to understand, and that she did not know because she was afraid that if she knew, she would hate herself and her life more than she did now. She swore that she would know many things soon and might know everything later on, and that time was not far away. The day she knew she would no longer be . . . herself.

In the last year of middle school Palestine's performance improved, with my help, and the teachers' insults decreased, but she still claimed that she did not understand a lot and knew only what she was required to know. She began to be with us almost every day. Her father had become more deeply entangled in his violence, and for Palestine fleeing to us temporarily was a need and no longer a choice. Some days her brother Aamer would come, not to spy on her but rather to seek our protection for himself, too, even though he still annoyed my mother by turning over her figurines to sneak a look at their private parts. Then some of her sisters joined her, taking refuge with us once a week. My mother greeted Palestine and her sisters with compassion, opening her arms and sending odours of meat, fried onions oozing sweet flavour, and seasoned stew to everyone's nostrils. The circle surrounding the tablecloth spread on the floor widened, with new bodies and arms crossing our own, as we made space for them to reach the dish of hummus ahead of us and eased their way to the Greek Kalamata olives. My father found in the new desires and fragments of coming defeats, temporarily added to our desires and our defeats, an opportunity to demonstrate his speed and skill in cracking hard-boiled eggs on new foreheads. They ate and laughed and so did we, knowing that little money remained, even in the secret hiding places. That did not stop us from spreading the cloth tomorrow and the day after, for a dinner that satisfied more desires and pushed the defeats away for a time.

Then, as I had feared, I lost Palestine. She and her family left the cramped house in al-Nuqra for a house that was no bigger in al-Fahahil, a distant, renovated residential area, in what seemed like exile to us. Their move meant that she transferred to a new school, and I began to come home from school alone, without Palestine beside me rushing to arrive ahead of me at our little house with its daily cooking, our noise that clung to the walls, and the constant sound of the toilet flushing, where she smiled at my father when he greeted her with reminders of her ugly form, her limping walk, and inexcusable references to rape. I visited her in her new house for a first and last time, and she did not talk much or laugh. Her father had become more savage and her mother more withdrawn; her sisters and Aamer hid in the corners of the apartment, which smelled of outdated furniture that had lost all humanity, as it had lost its ability to hold together during the rapid, unjust move from al-Nuqra to al-Fahahil. But Palestine's eyes seemed less lost and more penetrating. As we said farewell at the door, she hugged me to a body that had become tougher. I would not see her after that day, we both realised that, but I felt reassured, not miserable or deeply distressed. For Palestine had removed her scarf and showed me one side of her head, pointing with some delight to small hairs that had started covering her bald spots.

Our paths did not cross again. I walked on my path carrying my name as a burden, and a body designed by a ruler, as if it had become accustomed to the masculine name without any confusion, so its curves became straight and its swellings flattened, slipping easily into wide trousers. For fear that my arms would go where I didn't want them to, they withdrew to my sides and my hands plunged into my pockets, so my shoulders were raised and my walk took on the look of a boy who realised he was no longer a child and who wanted to catch up with the adults in form if not in fact. My hair was half long and half soft, lacking any identity, with thin waves that were neither rebellious nor attractive. I didn't know what to do with it, so I would settle for tying it in the form of a thin, dwarf tail that neither bounced nor was stirred by the breezes provoking it. Many times I would lift it up and fix it in the middle of my head towards the rear, in the shape of a bun. I would put many black pins in it without taking any care to hide their peculiar appearance, but by the time I got to the middle of the day most of the pins would have rained down on my shoulders and the bun would have collapsed like a block of sand that had lost its power to hold together. Most of the time my despairing attempts to gather it and rearrange it would be of no use. The bun annoyed my mother for years. At the door, when I was on my way to school, then to the university, then to work, she would stop me and say,

"Take that shit off your head!"

I was my father's first-born, and his hope. I succeeded in the *thanawiyya aamma* exam at the end of high school with a score a few tenths of a per cent over 90, and my mother's joyous trills circled out of the window and echoed in the building. The neighbour women joined her in the trills, their voices resounding tunefully to Abdel Halim Hafez's "By My Heart's Life and Its Joys", which sings out every year from the throats of home radios. The apartments in the building had opened their doors to receive joy or distribute it, along with sugar-coated almonds and improvised chocolates. The doors of the heartsore homes remained mute. Umm Hana' did not share in my mother's joy because her daughter Hana' had failed. Umm Husam cracked open her door, because Husam had passed with a score of 52 per cent, so she didn't know if she should be glad or cry. She did know that she could not trill in joy for him, though she did extend my mother the courtesy of one trill for my sake, which broke at the end because of the tears that choked her voice. My mother consoled Umm Husam, even if she did recite the Qur'anic verse, "Say, I seek refuge in the Lord of the Daybreak" in her mind five times in a row, following it with, "Say, I seek refuge in the Lord of Humankind" also five times in a row, to ward off the evil eye from Umm Husam. The eye could still strike me with a spark of envy because of her overwhelming

112

feelings of anger, without any actual intention of evil for me on her part. We pulled together a party in the house: my sisters belted their nightgowns and pyjamas with scarves for belly dancing, and my father danced as he loved to on our joyous occasions, few as they were. His dancing was more like the dance of a horse when it lifts its front legs alternately, but horses – without making the least comparison – are more stable, more elegant, more awe-inspiring, and more dignified. My father did not know how to follow a single pattern in his movements, either straight or circular; when he lifted his legs alternately he leaned to one side during his leap and nearly toppled over, so he would lift one of his arms in the air to compensate for the imbalance caused by lifting one leg, arching his back and extending his rear to gain his balance. In the end he would look like a lame or wounded animal trying to escape from the line of fire.

The joy ended quickly. My father announced, "Kuwait is your fate," as my score gave me a place in the department of English Language and Literature of the University of Kuwait, at the same time that I was accepted in the faculty of Engineering at Yarmouk University in Jordan. Enrolling in the Kuwait University required unattainable scores for expatriate students, so it was no easy or light affair for people like us. For my father the matter was settled, requiring no second thoughts or complicated calculations – Kuwait was "for free" and Jordan was "for money". The little money he got to feed us would never be enough for my education, in Jordan or anywhere else. He was sure that he would not come into a lot of money suddenly, and that there would be no uncle who would appear in the pages of unknown days to die in Colombia and leave him a factory for car tyres, as had happened to a Syrian colleague of his at work. The man left his job and left Kuwait's oil to the Kuwaitis, travelling to Colombia to monitor the process of transferring his uncle's factory to him. My father did not want to turn over in his mind the talk that followed, stripping the story of its early magic. It was said that his colleague ended up a prisoner of one of the criminal drug gangs in Colombia, as revenge on his uncle whose scores with them were not settled, and that the Colombian government liquidated the uncle's factory and sold off its assets to pay some of his bank loans. It was also said that some good people got together a sum of money to help his wife travel to Syria with her children, to wait for a husband whose chances of return or even of survival were diminishing. My father confined himself to enjoying the fantasy in the story of his colleague and his inheritance from his Colombian uncle, the part that came from the fables of impossible dreams. He took it as inspiration, in his own extravagant dreams, for remote possibilities of fate that would knock on stubbornly closed doors of fortune.

Why would my father go to Colombia? Demonstrably, luck was accustomed to jump away from him in his own places and streets, and even in what should have been the very heart of his luck. That had happened when it jumped from him to his childhood friend Uthman Fathallah ("God's Opening, Victory"), who had been his neighbour in the Wehdat Camp. They had been like brothers in their poverty and in the UNRWA schools, before God opened learning, money, and rank to his friend Uthman Fathallah, who specialised in a rare medical field in Germany and then joined the staff of a hospital in Saudi Arabia as a German expert. For years they chose a day during the regular summer vacations to meet in al-Wehdat Camp, the scene of their childhoods. They

114

would walk the streets of the camp, knocking on the doors of houses familiar to them, and then sit in a café in the market, talking over the details of their lives far from home. My father would lighten the aridity and harshness of his life, while Uthman trimmed some of the blessings and ease from his. My father usually bought a lottery ticket from a seller with a kiosk near the café; he and his display of lottery tickets, offered to those who wanted to buy hope and luck, were among the enduring landmarks of the street. Uthman Fathallah let out a light-hearted laugh when my father suggested to him that he buy a lottery ticket for himself. The German expert announced that he did not believe in luck, describing it as the excuse of the hapless. He tried to draw my father to a reasoned disbelief in the heresy of luck by means of a logical approach to the subject, but my father, who had never tasted any profit in the lottery of life generally, did not wish to embrace this disbelief. With the courtesy of the new European who developed finely within him, Uthman Fathallah bought a lottery ticket so as not to be split, in spirit or in thought, from his childhood friend, my father. He even gave him the honour of choosing the lucky ticket, since he was experienced in buying lottery tickets, and my father dedicated the essence of his failing luck to making the choice. He examined, inspected, and reflected on the numerical combinations of the tickets before withdrawing one in particular from the stack, one that had shone in his eyes for the hidden prospects inscribed in its numbers. My father knew that Uthman Fathallah would win, and it came about that Uthman Fathallah did win five thousand dinars, the value of one of the brackets of the lottery. His long laugh rang out on the telephone when he gave the good news to my father, who genuinely rejoiced at the win.

That angered my mother even more, as she added it to the long series of events she classified under the heading of "toxic frustration", a term she used for a major calamity that came to her from somewhere unexpected, something that could be summed up in the single word "Naeem!" Uthman Fathallah's win restored my father's confidence, which had been wavering for some time, in his ability to hunt down luck, even if it was for someone else. For days he called back the taste of the win inside himself, spoiled by a temporary conceit brought on by glee. My mother was shocked by my father's joy, and even more shocked by the fact that he was the one who bought the lottery ticket for Uthman Fathallah. "Your cleverness only benefits others!" She was grumpy all the time, though her bitter shafts did not touch my father's pride, which for once had increased. Then her anger reached an unforeseen height when my father admitted (though he did not have to) that Uthman Fathallah had offered to split the value of the lottery ticket with him, as he was the one who chose it, but that he had adamantly refused. He seemed pleased with himself, even arrogant; but here my mother's inner lioness appeared and she jumped on my father, as I threw myself on him in a vain attempt to pull him away from her claws and her teeth, scratching his neck and biting the end of his ear. When my father at last succeeded in getting away from my mother, with my help, he gathered up his rumpled person, pointed his forefinger in the air, and shouted:

"Listen to me! My dignity is above all else!"

My mother's only response was to lift her middle finger in his face and say, with all the fury of her agitated body pouring from her tongue and her eyes,

"Stick your dignity up your arse!"

On the evening before the first day of my first term at Kuwait University, my father took me on an outing he had carefully arranged. He wanted to discuss a momentous matter with me that would be hard, as he said, to speak about confidentially at home, where my mother caught the slightest whisper of a glance, and my siblings spread their existence in every corner of our house. For three evenings before that, evenings that stifled my spirit, he had dragged me to the balcony, along with a notebook, a pen, and long, flimsy apologies on his lips, some with no clear meaning, intended only to break my silence. In handwriting he took great care to refine and perfect, he divided the expenses of our existence on a clean white paper into large, prominent numbers, going over them more than once in ink, and writing the type of expenditure next to each number. In addition to the regular expenses he did not forget to add others that were variable, including, among innumerable other eventualities, the requests of my grandmother Fatima and my aunt Najah; the calamities of my uncle Muwaffaq; and the obstinacy of our Caprice car, which my father had bought not just used but abused, with its motor that coughed several times before turning over and with a worn-out body. It was a car handed down through four owners at least, each of whom had altered the body and the contents in his own way. Then he added an article to the paper concerning future expenses, "coming unavoidably", for the education of my siblings. The indications were that most of them would not achieve academic distinction, so they would not have the opportunity to study for free at Kuwait University. That meant that it was necessary to arrange for the expenses of their education in other universities, and therefore we had to start preparing now to bear the heavy burdens that would break our backs. Each time, my father sketched before me the frightening numbers of the regular expenses of our life, and the still more frightening numbers for the eventualities, and the expected numbers for a future that was terrifying, since beside those numbers were the faces of children who were growing and broadening, eating ravenously, their shoes and clothing wearing out quickly, their arms stretched towards his empty pockets. Then my father would add the huge numbers and subtract them from his shrinking income, and the result would be negative. It might be a little more or a little less, but the negative always dominated the final result. He would ask me,

"What'll we do?"

On the outing he had planned so that it would be decisive and revealing, perhaps preparing my way forward, my father stopped by Abu Musa's little shop in an annexe next to our building and bought two bottles of Pepsi. Then he called at the 'Ishsh al-Hana restaurant, located at the intersection of al-Nuqra with al-Hawalli and bought two sandwiches of falafel with tomatoes and tahini. We set off towards the sea. My father parked the car at the end of the beach and we walked barefoot to the edge of the water. The tide was low, revealing mud, pebbles, moss, the remains of creatures who had thrown off their shells, as well as litter and a stench that suggested the sea might not have bathed in its own water for some time. We sat on two jutting rocks. We ate and drank and threw our litter beside the rest, and we did not speak. The sea itself neither bellowed nor even babbled, listening to us with its calm body, and dozing when it grew tired of listening to our silence. The night was improbably black, and the sky was deep blue and glowering. The cars with headlights that usually rained jagged shards of light on the beach from afar did not appear, so our limbs plunged into darkness. Then it was as if something very heavy fell on the back of the universe, and our bodies bowed low.

My father smoked three cigarettes. Nothing was heard except our breathing, each one's breath careful not to touch the other's, and the sound of the tobacco's sigh. In the intervals between cigarettes a scene appeared to me, drawn on the canvas of the deep black sea and showing a person who seemed familiar to me, sitting on a rock on the shore. Suddenly the sea stood up, raising its giant arms and pulling the rock towards it while the person tried to shrink and contract, to avoid the squeezing arms of the giant. Then when he saw his shoes empty of him, floating on the surface of the water, rising and falling like little broken boats in the middle of an ocean, he knew that he had now become a corpse.

My father turned to me, his eyes searching my eyes. When our eyes pierced the blackness and met, in spite of me, he grasped my arms and pressed them tightly. Then he said, as if he had found the heart of the matter,

"Jihad, my child – you are the man of the house!"

I wanted your name. It came down to me, thin and diaphanous, in my wakeful, tortured dreams. It descended upon me from the heights of my spirit, venerable and venerated. With it came your captivating face, which took possession of me. Your grand stature lodged in my heart, taking hold of it and becoming its proprietress. Perhaps you were formed in my womb as a girl out of desire for the chosen name and not desire for the child. For your name, O majestic being, is everything I am not, everything I have not been, and everything I want to be. It is decidedly, O highest of all creatures, what I will not be. Your name, O marvel of inspiration, is absolutely what I do not dare to be.

I met you for the first time as a foetus in the fifth month of pregnancy. Your image appeared before me vaguely formed, indistinct in its features and dimensions, on the screen of the sonar device. Nothing in you gave any indication of you. In fact, nothing in you appeared alive or lifelike, except the intermittent pulsation of your form on the little screen. The doctor had me listen to your heart. All my senses strained to hear you. I couldn't listen too long for fear that your heart would tire of my listening to it, or that it would startle from my senses eavesdropping on you and stop its chanting. Then another, more realistic fear came over me, as I believed that some movement of mine – unintentional, I swear by the Lord of the Universe! – might cause a stumble in your pulse or a stutter in its rhythm. But as you swam in my waters and my blood, you extended your spirit to me as a lifeline to my coming salvation. As I closed my eyes in reverence for the greatness of the life that was being created within me, I saw you stretch out your hand, so recently planted, to my face, your breath kissing my neck, raining down fire. I opened my eyes, terrified, but your hands were still in place on the sonar screen, curled next to your face. I felt my neck; it was warm and moist, brushed by an air current seeping in from somewhere.

That was the second time I visited the doctor after becoming pregnant. The first time was the day he gave me the "good news". He thought he was giving me a reason to be happy as he announced that I was in the first month of a pregnancy. I didn't pretend to be surprised; the home test I had taken had revealed what I did not want to discover, but I wanted to be mistaken, I wanted my analysis to be wrong. I wanted my urine to be free of any signs of a human implantation that would extend the roots of the marriage and add to its branches rather than uprooting it. The doctor told me that I must take supplements to raise the level of iron and vitamins in my blood, which had low readings. "The foetus is nourished by your blood and its health comes from your health," he said in a clichéd manner, displaying the attention and serious-ness appropriate to the high price of the examination, which called for a medical explanation free of any meaning. The doctor assumed that I must rejoice. He waited for me to rejoice. He stopped speak-ing and looked at me, reading my reaction, a frozen smile splitting his face. But he soon returned to his indifference, as I gathered the fragments of the news. I fastened my shirt after many tries in which I missed the right buttonholes, and I hurried to leave. He wrote a prescription for me and I went out without stopping at the secretary's desk, as he had requested, so she could set the date for the next check-up.

On the way to my husband's very spacious apartment in al-Shuwaikh I turned onto one of the side streets. Smaller streets branched off from it, narrowing and crowding together, until I found myself stopped in front of our building in al-Nuqra. I switched off the engine and opened the window, then stretched out my arm to the air and the March branches, which had thrown off the remnants of winter, plucking from them echoes of my past, blooming days. Our apartment was on the second floor, and the window of the family room (which was also our room for sleeping, studying, and eating, the room for our life) was winking at the street. It was partly open and the curtain partly drawn back, the light somewhat filtered. Voices flaring with the existence of my siblings poured rapidly from the window opening into space over the street, mixed with the voices that rained down from other coloured life openings in the building. Their voices landed in my eyes, then drowned in my watery tears.

I started the engine and took off, unguided by any thought or feeling or even the road I should have known by heart. I opened the glove compartment and took out a cassette of Nagat El-Sagheera and put it in the tape player. In her voice woven with water, Nagat confided in me her love of the sea, the sky, and the road. It was nearing eight in the evening. The car went of its own free will to the shore that bordered the city and peered at it, looking over its shoulders. I searched for my rock and it beckoned me to come to it. I put on the night like a lilac-coloured shawl and knelt on the rock, one eye on the sea that turned its back to me, sleeping (or perhaps upset, or filled with silence), and the other on the uncaring sky, unforgiving, not studded with stars or joy. I wept. I believe I wept more than I ever had up till then. I wept all the tears allotted to my life. I wept openly, reassured that I was alone in the place, alone in my time. I was more reassured, perhaps, because the sea remained deeply asleep even when the sound of my sobbing rose, just as the sky remained distracted, distant, unsympathetic. But it seems that the sea awoke without my noticing it, as when I left my rock, one of its arms had stretched out to me, stealthily. On its surface floated the doctor's prescription, like an empty boat dancing lightly on the surface of the water.

I had an excruciating labour with you. Amid the flaring voices that surrounded me, I faintly heard the doctor saying to those around him that he might have to perform a Caesarean section. I pulled my body from the depths of pain and raised my head to him. "I want to see her come out of me!" I insisted. The doctor pressed my hand compassionately, saying, "The umbilical cord is wrapped around her. If things go on like this, she could strangle." He looked at my face, the features ravaged by fatigue, adding that he did not want my torture to go on any longer. I beckoned to him to come close. When his eyes were directly before mine, I pressed his shoulder and pleaded, "Don't cut me, for the love of God!" I told him to give you time to free yourself from the umbilical cord, and that I would wait, no matter how much time was needed. As for my torture, what did it have to do with him?

With the final push, the violent contraction of my body that split your being from my womb at last, you emerged from me with your head high, searching the heights. Your eyes were open avidly, turning to me, their piercing gaze coming to rest on the shores of my eyes. You exhaled the cry they were waiting for, you gave them the natural indicators of life they wanted to read, then you sought my arms. The nurse asked,

"Have you chosen a name for her?"

During cautious nights, I had slipped out of bed and moved quickly to the guest bathroom at the other end of my husband's large apartment. I mounted the seat of the toilet, then jumped onto the marble floor that shook under my body, weighed down by anger and hatred. The sound of my feet hitting the floor made the confined air in the room swirl around me before landing on my hot flesh in cold fragments. Then when I climbed onto the toilet seat again, I looked at the bathroom mirror above the sink and saw it fogged, reflecting the sallow colour of my face. I jumped and jumped, then jumped and jumped again, breathing heavily, the rivulets of sweat streaming on the mirror, until my face in the glass was slack under the accumulated fog. On the ninth or tenth jump my body was afflicted with dizziness and some "looseness" and cramping, so I was not able to lift my failing legs, while my arms were linked over my chest to defend myself from rapidly rising shivering. I would listen to my insides, hoping that the life that penetrated me by force had been spat out at last. But this life, your life, did not leave me in dark, clotted blood, as an aborted form – as I hoped – along with the faeces from the looseness.

On one incautious night, I mounted the edge of the toilet but one of my feet slipped out of place before I was standing firmly in position to jump. I lost my balance and fell, and my foot twisted under my body, taking the enormous weight of the fall. Pain reverberated inside me, but I repressed the scream that could have awakened all the oblivious worlds, had it emerged. I was soaked in pain and sweat; I dragged myself over the long distance from the guest bathroom to the bedroom. I think I fainted. When I awoke in the morning, my foot was swollen, and the pain had turned into a continuous, worsening drumbeat in every spot in my body. I told my husband, who was forced to take me to the hospital, that I had been taking a shower when I slipped in the tub. The doctor confirmed that I had multiple fractures in my ankle, that I must remain in a cast for six weeks, and that I could not walk for at least four weeks. But he seemed elated and grateful to God's decree and mercy, announcing that the foetus was fine. You continued in your formation, and your life was coming . . . coming without any doubt.

"Do you want me to believe that you fell in the tub after midnight?" My husband's laughter shook my being, in its state of collapse. It was the same laughter that had followed me to the bathroom and then surrounded me, crushing my heart, the day he consummated the marriage. On that day, and then on many later days, I stood under the shower's waterfall for a long period of pain, trying to scrape off his fluids that had calcified on my body. I rubbed hard, and then I rubbed harder. My body cried abundant water, but his water did not fall, it stuck to me. He wrote you with thick water, he planted you with lasting flesh and blood. He wove you as a settled spirit within me.

When my eyes, initially incurious, fell on you as a foetus in your fifth month, I felt as if I knew you. In the moment when your pulsing reached my ear, I was certain that you were speaking to me; it was as if we were meeting after a separation, over my cappuccino and your chocolate milkshake, in our familiar corner of the coffee shop, exchanging blame like two adults, without bitterness or any real reproach. Amidst the blame and fear, my fear over your violent pulse, it was as if you calmed my alarm. It was then that I decided I would entrust myself to you, no matter what was or what would be. It was then that I gave you your name. You deserved its noble meaning even when you were a gelatinous being with indistinct features; for I saw my coming days finding refuge in your royal court, I saw myself seeking sanctuary with you and you granting it. I saw myself as your poor subject, and you as my protector and my saviour.

Taking advantage of the relief on my face, the doctor operating the sonar asked me if I would like to know the sex of the foetus. I answered, not moving my eyes from their focus on you:

"She's a girl . . . my daughter . . . I know her!"

In the worsening seasons and darkening days, O my soul, you gave light to my spirit. I believe that because of Your Highness's grace and your great goodness to my being – to me, your hapless subject, seeking compassion – I survived. Who said that living is easy? But some lives are different, more truly lived, and you, O most noble of the generous, are the difference. You, O dearest of gifts, are Life, with a capital L. You snatched me away, you enveloped me, you ran in my blood, and the strange thing is that with you and by you I became lighter. As your life shackled me, I somehow became free.

You saved me from myself, from my own weariness with myself. One time, fatigue with life and with myself took me further: I bathed you, nursed you, and rocked you in my arms until you dozed. I breathed in deeply the aroma of your cottony face and kissed your sweet-smelling neck, clad in whiffs of jasmine cologne and talcum powder, and folded you into your bed. Then

I dissolved twenty aspirins, all there were in the packet, in a cup of water and drank it in three gulps. I stretched out on my bed, beside yours, lying there like someone who was dying, with the least possible posturing and drama. I waited to die. We were alone, you and I, in the house, my father's house, our new house. Things began to disappear from the room; the wardrobe, the bookshelf, the writing table all vanished. The clippings hung on the wall lost their strength and fell. The teacup with the blackened cinnamon stick left on the nightstand dissolved. The little coloured plastic nightingales that turned above your bed, singing, fled in fright. The colours in the room evaporated, and I floated above whiteness flowing over whiteness. I rose above the bed. The white sky shimmered through the ceiling of the room and became visible, drawing me to it. But sharp crying pierced the whiteness and drew me down from the ceiling. I tried to rise up again amidst the crying that pulled the cloud of whiteness from beneath me but I crashed to the floor, my head hitting the edge of the bed. I got up heavily, dizziness in all parts of my body. Little by little things and colours returned to the room, or some of them. You were crying, your cries like blades piercing my stupor. You turned over onto your belly and raised your head to me, still crying, the cries becoming panicked. I stretched out my limp arms to you and your whole being lengthened, stretching your body towards me. It was as if you threw yourself to me – my God, I don't remember completely, and I don't think that you could stand up in your sixth month. But still, it was as if you climbed the air to me, and you reached me before I reached you. I folded you to my chest and threw myself down with you on the bed, giving in to the tremendous giddiness that still enveloped me. You did not stop crying, and you were kicking my belly, where you were lying, with your feet shaped like fins. Then you stretched your hand to my face, and your tender fingernails, saturated with milk, scratched my nose and my chin. You put your hand on my mouth and pushed your little fingers inside it. At that point my chest rumbled violently, gathering my flood of nausea from the farthest reaches of my body and expelling it. I vomited. I vomited repeatedly. I spewed out a lot of vomit, intermittently, wrapped in white foam with a bitter taste that covered my chin and my chest and that ran down on part of your chin and your chest. At last you stopped crying, your panic stopped, and your mouth, broadening and relaxing just then, could have been read as the smile of God.

"What are you going to name her?"

The nurse wanted to take you away, but I pulled you to me. She told me that they were going to move me from the delivery room to another room. You called to me with your eyes. You whispered to my eyes to stifle my worry and doze. "Rest!" you told me. You patted my fear, you calmed me, you reassured me that you were with me. You crooned to me, "Go on, sleep, go to sleep . . ." I told the nurse who took you from me:

"Maleka," ("Queen") "her name is Maleka."

Then I slept. I slept deeply.

CHAPTER FOUR

Concerning the Naked Houses

It has reached me, O auspicious queen, whose vision wanders and whose wishes are winged . . .

Living in an oil-producing country like Kuwait did not make us Kuwaitis, as was said, accusingly or enviously, by the many relatives we left behind us in the camps. As a matter of fact our life in Kuwait was an extension of our life as it might have been in the camp, still marked by diaspora, with a few improvements and additions. We lived in an apartment building crowded with people and with contradictory, contentious feelings, due to the shrinking open spaces in al-Nuqra, which was among those residential neighbourhoods that had come to seem like camps for Palestinians in Kuwait. It had the mark of a ghetto, and the small, overstuffed apartments there were unsuitable for Kuwaiti families, despite the Kuwaitis' relatively limited capacity for multiplying, compared to the enormous reproductive capacity of the Palestinians. Our apartment did not differ much from my uncle Abu Taisir's house in al-Wehdat Camp in Amman. Each of the houses had the same picture of my uncle Mahmoud, who was martyred in the Battle of Karameh in 1968; later the picture was colourised, so my uncle's face looked clearer and his smile gentler, with cinematic features and a dreamy semblance. Likewise, in each house there was nearly the same wall clock that came free as a promotion for some Nestlé product, and there was the same kitchen cabinet, divided into two halves, the upper covered by glass and the lower by two wide, thick wooden doors that latched by hooking a bent rusty

131

nail over the edges. In the cabinet in each house there stood rows of boxes: loose tea, sage, dried mint, cardamom, green zaatar mix, and duqqa spice mix, as well as jars of pickled cucumbers (Armenian cucumbers and regular ones), makdous aubergines in oil, pickled turnips, green olives, black olives, and boiled Nabulsi cheese flavoured with black caraway seeds.

In each of the camps, al-Nuqra and al-Wehdat, the houses held three or four tin containers of olive oil, the yearly consumption of each household. My mother and my uncle's wife raised them on wooden planks so they would not be affected by humidity from the floor, and they both kept the prized containers in the holiest place in the house, their bedrooms (not least because of the ever-shrinking space elsewhere). Both were careful and frugal with the golden, full-bodied, richly flavoured liquid. The container of powdered Tang which my mother dissolved to make juice for guests did not differ greatly from the bags of juice powder that my uncle's wife dissolved for her guests. The Singer sewing machine covered by a prayer rug in the family room of my uncle's house (a room used triply as a living room, a room to receive guests, and a bedroom) did not differ much from the Butterfly sewing machine in our house, also found in the family room that was used for sleeping, for eating, and for study, although my mother had sewn a cover for her machine, matching the curtains in the room and edged with lace.

My cousin could kill a cockroach scuttling under the television table with one of his sandals, with such skilled aim that the eyes of his family never swerved from Abdel Halim Hafez as he flirted with Faten Hamama, gently harassed her, and pursued her with "Lovely and a Liar". Likewise, my brother would assassinate a gecko crawling along the wall with a blow from one of his shoes, hitting the target on the first throw, while our eyes remained fixed on Abdel Halim Hafez asking "Why Do You Blame Me?" when in fact we did not blame him for falling in love with Mariam Fakhr Eddine, enchanted by her eyes. My sisters sewed dresses for their dolls from fabric scraps my mother gave them, leaving behind needles and pins on the tile that pricked our bare feet, so we sealed our existence in blood on land that was not ours. Likewise, my cousins sewed creative fashions for their dolls, although their dolls' clothes were prettier, and they did not scatter pins, needles, bits of thread, or remnants of fabric, as they faced living conditions which were much harsher than our own. Still, needles would get away from them and puncture their fingers; they would suck the blood and not let it stain their clothes or their dolls' new clothes. My uncle would lie back on the long floor cushion to listen to the eight o'clock news on Jordanian television, sipping tea with sage; likewise my father would sit cross-legged on a thin cushion to listen to the eight o'clock news on Kuwaiti television, drinking tea with mint. When some Arab leader would start to speak in each newscast about the prime issue of the Arabs, warning of the consequences of neglecting the rights of the Palestinians, then neither my uncle nor my father would shrink from aiming the middle finger at him. They might add a curse targeting the private parts of the leader's mother or sister, if he plunged into the dusty verbal battlefield with too much enthusiasm.

My uncle was blessed with ten children and my father with eight, but there were two essential differences between the two lives, that of my uncle in the Wehdat Camp and ours in the Nuqra Camp. First, my uncle's house belonged to the family, because their status as refugees had taken on a permanent cast. Abu Hamad did not descend on them at the end of the month, like a wind wrapped in dirt, demanding the rent that was due to him.

"Open the door, Abu Jihad, open the door! Don't make me break it down."

Abu Hamad's knocks poured down continuously on the door of our house, and the convulsions of the door climbed the walls that surrounded our life, halted on the inside. They clung to the droplets of sweat that clouded our anxious faces, then filtered into our bodies, so that we shuddered and froze. Even the cracks in the gloomy walls seemed to extend in new veins with the rhythm of the convulsions. The temperature would climb in the front room, separated from the outside world by a wooden wafer called a door. The heat rose from our bodies, which suppressed their fidgeting and put on the clothing of a narrowed life, and from the air trapped in the house because the air conditioner was turned off. From the type of knocking, its intensity, the speed of the blows, and the increase in their speed, we could measure – with some intuition and more experience – the degree of Abu Hamad's anger (or that of Bu Hamad, as his people called him and as others also came to call him). Our silence increased his resentment, so he did not scruple to use both hands in heaping still more blows on the door. His wrathful hands were solid rocks thrown at us with rancour, as we scurried to our den to hide.

"Open up, Abu Jihad! Open the door!"

As usual my father was late in paying the rent, for no reason other than that he simply "didn't have it". Over the span of a week, Bu Hamad would attack us daily. "The sandstorm's upon us!" my mother would say, hurrying to turn down the television, so that mute faces looked out from the screen. My father would ask us to freeze in place, so we would not move a muscle or make any sound, swallowing our breath, which struggled against the noise of fear inside us. Silently we also thanked God who had guided us to lock the door, guidance God bestowed on us the first week of every month, the time of the sandstorm. That was because the hands of neighbour women were accustomed to open the door without any "ahem" or asking permission; the women did not believe for a minute that they were violating a life that was public to a large extent, as their lives were. My youngest siblings were the best at freezing, standing like stone statues, or like beings suddenly enchanted, imitating cartoons. They might exaggerate in performing the frozen scene, challenging life by enjoying playing dead, even after the sandstorm subsided. For them, freezing was a game; for my mother and father, and for me, specifically, it was a terrifying threat.

"I swear to God I'll break down the door, Abu Jihad!"

I would close my eyes to drive away from my sight the prospect that the door would collapse at any moment, its hinges in pain, groaning, weakening, and coming loose. That would turn us into a spectacle not very different from the scene of a woman with a repulsive body whose towel has fallen outside the bath precisely when the walls of her house are collapsing, so her nudity strikes people's eyes, and she doesn't know whether she should hide in shame from becoming a spectacle or from loathing for her nudity, amply endowed with all elements of ugliness. That's what came to my mind every time the door shook under the merciless blows of Bu Hamad: I would see the front room where we gathered, unmoving and unspeaking, revealed in the public square as if its walls had come down on all sides like a banana peel. I would be alone in the room, standing naked in the middle, and what would bother me more than anything else would be that my hair was messy at that moment, or parted on the wrong side, or that the traces of a purple bruise at the top of my thigh, caused by colliding with the furniture crammed in our house, would still be visible, or worst of all, that the stubbly hair on my legs would be clear to see for the spectators in the square. That would make me curse the day when my father became my father.

During the moments when we were frozen I would blame myself for many things, including not having removed the hair from my legs with sugar paste or with my father's electric razor, without him knowing that his razor was used for this purpose. I would blame myself for not having bathed, or for wearing plastic sandals scuffed from daily use. Still, these repeated moments gave me the opportunity to recall other free, ignoble, indiscreet spectacles of nakedness, such as that of Sukaina, scenes that reassured me that my possible nakedness would be more bearable and easier to absorb. For Sukaina's nakedness was very hard to take in, open to viewing many times, because of all the reasons for divine intolerance of the frailties of the human condition. This turned Sukaina's body into raw material for our temperamental imaginations, so we would visit upon it deformities greater than it had and persist in playing with its details.

One time, Sukaina was sitting on the threshold of her apartment door opposite our apartment, wearing a beige slip of cheap nylon, stretching her legs in front of her. The colour of the slip, which was nearly transparent, was a little darker than her beige flesh, tightly packed in every part of her body. The slip was trimmed with cream-coloured lace, the colour age-worn and faded. A small, half-hidden hole moved with the skirt of the slip, and Sukaina put her finger in it and widened it. From beneath the slip the edges of her bra were visible, white yellowed by sweat and humidity, strangling her weary breasts. The slip was raised to the top of her knees, so the flesh of her thighs was directly on the floor, the object of avid, curious glances. Protruding varicose veins made blue-green clusters that massed in some parts of her legs. The neighbour women were not about to miss a sight like that. Claiming compassion for this poor creature, they hurried to bring covers from their houses to conceal Sukaina's exposed flesh. The voices entwined, holding the smells of reckless layers of flesh and thin desires, as the women repeated, "God cover you and cover us!" But Sukaina was not concerned about being covered up, nor did it seem that the sight of her flesh alarmed her as it did the others. She had found the key at last, as she always did, so she had opened the door of her house, ignoring her husband Jamil who was relaxing in his siesta, and had gone out barefoot and nearly naked. She had locked in Jamil, who usually locked her in together with her mind wandering in its own world, and had sat down on the floor. Even when Sukaina had her first child, she would find the key Jamil had hidden and open the door, then lock it on Jamil and the baby. Her little one would cry while Jamil remained deeply asleep. Then when there were more little ones, Jamil decided to bring his mother to keep her eye on them when his wife's mind wandered. Sukaina would respond to my mother more than to any of the other neighbours. My mother would kiss Sukaina's head and take her wan face in her hands, steeped in the mists of our compassionate house, and kiss her cheeks, inflamed with sadness. She would placate her and mollify her, as if she were the one who had irritated her. Then she would make her a cup of hot cocoa, not giving it to her until Sukaina opened her mouth and spat out the house key she had kept under her tongue and put it in my mother's hand.

The women would delay in covering Sukaina. Watching an ugly scene amused and comforted them, though that did not mean they were gloating, or harboured any lasting ill will. Sukaina's open nakedness was like their own concealed nakedness, which they hated and which sometimes disgusted them. At times, in a kind of self-revelation, they might express their disgust in their own way. Mahdiyya would arrange the time for her nearly daily visit to my mother, in the afternoon, to coincide with her husband Abu Muaadh's departure for work in the carpentry shop and with my father's departure for his shop, where he went more out of habit than in any hope of income. In our house, with its many mirrors, Mahdiyya could see herself and what was behind her. My mother sat cross-legged on the bed in her bedroom, smoothing out the pile of washing she had gathered from the clothes line, shaking the crackly dryness from its joints, and folding it. Mahdiyya would stand in front of the dressing-table mirror, or she might open one of the doors of the wardrobe with a mirror inside. Then she would lift her dress above her belly, inspecting her nudity fully. The enormous block of fat gathered all around her waist created a bewildering chaos in the mirror. Her dark, concave belly button seemed like a single eye, struggling to see in the midst of the billowing seas of flesh surrounding it. Mahdiyya's legs were bowed, with thin calves compared to her oak-like thighs and her expansively fat belly, where years of repeated pregnancy intersected with the flabbiness of passing time and with the effects of clarified butter. "Just look!" she said to my mother. "Just look at how ugly

I am!" My mother left the laundry in compassion for her neighbour, trying to alleviate some of her resentment of her body, and stood next to her in front of the mirror. She lifted her dress to her belly and showed Mahdiyya her own flesh, no less folded and broken, her fingers passing over the stretch marks below her belly, which threatened to crack even more and become worse. Then the two women, hugging their bodies in the mirror, became perplexed over the very dark black lurking at the top of their thighs, at the source of their fleeting, hidden pleasure. My mother admitted to Mahdiyya that this was the first time she had discovered the darkness of her flesh in that area, which harboured their sheltered, usually stolen desires and where their many babies slipped into the world. My mother laughed as she compared her flesh and Mahdiyya's, and then arrived at a conclusion she had not expected: "You know, Mahdiyya? We really are ugly!"

"Open up, Abu Jihad! Open up now! By God, I'll break down the door!"

But our door did not knuckle under, it did not submit to the threats of Bu Hamad. Our door remained locked, standing, bearing up under the bruising blows. It remained steadfast, deriving its steadiness from the creed of adapting; it remained invincible as things and beings do when they are in harmony with their owners, so that they feel their emotions and know their thoughts. That's because over time they grieve with them, they cohere with them, they become an organic and psychic extension of their states, their very being pledged to that of their owners and dependent on it. Our door was compassionate with us, and its wood – where moisture and the storms of the ages had settled, with the troubles of the times and the rifts of spirit – was tender with us. It defended us from the wind of Bu Hamad and from many other winds that left their debris on the thresholds of our life.

The second difference between my father's life in the Nuqra Camp and that of my uncle Abu Taisir in the Wehdat Camp was that my uncle lisped, pronouncing the letters *siin* and *saad* as if they were *thaa'*. So my uncle's telling a leader *your mother thuckth* had a different ring to it from the same insult coming from my father.

We lived in our houses as if we would live in them for ever. Even when Bu Hamad was threatening to break down the door of our apartment, and the doors of other apartments in the building, we did not imagine that in reality anyone was capable of pulling our floor out from under us or of stripping away our walls – walls we had painted dozens of times during our seemingly everlasting existence in the apartment, walls where we had hammered in dozens of nails to hold dozens of framed pictures. We had also changed the window curtains several times, when they were worn out by the sun, by the dust of days, and by our bodies that grew in secret when we hid behind them in successive seasons of hide-and-seek. We upholstered the sofas of the front room twice, then we changed them once. We took our wooden tea tables to our neighbour Abu Muaadh many times, so he could fix their wobbly legs.

Our apartment was made up of two bedrooms and an open front room overlooking the street, something that made it more like a wide hallway in fact, big enough for a set of small sofas and a set of tea tables, with a side corner for a modest buffet. My mother and father's bedroom opened onto the front room with a wide double door, so if any guest came unexpectedly, we delayed welcoming them and left them standing at the door until my mother closed the open door to her bedroom. Our bedroom was also our living room, as there was a television in it and a sofa with

141

a storage compartment which my mother used for our blankets. There were also two wardrobes, the large one for the girls' clothing and the small one for the boys' things. Then when the clothes multiplied for us girls, as was to be expected, we took over a growing space in my mother's wardrobe.

My father commissioned Abu Muaadh to make us a bunk bed with two levels, followed by another of three; two of my brothers slept on the two-level bunk bed while three of my sisters slept on the three-level bed, the lightest one climbing up to the top bunk. Those left were distributed on the floor and the sofa, which was unfolded at night, while the nursing infants among us would be next to my mother and father in their room, on a small bed repaired many times by Abu Muaadh and repainted pink or blue, according to the sex of the newborn. When the baby was bigger he joined us in our room, which was shrinking around us, and a new infant would take his place in my mother and father's room. When some of our bodies became large, our legs lengthening and our arms stretching out, cramming the small room with our extremities and our appendages, my father had recourse, as usual, to Abu Muaadh. He closed off the balcony, which extended outside our room like a narrow appendix, placing wooden boards on all the open sides, so that it turned into an extra room. He made it possible to open the side next to the clothes line by means of two wide wooden planks which could slide sideways to open and close. The new room was used as a study corner, with those of us in their final year of high school given priority to stay in it. At night it turned into a bedroom, big enough for two of us at least. It was warm in the winter, while stifling summer nights required the use of a rotating electric fan, with the door to the balcony kept partially open, in the faint hope that some of the air conditioner's chill would seep from our room into the closed appendix.

During extinguished nights our bodies resisted sleep, our breath tossing and turning. We would talk, mumble, pinch, kick, tickle, grunt, punch, tussle, ache, and laugh, the bodies near each other whispering amid the anger of the more distant ones at being excluded from the rustling speech. A fart would ring out, piercing the calm of the night. We would yell at the farter, who would swear, lying, that he had nothing to do with it. But a "blank shot" noisy fart was easier to take than a scheming, malicious, noiseless one; we would breathe its rotten smell coming from under the blankets, especially on the days when my mother made cauliflower maqlouba, as it spread in the confined air like nuclear fallout. From experience we came to link the fart, loud or silent, to the rears of the ones who produced it, even if they denied it, and if the smell got worse we would pounce on them, doing battle with pillows. On secret nights, our desires, curled under the blankets and covers, could not resist stretching out and circling beyond the ceiling of the room. Our cocoons would split open and the butterflies of our wishes would emerge, our branches would flower, our fruit would hang heavy on our bodies, which grew larger hastily and avidly, with a touch of rashness, during our troubled, tossing sleep.

On days overflowing with our lives we would spread out our bodies, which would collide with each other. But we did not mind our nudity, or some of it, which might escape us. At least, we did not cover it completely, just as we did not attempt to contain our flesh when its size overflowed the meagre spaces available to us for privacy. We would dress and undress with the smallest measure of reserve, without completely hiding from each other's eyes, on the basis (perhaps) that our bodies, growing next to each other, resembled one another. My father would roam between the rooms of the house in his white underwear, stained here and there by the laundry blue used in the wash. Abu Muaadh would open the door to the boys and girls of the building, sent by their mothers to ask for Umm Muaadh's large cooking pot, wearing pyjama bottoms and a vest, the cotton fabric softened and nearly transparent from repeated washing in boiling water. Our neighbour Abu Husam would sit on the balcony in spotted underpants, smoking a water pipe. If we lost a blouse (or a skirt, a dress, a shirt, or trousers), we would wander around the narrow spaces between the furniture in T-shirts and underwear and slips, looking for our things in our messy existence, too cramped for individuality. Then we would open the door of the bathroom, not off limits whatever the activity of those who occupied it, and there would be my mother, naked in the tub, using a pumice stone on her heel, gathering in the tissue of her flesh, which exhaled soapy vapours, while the foam of the shampoo formed a white cloud on her head. We would ask her about our missing clothes, and she would ask us to scrub her back where her hands couldn't reach. Then Sukaina might surprise us, leaving her apartment unnoticed by her sleeping husband Jamil, coming barefoot, in a light-blue slip, its white lace unravelling in several places. As usual Sukaina would enter our apartment, the door open to all by its nature, without knocking. She would call for my mother to make her a cup of hot cocoa, so my mother would hurry out of the tub, wrapping her body in a small towel which concealed only fragments of her round flesh, glowing as if lit by the water. She would shout to us to bring something to cover Sukaina and ask one of my sisters to put the milk on the stove. Then Umm Husam opened our door and took off her dress, trusting the discretion of our house to hold her nakedness within it; she asked my mother to lend her the black uplift bra, so she could wear it to the wedding of her husband's cousin. Meanwhile Bashar, Mahdiyya's youngest son, ran naked into our house and threw his small body on my mother after fleeing their house as his mother was bathing him, in preparation for a historic event; he had covered the relatively long distance to our house nude, and implored my mother to hide him in her house from the circumciser, his crying entwining with our voices asking about our missing clothes. The scenes of abundant flesh running through the corners of our house seemed like part of an orgy, not planned, not artificial, and not indecent . . . completely.

When our nakedness and that of our neighbours was concealed outwardly, it showed itself implicitly, appearing through enquiries and rhetorical questions. My mother, for example, was always asking Mahdiyya the question that bothered her, as it did all the neighbour women: "Umm Muaadh, how do you sleep with Abu Muaadh?" (My mother would give Mahdiyya a look that told her that the "sleeping" she meant was having sex.) The second question, almost as insistent as the first, was, "When does Abu Muaadh see you naked?"

Mahdiyya had five boys and seven girls, and she lived with her husband and her children in an annexe, made up of two rooms plus a kitchen and a bathroom, next to our building in al-Nuqra. In addition to his work in the evening in Hawalli in a private carpentry shop owned by an Iranian furniture merchant, Abu

Muaadh worked in the morning as a carpenter in the Kuwaiti Ministry of Public Works. He used his skill in carpentry, even if it lacked the slightest aesthetic touch, to build many wooden cabinets with drawers, shelves, and doors all round the walls of their cramped annexe, to hold their enormous family's clutter. He also divided the kids' bedroom horizontally by designing a wooden ceiling on supports, so the room in fact came to have two floors. The lower floor, which reached two metres in height, was for the boys to sleep in or to stand upright. The second floor was a metre and a half high; it was reached by a movable wooden ladder, and it served as a room where the girls lived, studied, and slept, and where they spent most of their time. They hunched over when they stood and moved across the narrow space with their backs bent, or else they crawled on all fours. The boys on one floor and the girls on the other all slept on disintegrating mattresses or light floor cushions which were folded in the morning, rolled up, and stuffed into the cabinets. Abu Muaadh and Umm Muaadh slept in the other room, which was used as a front room, a family room, and a dining room, and sometimes as a temporary carpentry workshop, if someone asked Abu Muaadh to restore or repair a piece of furniture. Some years after they were married Abu Muaadh's mother and father came to live with them, so they shared this front room with them as a bedroom.

Mahdiyya told my mother and the neighbours that she did not remember the last time she was naked in front of Abu Muaadh, as she slept in her daytime clothes – they were also her nightclothes, with a design that allowed for multiple uses. As for Abu Muaadh, Mahdiyya asserted that she could not imagine him completely naked, perhaps because of a natural shortcoming in her powers of imagination, and because of a shortcoming of his also, which was that he had simply not stripped in front of her in ages. Mahdiyya could also not taste Abu Muaadh's body, admitting that their bodies barely touched or rubbed together. Then a laugh bubbled up, as she recalled surreal scenes of her sex life with Abu Muaadh. Once he had sex with her standing in the bathroom while she was boiling the white wash in the huge aluminium pot on the Primus stove. Mahdiyya went on stirring the laundry with big wooden tongs with one hand, while she supported herself with the other on the edge of the sink, lifting her dress and relaxing her underwear enough to allow Abu Muaadh to slip into her easily, without giving her a word or a breath, a gasp or a gulp. For her part she made do with the croaking of the stove and the exhalation of the hot water on her face in place of absent expressions of desire. Abu Muaadh might slap her broad rear if she tried to adjust a position of her "arse" that was uncomfortable for her, then he expelled his fluid into her, left her, and disappeared. One night, while she was sleeping in the front room next to Abu Muaadh, not far from where her in-laws lay, Abu Muaadh's penis crept out of his pyjama bottoms (which only needed one button to open) and beneath her dress, moving under her panties, which had slipped a bit. Mahdiyya had to stiffen when her mother-in-law suddenly woke up and asked her for a drink of water. Abu Muaadh had thrust into her from behind while she was lying on her side; her face was towards her mother-in-law, so she feigned sleep as her mother-in-law kept asking for the water. She was depending on the darkness, the other woman's weak sight, and Abu Muaadh's sexual technique, which preferred rapid thrusts and ejaculation with no tremors or vibration, amid absolute silence, contained breathing, and sweat coming from the heat of the covers rather than the heat of desire. When he had finished with her, she got up and took the water to her mother-in-law, who chided her for her deep sleep.

For years, Mahdiyya, together with the neighbour women, trusted their bodies to my mother on the afternoons when their husbands were thankfully absent from their lives. Their nakedness remained clearly expressed in their stories, out of love for it, rarely, or out of rancour over it, usually. It was expressed eloquently and creatively at times, and more often in trite clichés. The mirrors of our house, on which our nakedness and that of the neighbours had been imprinted, continued to turn over the pages of their memory of rich flesh that had been entrusted to them, and did not reveal its secrets. But then our nakedness left us, as if we had gone to sleep and then wakened to a new religion that was the enemy of all manifestations of human flesh, however expressed.

My sisters all began to wear the hijab in the years when the naughty body began to burst out, going through life with yearning gazes lowered, covering their chests with their arms, chests that were no longer a whisper but a shout. My mother was angry over the humps of shame that grew on their backs, as their height was shortened along with their gazes, as their ambitions diminished and their hopes receded. Reema, the third girl, was the first one to wear the hijab, inaugurating the era of covering bodies and confining them under wraps. She had not yet bled as a woman for the first time when she made the decision to wear the hijab. She was eleven years old, obediently following the guidance of the Islamic Education teacher in her efforts to curb the bodies of little girls in elementary school early, before they could contemplate their own devilish potential. My father tried to turn Reema away from the imported guidance, or at least to put it off until her awareness formed alongside the forming of her body, but she stuck to her position with the support of the teacher, on loan from Egypt. The teacher's hijab was composed of vivid sets of clothes and head coverings like over-decorated hats, with large brooches or bright flowers ornamenting them on the side. She allowed her ears to appear, as no affirmative religious text had come down stamping them as "*Awrah*" to be concealed, so golden earrings hung from them, their common designs suggesting that they were bought for the purpose of storing her money. My mother was not enthusiastic about Reema's hijab, because it meant buying new clothes for her, and that meant an extra burden on the household budget, always in a state of collapse. But Reema dragged my mother over to her faction less than a year after she began wearing the hijab, as it no longer seemed acceptable for a mother to walk in the street bare-headed while her young daughter was covered by a full hijab. Reema's dress was stricter than that of the Islamic Education teacher, since Reema avoided bright colours and preferred long, loose jilbab coats that subdued the features of her body, along with all-encompassing head coverings that concealed the hair, the shoulders, and the chest. This was after she placed herself in the hands of another Islamic Education teacher the next year, who was among the supporters of almost total restraint of the body.

My mother conformed to the reality of the hijab, although she was less prim and committed to all its fine, strict regulations than Reema was, since she hated dark jilbabs of a single colour. She allowed herself to wear baggy dresses that gave her body, inclined to plumpness, both breadth and depth, so she did not feel guilty when she ate, nor did she feel embarrassed by the extension of her areas of fat, which knew no restraint after that. Then my sisters followed Reema and my mother as their bodies matured and their expectations in life subsided.

The contagion of obligatory covering passed to the neighbours, though they were already covered by the conditions of their lives. Umm Muaadh, for example, was not very different before the era of the hijab than she was afterwards, since she previously wore long dresses and jilbabs without a waist, with fabric flowing in every direction, and gathered her curly hair in a kerchief to keep it out of her way, not to cover it. After she entered the era of veiled Islam she began to visit us with the same dresses, wearing a prayer scarf over her hair; then when she took her place on the sofa in our room she took off the scarf and remained with her kerchief, not rushing to absolute concealment in the presence of my father. This was on the basis of a personal fatwa she had issued, to the effect that the men of the building – those we see daily, entering their houses whether the men are present or absent, inspecting their bedrooms and looking stealthily at our bodies in their mirrors, if possible; those to whose wives we offer advice about restoring the whiteness of underwear yellowed by the remains of urine or traces of wet dreams, helping them hang out the washing or sew zippers in trousers or chop onions or prepare trays of Eid maamoul sweets large enough for a tribe – those men, because of their shared, intimate association, can licitly become our *mahram*. No-one would ever hold anything against Sukaina, either, who continued, right up until we left the building and its people, to take advantage of Jamil's naps and to flee to our house whenever she could, in her slips with their ravelling lace.

I, for my part – and I won't entirely seek refuge from my own

I – I was off the table, beyond questioning, incomparable. That's because I, from the time I was first brought into the world (not from when I was brought up), came out to different expectations and conditions of nakedness, going beyond our safe, trustworthy mirrors to others that shamed and revealed.

In most of life, it was enough for me to dress as myself for me to be naked.

I never for a moment imagined that those days would be my last in Kuwait. I was brimming with confidence that we were established in our place, despite the legacy of displacement. Even when the anxious path of departure snatched us, you and me, so that we were enfolded by dry desert and a one-eyed sky, I persisted in my sinful certainty that with you and through you, I would be back. From my boundless confidence or overflowing sin, I even left the novel *The Unbearable Lightness of Being* on the bedside table with a bookmark in the middle, so I could finish reading it after we came back. Shall I tell you the truth, O my queen? I think I faked certainty; I seized it from the maze of my life, and I ended up wandering even more, one sin begetting others.

Aside from anything else, the matter of our house in the ghetto of al-Nuqra, the house which had held an emotional space in our lives (one that now seems ghostly), was settled as far as we were concerned. We had to leave it at any cost. I returned to it from the hospital after I gave birth to you, coming to the same house I had entered as the first baby and the first wish at my mother's breast. I carried you as a new life attached to my defeated life, and as I hugged you to my chest I strove to keep you from being an extension of my defeat. A month after your birth I got my divorce, and then a week later we moved from the Nuqra ghetto to al-Farwaniyah, to a large apartment with three bedrooms, a large front room, a family living room, two bathrooms and two balconies, one off the kitchen which Bella used to shelter his pigeons. The new apartment was on the third floor of a recently constructed building, and its rent was more than double the rent of our historic apartment. That did not prevent us, however, from gathering up our extensive clutter over days whose brightness was aborted behind our drawn curtains, and on concealing dark nights. We left the apartment and the building and the ghetto without any farewell, as if we were "committing a crime", as our neighbours gossiped. For my mother, my divorce was the "crime". She went to sleep and woke up crushed, and sometimes she remained lying on the bed, unable to sleep or to wake up. When she did sleep, worry for me crouched on her head, along with an additional worry (you), as she kept saying, so she would wake with a heavy headache, one that brought her down whenever she tried to get on with life. My mother did not find in our comfortable new apartment, with its space and conveniences, any compensation for the long, overcrowded years in the Nuqra apartment; she found only a place to flee from the faces of the ancient women of the building, who besieged her with questions about the circumstances of my divorce. Umm Muaadh and Umm Husam visited us in our new apartment, carrying with them the gossip that had lingered after us. My mother hurried them away with a meagre reception, offering them only bare tea followed by coffee that clearly said "goodbye". The women's eyes roamed over the large front room, without daring to look at the bedrooms or join my mother in the kitchen. They realised that their era with Rauaa had ended, the era when they sat together to make savoury pastries, Eid cookies, and maamoul sweets, accompanied by the uncoordinated rhythm

153

of the cookie moulds which we children raced to bang on the table with great excitement. For our part, yours and mine, our era had begun.

I loved our new apartment, despite its unsentimental air, the pale walls with their cheap paint, and the absence of our pictures, which remained in boxes; we only hung some of them, at distant intervals, as my mother's mood allowed. She had also lost her interest in acquiring figurines of flirtatious men and fiery women. You and I occupied the main bedroom, with an attached bathroom and a small hallway large enough for a little chest for towels and shoes. It had a main door that separated the passage from the rest of the rooms, and an inner door that separated the room from the bathroom and the hallway, so it was like a house within the house. It became our space, yours and mine, just right for us; I could shut the door and we would be in our own domain, alone but not lonely. I bought a single bed for me and a small bed for you, fenced on all sides like a cage, though its wooden bars did not keep you from standing up in your seventh month and jumping from your bed to mine. I also bought a desk and two bookcases, which I stood along one of the walls. Finally I acquired the armchair that I had imagined during our long, overcrowded past in our apartment in the Nuqra ghetto, when it seemed like a dissolute dream – I would plunge into its ample foam and read, going through the twists, turns, and steppes of the pages without the words falling into our crowded life, amid our tangled bodies and colliding voices. It was an armchair with a high back and a wide, oblong seat, the ends sewn up by the personal possessive pronoun: my chair, against my wall, in my room, in the space designed for it between the desk and the clothes closet, not budging and not shaking. That gave it something of the character of an unrealised homeland. When I sought shelter in it, it was as if I was seeking shelter in . . . a chair, to the extent that a chair can become an embrace and a source of warmth.

When I closed the doors of the room on us, both the main one and the inner one, you and I were in our own home country, while the others – my mother, my father, my sisters, and my brothers – lived in the diaspora as refugees in the new apartment, bigger than our nearly eternal apartment in the Nuqra ghetto. Despite its size, the new diaspora apartment was choked with our clutter, which we brought with us from our old apartment. We were amazed at how our existence, during all these past years, had been squeezed between all these things. Yet even though we only lived a few months in the apartment of our renewed diaspora, it nonetheless saw us add more clutter and pile up more things. Perhaps we assumed in our feverish unconscious that they would provide legitimate evidence of us in the place and in our shaky existence, as the empty spaces in the apartment shrank and our bodies, which had escaped each other for a time, came close together again. We bought a cheap dining table with ten chairs. Its thin, sensitive wood shook under the weight of our bodies, suddenly raised from a cloth on the floor to the table; we needed some time to get used to sitting on the chairs. We also bought a set of used sofas in the shape of an L for the family room. But the trait of being confined and crowded, flesh sticking to flesh, prevailed over the newer, transitory trait of space and expansiveness; we sat cross-legged on the dining chairs, yearning drawing us to the floor beneath us. We spread out on the floor in front of the television set in the family room, which within the first days had turned into a room for sleeping, studying, and eating, as we came down from the high dining table and the uncomfortable chairs to the floor. If our days in Kuwait had been longer, perhaps we would have cloned the apartment in the Nuqra ghetto, with its tight space and human flesh pushing against itself, in the new diaspora apartment. In fact our bodies had decreased in number and extent, with the departure of Rima and Jamal to study in Jordan, and with the marriage of Rania. But the bodies of those who remained grew bigger. We were always many, and any space, however large, was always tight for us.

When you gurgled and babbled and tried to pull out the bars of your crib, calling for me, I would leave my writing, which was trying to form itself in my secret nights in our room, yours and mine, our home country miraculously emerging from the diaspora of the rest. I would go to you, lift you out of your cage, hug you to me and lie down with you on my bed. I would stretch you out on my belly, your soft cheek resting on my chest, your breath, mixed with burps of milk and Miloba children's tea, condensing on my neck. I would massage your back, and the gurgles of your tender stomach would tickle my belly. Then you would let loose your winds, so the calm of our retreat would be broken by a quickly unravelling string of farts. Then you would smile, draw a deep, long breath, and sigh, your breath a rustling breeze, a butterfly, a playful bird, and fall asleep.

Then we went to sleep and woke the next morning to find that Kuwait had gone. The three of us: you, my father, and I were in our new house, in our Kuwait. At first we tried to manage our affairs as if the Iraqi invasion were an action that did not entirely concern us, and Iraq's swallowing Kuwait most certainly did not put an end to my home country, a room large enough for our two lives, yours and mine, and a bathroom and a hallway and two doors, each with a key, in our apartment in al-Farwaniyah. We continued in our certainty, richly mixed with delusion, that nothing would affect the condition of our diaspora, even during the first weeks of the invasion: our money, which had historically been meagre, was still in its hiding places, and our store of food, which had historically been ample, still filled the kitchen cabinets and the drawers of the refrigerator. Then after two months we discovered that we were living a peculiar life not subject to any interpretation of any kind, inexplicable. We realised that even if we were in our place, our place was no longer completely in its place. Our worry, my father's and mine, was in the end not for ourselves so much as it was for the rest of us, stuck in Jordan in a summer vacation that had gone on longer than planned.

My mother and some of my brothers and sisters had gone to Jordan for the summer vacation. Rima and Jamal were already there, continuing their university study, registered in the summer term, while Rania had left our house and our calculations early. After her graduation in business administration from the University of Jordan, Rania had returned to Kuwait and worked at the National Bank of Kuwait, earning a salary that allowed her to buy a used Mitsubishi, and hijabs with extravagant patterns. Then she became engaged to a colleague of hers and got married three months after starting at the bank. She did not take some of the burden from me, as we had assumed – or rather, as I had assumed. My father discovered Rania's plans to remove herself from our calculations from the beginning, specifically from the day she came home carrying many shopping bags, after receiving her first pay cheque. She spread out the contents of the bags on the table, taking time to reveal her treasures before us: blouses, shirts with printed designs and sequins on the chest, skirts with a mermaid cut that brought out the details of the figure (one that wore a hijab but did not abide by the spirit of the veil), shoes, and obviously cheap handbags of every colour that was not neutral. When Rula wanted to try on a purple shoe with many metal rings, Rania snatched it from her like a wolf.

At the beginning of the school holidays my father had loaded the family into his car and driven them overland to Jordan, to stay in Grandmother Radiyya's house. He returned after two weeks, on the one hand because he didn't think he should close his electrical repair shop for a long time, and on the other because it was hard for him to think of leaving me alone in the house with you. A month after the invasion, one of my father's acquaintances came from Jordan with a letter from my mother, saying that the money she had with her had run out and she had borrowed from people she knew there. She was thinking of putting herself and my brothers and sisters on the next bus and coming back to Kuwait – at least she would be in her own house, and if the worst happened (meaning war), she would die in Kuwait, the country where she had spent her life. It didn't seem to us as if the worst was likely to happen. Even when the news reported daily on the huge numbers of American troops advancing on the Gulf (cloaked as a precaution with the adjective "international", to avoid the appearance of bullying), together with naval fleets gathered as if for doomsday in preparation for the war to liberate Kuwait – even then we were confident that the war would not happen. In no way was the source of our confidence any doubt about the American readiness for violence; it was rather doubt about the competence of Saddam Hussein himself and about how serious he was.

By two months after the Iraqi invasion of Kuwait, the momentous event receded from the news broadcasts, no longer the only event. Over time we had got used to the unusual situation, becoming familiar with a condition that was neither invasion nor occupation nor siege nor expulsion, completely. The condition was the closest thing to incomprehension, laying out possibilities for coming days all of which might be possible just as they might be impossible. On evenings wrapped in radio frequencies, we would sit on the balcony, my father and I, counting the apartments in the neighbouring building emptied of their occupants. The façades of some of the buildings, which had been stripped of their air conditioners, looked like faces with their eyes gouged out. Our own eyes were on the cats gathered around an overturned garbage container next to the chassis of an old Volvo. My father commented that Saddam did not want Kuwait, or at least did not want to stay there for long. For him the operation amounted to an armed robbery, as it was illogical, according to my father's theory, for someone – Saddam – to pull out the windows and the floor tiles from a house he had taken over in order to live in it! My father thought it was a matter of time, and that it wouldn't be long before Saddam decided to withdraw from Kuwait, satisfied with what he and others had looted from it.

Nonetheless, it did not seem advisable for my mother and my siblings to come back, even if Kuwait, the only country we knew, were to be returned to us. My father and I sat in the front room, spreading out on the floor green zaatar, olive oil, some canned food, and some possibilities. A few days after the television broadcasts were cut off, an inevitable result of the invasion, the Iraqis had begun broadcasting from a station in Basra, so we became less subject to boredom, thank God, and less addicted to waiting. We watched some American films that brought back America's foundering in the swamp of the Vietnam War (of course not in order to gloat), and the play *Bye Bye London*, which reminded the Kuwaitis, by the confession of one of their own, of their revels in Western countries. We also watched the daily programme *Hello!*, which seemed to be prepared in haste by the Military Media Division; it examined the very high morale of Iraqi troops on the front and dispensed charges of enthusiasm to the tune of "Ha khouty ha, my brothers!" It also played long news clippings of demonstrations led by the oppressed of the earth, along with remnants of the fragmented left, confused enemies of capitalism, and those who hated, without any suspicious agenda, the interference of international imperialism with the fates of peoples and states, all of them condemning the war which the coalition forces, led by the United States, claimed to be waging on Iraq for the sake of the liberation of Kuwait. In the intervals between news broadcasts, improvised programmes, and films making a point, my father and I were surrounded by the incomprehensible – so we could not resist dancing to the rhythm of "Hiya wa-hay, ha ha, today the charming one came to us, so welcome him, my family!" I would tilt my head, bend at the waist, and shake my buttocks, like the full-bodied Iraqi women, while my father inclined his rear, lifting one of his legs, performing his famously lame form of dancing.

Where was America with respect to Israel's occupation of Palestine? Why did it not summon the coalition forces to liberate

Palestine? Angry Palestinians in the Jordanian camps were asking those questions, their faces grim, on television one evening. Palestinian university students also marched in a mass demonstration on one of the streets of Delhi, denouncing the coming war; one news agency covered it and Iraqi television rebroadcast it time after time. They raised Palestinian and Iraqi flags and pictures of Saddam Hussein and Abu Ammar, and as usual they burned Israeli and American flags and effigies of George Bush, demanding the liberation of Palestine first. My father moved his eyes between me and the throngs of demonstrators, and said, as if he had reached an inescapable conclusion, "We ate shit!" The collective, gathering "we" encompassed him and me and all the Palestinians.

One of us, my father or I, had to go to Jordan to support my mother and my brothers and sisters, to provide them with a house and money and food, even if it were in lesser quantities than they had been accustomed to in the past. My father explained to me that it might not be easy for someone of his age and in his field to get work in Jordan. When he saw my panic at the idea of leaving the homeland I had recently furnished in our new, diaspora apartment, where we had settled only a few months earlier, he suggested that we cast lots. He wrote our names on two pieces of paper which he folded several times, then he asked me to draw the paper with the name of the one fated to be displaced. I unfolded the paper slowly, in no hurry for the result. My father's face became sombre. I shook my head in agonised acceptance. My father spoke, guilt tinging the edges of his tone:

"Forget the lots! I'm going to go."

But I knew that his offer was more emotional than real, for I was the difference in life, I was the one who made a difference in our thorny life. Naeem's life was broken down during most seasons, working only to stop, exposed, and patched only to come undone, until I spread out my life over his, and over all the lives gathered under his and around it. When I graduated from the University of Kuwait, I worked in a private school with limited resources, teaching the English language, for a period of one semester. Then I took a position at the International English School teaching Arabic–English translation and the Arabic language to non-native speakers, beginning with the second semester. I was hired after responding to a newspaper advertisement seeking a teacher to begin immediately, and that meant that they disregarded my limited experience. I understood that the teacher whose place I took so rapidly and without much scrutiny of my qualifications had fallen down dead in one of the classes, so they wanted me to take his place temporarily and pick up where he had left off. When the new academic year began the school chose not to do without me, even though they had many applications from teachers more experienced than I was. Instead they increased my salary and then doubled my yearly rise after I lightened the emphasis on the sacred revelation of Arabic, and made way for contemporary Arabic, more spoken in character, in which my students progressed more smoothly and with fewer stumbles. In the later afternoon I worked at the Horizon Institute for Languages and Tutoring, giving supplementary classes for the English language curriculum to high-school students at all levels in the state schools. At first I was paid a fixed salary, then when students began flocking to my classes, I stipulated to the administration that instead I take 50 per cent of the fees of every student registered with me and they agreed, especially after they were forced to set up a waiting list for my classes, requiring students to register early to guarantee a place. During the summer breaks I gave English classes, through the same institute, to employees of companies, banks, and organisations in the private sector.

My income was more than double my father's, so I shared in covering Rania's university fees, and took charge of the fees and expenses for Rima and Jamal's university educations. From time to time I sent some money to my grandmother Fatima, which might beautify my aunt Najah in the eyes of prospective grooms, who were not attracted by the gold bracelets that weighed down her wrists. I would also send Grandmother Fatima cool linen fabric so she could make herself knickers with many hidden pockets, and I would ask those who travelled regularly to take Grandmother Radiyya shampoo, conditioner, hair dye, and foreign, perfumed moisturising creams for her face. Since my uncle Abu Taisir had begun to spend more time at home than at the vegetable stand, venting his feelings on his wife and kids and aiming his finger indiscriminately at the faces that appeared time and again on the news, I set aside something like a monthly allowance for him, which would allow him to preserve his "dignity". He then could break a tomato crate over the head of a customer with no great deterrent, or throw it in the face of the shop owner in a greater outburst, and at the same time continue giving his finger to the television as a public political position, even though with less convulsive anger. Rauaa, for her part, stopped stealing from Naeem and began to feel less guilty about buying her figurines, though after my divorce she lost her passion for them and became an apostate. My father's money, hard earned, went to the rent for our apartment in the Nuqra ghetto, and then for the apartment in

163

al-Farwaniyah, so Bu Hamad no longer burst upon us like a sandy yellow windstorm, threatening to uproot us from our established homeland suspended on the second floor of the apartment building. The rest of my father's money went towards our food, which increased, increased a lot. Nonetheless affluence still eluded us, and our feet still could not stretch out much from under the covers of our life. Every extra penny that entered our house found a patch waiting for that penny to sew onto the fabric of our existence, if not a disaster to be dealt with.

I folded my name in my hand and went to our room, yours and mine, our independent homeland, our own geography that held itself aloof from the possibilities of perishing, or so I thought. I gathered some of our things, leaving most of them in place; we might return to them someday, any day, since not all homelands are necessarily fleeting.

It was in the afternoon, and I was alone with you. My father had gone to his shop, for even though he had refrained from going to his government job, deferring to the wishes of the Kuwaitis, nonetheless he chose to open the shop and sit in it, if only for appearances' sake, so that the electrical equipment being repaired in it would not be plundered. In fact, his shop saw unexpected activity during the months of the Iraqi occupation. People brought in devices in which all life and electricity had stopped circulating, and Iraqis flocked to him as well, carrying dusty radios and televisions assumed to be extinct, so he could repair them. The shop which had not fed us when it was in Kuwait now began to feed us and others with us after it became part of Iraq, in some nightmarish sense. I was in the family room looking for your teething ring, when my eyes fell on a small, folded piece of paper near the leg of the television table. It was the second paper from the draw that had determined who would go and who would stay. I unfolded it and read the name of the person who was not to go. I thought I had not read what I read. I went to my room, opened the desk drawer, and took out the first lottery paper, the one bearing the name of the person fate had chosen to make the trip. I verified that I had indeed read it correctly. You were standing in your bed, babbling sweetly, laughter and fresh drool flowing from you. I picked you up, sat on my broad armchair, and sat you down in my lap, holding your head to my heart. My eyes were following a new crack in the wall, caused by a recent yawning of the bricks and stretching of the paint. The crack spread and worsened at the top of the wall and at the bottom, branching to the left and right; then the wall split, cracking open my homeland.

Next to each other on the desk were both papers from the lottery, unconcealed. Jihad . . . that was the name that lay, forsaken, on each of the two papers.

I left my room with you and two suitcases. One contained some of our clothes, yours and mine. The other, smaller case held a framed picture of you on the first day of your life, a being with enchanting senses; an album of pictures tracking your days, threaded through mine; and your teething ring, two bottles of milk, half a dozen packets of Similac milk, four packets of Cerelac (wheat and rice), three packets of Miloba children's tea, a bag of nappies, and four bottles of mineral water. From my shoulder hung my leather university bag, containing the first stories I had written, a file of papers, documents, and certificates belonging to me and my siblings, and some money for the unknown time ahead. If only, O queen of my heart, we had been able to take our homeland with us, in my father's used red Nissan, in which he took us and my rupture to Basra!

On the mournful road to Iraq, the possibilities of Kuwait remaining or returning began to fall from my hand, though I tried to gather what I could of their scraps. I was frightened because the places there, the faces, the long time it had belonged to me dissolved like fresh ink in the water of my eyes. My father did not speak much along the way, and his eyes avoided mine. I brought the two pieces of paper along with me, each one with "Jihad" as the first and only option, though I did not show him the other copy of my name that I had found. According to the plan my father was going to take us to Basra, and from there a taxi would take us to the Hotel Sagman in Baghdad, which was among the few hotels that accepted payment in Iraqi dinars from non-Iraqis, rather than only in precious American dollars. I got the name of the hotel from a colleague of mine who was the director of the school's library. We had agreed that he would go ahead and then wait for me there, and that I would accompany him and his family to Jordan.

A week before our trip I went to see Rania in her apartment in al-Salmiya, to say goodbye. Rania, who was pregnant, and her husband Ala' had made their decision: they would remain in Kuwait whether or not war broke out. If Kuwait returned they would remain in it, and if it turned into Iraq, they would live there. She had stopped going to the bank, in compliance with the orders of the Kuwaiti government in exile, since she did not wish to anger the Kuwaitis, who might return and make reprisals. She had improvised a hair salon in her house, setting aside one room for it, and began receiving women bored with waiting and brides who had put off their weddings and now decided to go ahead with them, as the likely war did not disrupt the natural life cycle. She set their hair, applied make-up, and rented them her wedding dress. Ala' continued going to his job at the bank, in accordance with orders from his Kuwaiti manager, who remained at home. Ala' secretly assembled papers and documents the Kuwaiti manager asked him for, keeping them in files in his apartment. If Kuwait returned he would give the files to his manager, and if Kuwait remained Iraq, he would burn them and find himself working in an Iraqi bank. Rania apologised because she could not give me any money to help the family in Jordan until I found a job. Inwardly, I was surprised by her apology – never before had she offered me or anyone else money, nor had I ever asked a penny of her. I realised then that Rania made more money, in this state of non-war, than we had thought or ever could have imagined.

I gathered up my books and your toys and put them in cardboard cartons, to protect them from the dust of abandonment. I placed them in a corner of my room and spread a large waxed cloth over them, so they wouldn't be eaten away by humidity. Everything was ready for my departure; all I had to do was to take care of Sheila and her friends. Sheila was the Sri Lankan maid whom I hired at the beginning of the summer vacation, when my mother and siblings went to Jordan; she stayed with you and took care of you while I was out. After the invasion, when the Iraqi attack had become a reality (however confused), the institute was closed and I no longer went in. I apologised to Sheila for having to end her service, since I was now without work and without any prospects of money.

I woke terrified to the breathless ringing of the doorbell, after 1 a.m. It was Sheila. She was crying, standing before me with eyes open wide, looking over her shoulder to make sure that no-one was coming after her. She was barefoot, wearing a dress with an uneven hem and a light jacket. We were in the first week of the second month of the invasion, of waiting. From her hybrid language, a mixture of mangled English and worse Arabic, I understood that Sheila was staying in an apartment in a building near ours, with a group of Sri Lankan and Indian maids who worked by the hour or by the day. Some of them had fled from their Kuwaiti sponsors and they were stranded after the Iraqi invasion. A few days earlier, the doorman of her building had started going to them, sometimes trying to seduce them with money and sometimes threatening to take them by force to the commander of an Iraqi military unit headquartered at the head of the airport road. When he came to Sheila she put him off by giving him a gold chain she had bought for her daughter, for whose marriage she had been saving over many years. The doorman left her alone for a few days, but he kept sniffing around her, looking for any other gold in her possession. Sheila swore to him that she had given him everything she had, but Padmavati, an Indian flatmate, told the doorman that Sheila was hiding earrings in a place no-one would ever think of. The doorman left Padmavati alone and pounced on Sheila. He turned her over and put her in the position of a stooped rabbit, removing her pants and inspecting her rear until he brought out the earrings she had hidden between her buttocks. He wasn't satisfied with the gold earrings, for Sheila's small, cocoa-coloured rear aroused his water and his blood, so he bit her there. She screamed in pain. Then he hammered his penis into her with a burning, violent blow that tore her body. A day after it happened – a day Sheila had spent stretched out in bed, sweating and bleeding – the doorman became afraid that something bad would happen to her, so he threw her out of the apartment and threatened that if she came back, he himself would take her to the military unit. Sheila begged to stay with me. I asked her about her passport; she took it out from under her dress and gave it to me, then fell to the floor. My father picked her up and put her in the tub, then closed the bathroom door on us. I took off her clothes. Her pants were nearly stuck to her bloody rear. I put the plug in the tub and filled it halfway with water, then I poured a packet of salt into it. Sheila squirmed in place, in pain; I told her that the salt would disinfect the wound. I bathed her, dried her, and dressed her in pyjamas of mine, then I stretched her out on a bed belonging to one of my sisters. My father had made her some instant chicken noodle soup and put bits of bread in it, and I gave her an aspirin and an antibiotic capsule. Sheila went to sleep as we heard the call for the dawn prayer. My father prayed; I sat before him, waiting until I heard him recite the formula ending the prayer in a rhythmic chant, so we could drink coffee together.

A week later, when Sheila had recovered and put a little flesh on her bony frame, the doorbell rang calmly. It was eight in the evening. At the door stood three Asian women who asked me about Sheila. They were her flatmates in the apartment, all of them Sri Lankan and one from her village. They introduced themselves to me: Nimali, Chandrika, and Chanti. Each was holding a bundle of clothes in her hand. When Sheila saw them she rejoiced, and asked them how they had got rid of the doorman. The women looked at each other, then Chandrika spoke for them. She said that the doorman's conscience had awakened; he had wept and made them weep, and left them alone and gone off, even giving them the gold he had taken from them. Chandrika opened her bundle and brought out a chain and earrings, which Sheila recognised immediately; she hugged Chandrika warmly. The women's eyes clung to Sheila, who showed the effects of our food and our peace. I asked them to come in and have dinner with Sheila; they took off their sandals at the door and followed their friend, heads lowered and backs bent, to my sisters' room, which had become Sheila's room temporarily. They ate and talked, and when it was time for them to leave, they lingered at the door. Nimali said that everything they owned in this country was in their bundles, that their apartment was lonely; it had no food or water and people often knocked on their door at night, frightening them. Sheila asked if her friends could stay with us for a while. My father's voice came from behind me:

"There's plenty of food – let them stay!"

Sheila and her friends took delight in cleaning the house, in a futile daily rite. I tried in vain to dissuade them. They seemed happy, talking all the time and laughing for no reason, at least as far as I could tell. I had asked them about their passports and they had told me, without hesitation, that they did not have them. The passports were in the possession of their Kuwaiti sponsors from whom they had fled, and who had now fled Kuwait themselves. They lived in our house as if it were their own, moving around it as if they were moving in houses they had built in their dreams, in their distant villages, not threatened by being swept away by monsoon rains. They wiped away the little dust on the furniture with care; they opened the curtains and closed them gently; they polished the windows conscientiously; they washed the dishes carefully; and they brought down the large aluminium cooking pots, rarely used, from the kitchen cabinets and polished them scrupulously. They rocked you tenderly, as they would their own daughters, whose pictures were folded away in their bundles. In the evenings they sat in my sisters' room, which had become their room, eating a lot and talking more, confident that even if war broke out, they were safe and secure with their bundles and their gold in our apartment, their alternative homeland, nearly permanent. They were immersed in their lives, which seemed to them a beautiful dream that they saw with their eyes open, during the day.

In the lift I met a neighbour whom I knew by sight, though I did not know her name or anything about her. My mother had taken care not to form relationships with our new neighbours, nothing that went beyond, "Good morning, friend (*and that's the end*)," as the saying goes. But this neighbour, who lived on the fifth and last floor of the building, would catch me in the lift and keep on talking to me until I got to the third floor, where our apartment was. She would then hold the door, preventing it from closing, while I feigned interest by altering my facial expressions. After the invasion our encounters in the lift increased, going up or going down, and so did her talk. She told me the story of a well-known Palestinian obstetrician-gynaecologist who was killed, shot in a car chase on the streets of Kuwait, like the chases in foreign films. He had been involved in an affair with the wife of one of the important men in the Palestine Liberation Organisation, and it was said that her husband was behind the operation, seizing the opportunity of the eclipse of Kuwait to avenge himself on the doctor known for his romantic adventures with two kinds of women, married ones and Filipino servants. But that day, I was the one who held the lift door open, when my neighbour asked if I had heard about the killing of a building doorman in our neighbourhood? He was found dead in his room, stabbed a number of times in the heart. It was said that the killer stole all the gold jewellery he had. "Most likely it's his life savings . . . how awful!" She waited for me to respond, so I repeated, distractedly, "How awful!" Then the neighbour said, with some resignation,

"I mean, if one of us dies in this situation, nobody cares – there's no law or anything!"

Chandrika was carrying you back and forth in the front room, your head relaxed on her shoulder, singing to you in a tender voice embroidered at the ends with a crystalline fringe, while her eyes floated in an overflowing sea of feelings. I was standing at the door, carrying sacks of bread and contemplating her. She looked at me and said, joyfully,

"Maleka goes to sleep to my songs."

I bought Sheila and her friends suitcases, where they put their bundles. I opened my closet and my sisters' closet for them, and told them to take what they liked of the clothing. I gave them some canned food, which they stuffed into the sides of their suitcases, but when I offered them money, they refused. They embraced me gratefully and kissed you tenderly, four oppressed mothers; they humbly bent over my father's hand with kisses, but he snatched it away. They took leave of the house, their house, and got into my Mazda. I drove them to the Sri Lankan embassy, which had opened its doors to receive Sri Lankan workers, most of them maids, and to take them out of Kuwait in buses. Sheila sat next to me, and her friends took their places in the back seat. Chandrika asked if you could go with us, and that was what you wanted, too – you jumped from my father's arms to Chandrika's when she opened them to you. You hugged her and curled up in her lap in the car, as she caressed your soft hair with her chin. She sobbed all the way, and when we arrived at the embassy building, the faces of all the women had disappeared behind their tears.

My tears stayed behind my black sunglasses, in my father's car, as my eyes followed the disappearing geography of Kuwait. When the tears crowded behind the glasses' frames, then spilled down my cheeks like a sweeping revolution, I turned my face to the window as my father settled into his silence. We stopped at the Mutlaa border post for inspection. Members of an Iraqi force headquartered there looked at our papers and made way for us, without inspecting our few suitcases, which clearly seemed to them not to contain any Kuwaiti treasure. In Basra my father searched for a taxi driver heading for Baghdad, until he discerned signs of kindness in one aged driver; he paid him two hundred Iraqi dinars to take us, you and me, to the Hotel Sagman in Baghdad. The time had come to say goodbye, a moment I had not thought about, or not wished to think of. My father took you in his arms and kissed your head, your face, and your neck covered by snowy powder, then he put you in the back seat of the taxi. I stood at the car door, while the driver sat behind the steering wheel and started the engine in preparation for leaving. I took off my glasses and our eyes met. He said, sadly,

"Time for goodbye, then."

"Yes . . . goodbye."

He directed his eyes, where an awareness of guilt hovered, everywhere except towards me, but in the end our eyes had to meet. I aimed a look of reproach at him; his body trembled, and he raised his hands to his face and covered his eyes. "I have to confess something to you," he said, tears constricting his throat. I collected my father in my small arms, which encircled him completely as he shrank onto my chest.

"I know what you want to say."

He looked at me enquiringly, avoiding the knowledge, or as if he wanted to withdraw his confession before he made it. I said,

"I know you're afraid for me." I reassured him: "Don't worry – I'm the man of the house, aren't I?"

All the way from Basra to Baghdad, my father's face remained projected on the taxi's windscreen, worn down with guilt. When at last the car stopped in front of the Hotel Sagman, my father's face disappeared and my heartsore weariness retreated a little. Kuwait dissolved, and my spirit was relieved, for a time, of the weight of its days. At the hotel desk I was welcomed by a beautiful young woman with honey-coloured eyes who was from Mosul, as I later learned. I asked her for the room number of a hotel guest, Rasem Aayyad, who should have arrived yesterday with his wife and two children. The young woman seemed to know me and asked,

"Are you Jihad Naeem?"

I relaxed and gave her my passport so she could verify it, but it seemed she did not need a document to establish my identity. She opened a drawer in front of her and gave me a letter, folded in a small white envelope bearing the name and emblem of the hotel, with my name written on it in a hand I knew. I opened the letter, my face darkening before I read it, as I had seen the likely content in the disappointment on the hostess's face. "I'm sorry," wrote Rasem, "I was not able to wait for you. I had to leave . . . I hope you will understand. Good luck." The young woman told me the man was polite, then she came out from behind her desk, sensing I was on the verge of collapse. She took you from me and asked one of the employees to bring me a glass of water, then she led me to the lobby and seated me on a leather sofa. I learned from her that Rasem had arrived yesterday morning, and that his wife was cross the entire time – she was not even ashamed to fight with him in front of the guests in the lobby, insisting on leaving, threatening to take the children and leave him in the hotel if he did not go with her, so he had bowed to her wishes. The young woman asked me if I intended to stay at the hotel. The driver had helped me bring in my few things and had left, and I did not know

175

of any other place to go. She asked me how many days I planned to stay, and I answered, my eyes lost,

"I don't know."

The room was small and comfortable. We bathed, you and I, and from the soapy foam in the tub we made sparkling crowns for our heads, forgetting about what was waiting for us tomorrow. Then I made you a meal of milk followed by a dish of Cerelac, and I gave you a little water from one of the bottles of mineral water I had not used on the way. I sipped a little of the water, and ordered a cup of tea from room service. I took a packet of salty white cheese out of the suitcase, as well as a loaf of pitta bread I had brought for the road but had saved. I ate a quarter of the loaf and a little white cheese, and hid what was left of each in the "minibar" fridge, not touching its contents. Then we slept on a large bed, your radiant face turned to my faded, hungry face. You stretched your tender arm towards me, planting your fingers, with your pink fingernails, in my neck, and went to sleep. When your breath condensed on my eyelids, I also slept.

In the morning a young man greeted me at the reception desk, handsome and neatly groomed. I asked about the young woman who had been there the night before. "Do you mean Ghusun?" I understood from him that today was her day off. He asked me kindly if he could be of any service so I thanked him, then he suggested I go to the breakfast buffet. I told him that I was not hungry and that I preferred to take a walk. (Later, as I checked out, I discovered that breakfast was included in the price of the room, and that I could have hungered less.) I strolled in the block near the hotel, and went into a shop where I bought a fresh bun. I sat on the sidewalk and ate half of it, feeding you the other half.

We spent the rest of the day together in the lobby, watching the temporary faces. That night, we watched an old Egyptian film on the television in the room, and I fixed you a bottle of milk, then a dish of Cerelac, and gave you some water. I ate the second quarter of the loaf and some of the salty white cheese. I ordered a cup of tea and drank it slowly . . . extremely slowly. On the evening of the fourth day, the packet of cheese was empty, so I dipped the remains of the bread in the tea and sprinkled sugar over it. There was a light knock on the door that pulled me from my pensiveness. I stood up and nearly fell over from dizziness. I picked up the cup of tea and the bread and hid them under the bed. It was Ghusun, carrying a large, covered platter in one hand and in the other a bag with three bottles of mineral water. I told her that I did not want the hotel food, and she told me that the food was from her house, from her mother, and that the water was from the hotel, where they would not miss it! She told me that I had a long way to go, and that I would need the water if only for your milk. Then I learned that she had met a Jordanian who had come from Kuwait with his son, and who was visiting relatives living near her family. She explained my situation to him and agreed with him that he would come to the hotel in the morning to take me with him to Jordan for one hundred dollars. I had left word with Ghusun and her colleagues at the reception desk that I was looking for someone to take us, you and me, to Amman. I had also hung a note concerning that on the bulletin board, and I tried to fathom the faces that arrived in the lobby, where I spent long watches of the day and intermittent periods at night, looking for travellers who would accept me as a companion on their journey. During this time I minimised my expenses, not wasting the money

I had on any unnecessary food or water, until tremors of hunger nearly shook loose my arms and legs.

I took the cover off the dish and found a mound of rice with two pieces of chicken on it. On the edge of the platter sat two small plates, one with salad and the other with cubes of aubergine cooked in tomato sauce. I tore into the food and devoured it.

In the morning, Ghusun introduced me to Abu Aiman. He was a man in his forties, square-built, who had his son Aammar with him, a boy who was not yet thirteen. I understood from Abu Aiman later on that he owned a shop selling inexpensive clothing in Hawalli in Kuwait, and that he had three other sons, in addition to Aammar. He had made the trip between Kuwait and Jordan, across Iraq, five times since the Iraqi invasion, taking one of his sons with him each time, in order to transfer the merchandise from his shop to Jordan in batches. Abu Aiman picked up my large suitcase and put it with a collection of other suitcases and boxes that clung to a basket on the roof of his Toyota Cressida, tying the suitcase down with a strong fibre rope. I asked him if I could keep the smaller suitcase with me in the car, the one that held your water and food, and he agreed. I had to share the back seat with another man who was going with us to Amman. Abu Aiman addressed him as "Mister Ali", and Mr Ali spent the whole trip puffing and kicking at the stifling air in the car and voicing his annoyance with my suitcase. When I asked Abu Aiman to stop the car twice, so I could change your nappy, the man grumbled openly, addressing Abu Aiman with comments like: "This isn't what we agreed on, Abu Aiman," and, "If I had known that I was going to get involved in something like this, I wouldn't have ridden with you, Abu Aiman," and, "I have a right to be comfortable, Abu

Aiman – I'm paying you money for this ride." At that point, Abu Aiman gave him the hundred dollars he had paid, and offered to set him and his suitcases down in the middle of the road and leave them, so Mr Ali held his tongue after that, though his eyes were still puffed up with anger. Then Aammar, who was playing with you, suggested that he sit in the back seat next to us, you and me, and that Mr Ali sit in the front seat alone, and the suggestion appealed to Mr Ali. Aammar took your bottle of milk from me and picked you up, like a little father, and began feeding you. I rested my head on the seat and slept, reassured.

It was almost sunset when I opened my eyes. I found lines of civilian cars, most of them bearing Kuwaiti plates, stopped in the desert on both sides of the road. I asked Abu Aiman where we were and he told me we had reached Trebil, on the Iraqi–Jordanian border. Aammar had already got out of the car, carrying you, and you seemed elated by the fresh evening falling on your face. Abu Aiman also got out, to ask about the reason for the stopped cars. He learned that the Iraqi command had decided to close the Trebil border crossing to Jordan indefinitely; some of the cars had been waiting for more than a week. "What do you mean, indefinitely?" shouted Mr Ali from inside the car. "Are we going to stay here our whole life? I've got work to do!" Abu Aiman suggested that he eat shit and shut up. That night we discovered a lot of shit behind the little hills where the people stranded in the desert squatted to relieve themselves in the open air, whipped by dirt and wind on all sides. We walked through it like someone playing hopscotch, to keep from stepping in it. The cars gathered haphazardly in rings and circles, their owners sleeping in them. Some of them lit fires in the middle of the circles, which they fed with bits of wood and boxes discarded in the desert; they sat around them guessing how far they were from the hyenas and other animals lying in wait, whose voices pierced the emptiness of the night. But the cold of the October desert did not allow us to stay up long, outside, so we went back to our cars early, cracking the windows a centimetre or so, just enough to air out the insides of the cars. When morning came, I made a trade with a woman who had run out of water – a bottle of mineral water for a pitta loaf, two tomatoes, two cucumbers and a green pepper. I wiped off the vegetables with my blouse, cutting them up with a pocket knife I borrowed from Abu Aiman, and I divided the bread into three pieces, making a sandwich for myself, one for Aammar and one for Abu Aiman. I had two bottles of water left, and I hid them under the seat of the car. I would slip into the car and ask Aammar to stand with his back to the window, so that he acted as a curtain hiding me from others' eyes; then I would prepare your meal and feed you secretly. When the women noticed your good health and asked me about your milk, I pointed to my thin chest, and they went off shrugging their shoulders, unconvinced. Abu Aiman and Aammar drank from two gallons of water they had brought with them from Baghdad. Mr Ali would get out of the car, carrying his backpack with its many zippers, and walk some distance away. Then he would open a zipper and take out a cookie or a piece of chocolate, eating it out of sight of hungry eyes. From another opening he would pull out a small water bottle and drink from it, rationing his sips.

Our second day was more blazing than the one before, and that night the cold was harsher. I gave a woman a packet of wheat-flavoured Cerelac, and she gave me two loaves of bread; Aammar ate one entire loaf, and I divided the second between me and Abu Aiman. In the afternoon we spread some cardboard on the ground and sat on it, our backs to the car. Aammar walked further than the previous day, gathering wooden boards and sticks to feed a fire that would soften the desert night, where we could warm ourselves until the fuel ran out; then we would climb into the car and sleep sitting up, in the worn-out seats. I tried to stay outside the car the longest possible time so I could stretch out my legs, stiff from sleeping upright. Mr Ali got out of the car and headed towards us, so Abu Aiman invited him to sit with us. "What do they call you, Abu what?" Abu Aiman asked him, enquiring about his *kunya* name. Mr Ali was trying to embrace the fire, drawing it to himself with his two huge arms; he answered,

"Abu nothing! I don't have kids."

A scream rang out, arising from a deep wound. The night was quiet except for the crackling of the dry wood being devoured by the fire. Other screams followed, bleeding sharply. People hurried towards the sound. A woman was sitting on the ground, her legs spread, between them her child of seven months, dead. "There is no power nor strength save in God. Only God is eternal." Voices mixed together. "There is no power nor strength save in God. Only God is eternal." The woman had taken off her scarf and rubbed sand in her hair and on her face, and she was digging her fingernails into her bloody neck. I hugged you tightly to my chest, and you moaned from the pain. I kissed your hair, your forehead, your face, and your neck; I planted kisses on your hands, and counted your fingers more than once, and cried. Abu Aiman and a number of other men dug a small grave, choosing a spot free of human droppings. The woman went on holding her infant to her chest, refusing to give him to the men, who tried to tell her about the beautiful life of the little one as a bird in paradise. When she was not convinced, they took the bird from her by force. He was wrapped in a heavy wool blanket. I went up to the woman, kissed the sand in her hair, and begged her to give me her infant's blanket for my infant. The woman stopped crying, looked at me, and then spat in my face.

Aammar climbed up to the roof of the car and mounted the carrier, then, following his father's instructions, he freed one of the boxes tied on top with a pocket knife. He took out two dark-blue jackets, the kind of wool jackets that were distributed to pupils in schools. I put on one and wrapped you in the other like a blanket. Once the fire found nothing more to consume it consumed itself, and we got in the car and went to sleep. Aammar could not sleep sitting up, so he put his head on my lap and lifted his legs onto the back seat. Abu Aiman wedged my small case in the empty space between the front and back seats and covered it with a piece of fabric, making it into something like a mattress, where you slept.

On the third day, we didn't find anything to eat. I still had three-quarters of a bottle of mineral water, so I made a meal about the size of half a teacup out of Cerelac with rice. I put it in the cover of your milk bottle for Aammar to eat. I kept the rest of the water for your milk. Abu Aiman offered me some of the water from the gallon containers, so I could wipe you over. I tried to save the nappies by keeping them on you as long as possible, so the skin between your thighs became chapped. It was as if you had grown in these three days, I said to Abu Aiman – I couldn't pick you up anymore. He said, "You're tired." I stayed in the car most of the time, fighting off the pinch of hunger and exhaustion. It was as if the screws fastening my arms and legs to my fading body had come loose, so my limbs relaxed onto the seat like leaves clinging to a tree though the autumn had worn them down. I did not respond to your efforts to play with me. When your active hands rained down on my listless face, I exerted a lot of effort to kiss them with my trembling, cracked lips. In the afternoon, shouts from Aammar spread out over our waiting area:

"Maleka's walking! Maleka's walking, she's walking!"

You stood cautiously, as if you were evaluating your courage. Aammar held your arms to steady you, then let them go. I opened the door of the car to go to you, but I could not get my legs out. You stood a few metres from me. I called you. You flapped your arms in the air, I stretched out my arms to you, and you took the first step towards me, amid the jubilation of Aammar and Abu Aiman, standing at the car door encouraging you. Then you took the second step more surely, followed rapidly by the third and the fourth, before your tender, inexperienced legs collapsed. Aammar hurried to you and helped you stand up again. Three steps separated you from me. You flapped your arms with greater excitement and went on flapping them rapidly, covering the rest of the steps to me half walking, half running, half dancing, half flying, and threw yourself into my arms.

As darkness fell, I remembered that I had not gone behind one of the hills to pee before sunset. At night, when we heard a car engine turn over, we would surmise that the occupants, and especially the women, wanted to relieve themselves. Their men would guarantee them a safe place to pee by going further into the desert with the car, far from the camp of cars. Then they would open the front and back doors of the car, as screens against wind and fear, leaving the front headlights on, to swallow up any predator led by its instinct to approach. I could not ask Abu Aiman to go with me to some distant spot at the end of the night so I could pee in safety, so I was careful to empty my bladder behind a sandy hill before night descended on the desert and the voices of wild animals rose from afar, where they crouched in ambush.

I found it strange that my bladder was full even though my belly was empty. The snores of Abu Aiman and Mr Ali mixed together; your breathing was regular as you slept on your mattress, and Aammar was tossing in his sleep. I tried to think about anything except the fact that I was cramped and that my bladder was about to explode. I forced my eyes to close, and in the dream of someone very much awake I saw the man who was my husband pulling me by my arms, tearing me out of bed and dragging me on the floor in the long corridor between the bedroom and the living room. Then he dragged me through the longer corridor between the living room and the door of the apartment, our marital apartment. At times I was trying to hold on to the floor to keep from moving, and at times I bit his hands to free myself from them, but he kicked my belly and my teeth lost their grip on his hands. Then he opened the door and threw me out, closing it behind me. I was in a nightgown, barefoot. The blind doors of three apartments examined me. The time was close to dawn. I spread my arms over my shoulders and bare chest, folding my legs underneath me, spreading the light chiffon fabric of the nightgown over my exposed flesh. I retracted my body so that it occupied the least possible space as I sat in a heap on the doorstep, waiting for daylight.

The engine of a car standing behind ours shuddered several

times, and its headlights came on. A beam of light poured into our car, sketching my face clearly in the rear-view mirror. My features were worn down, my cracked lips trembled, my cheeks were sunken, my eyes were deep in their sockets, my forehead bulged, and my jaw protruded. My face belonged to a head that had begun to shed its flesh. The car withdrew its lights and moved away, its occupants looking for a spot in the revealing desert that would give them the privacy to relieve themselves. The stream of light was cut off, but my face continued to look at me from the dark mirror. My face cried. It cried violently, completely overwhelmed.

When dawn broke, O my queen, and the desert shook off some of its desolation, I had wet myself. I had wet myself, Maleka, right where I sat.

CHAPTER FIVE

Concerning Irrational Love, and
Still More Irrational Life

It has reached me, O most auspicious queen, whose ideas are wilful and rooted deep, and whose heart trembles, where baffled butterflies leap . . .

Jordan is a dry land, a stretch of geography largely deprived of any variety of streaming or fluidity. Its water is distant, even from its original inhabitants; its air is stifled and its misery unrestrained; its sorrows are not disclosed nor its yearnings plucked. Its roads devour feet, its sun melts faces, its cold bends bones and hardens the spirit. The features of its money have faded, rubbed by many hands, their fingers austere and their fingernails roughened, by endurance often and less often by lost patience. It is a house open to the wind and the sand, and to the neighbourhood thieves, not dangerous or very skilled, who snatch fruit from trees of plums, peaches, and loquats from atop the low wall of a house on a mountain, alluring for what is not within.

Three years before the Iraqi invasion of Kuwait, and more precisely, when I went to work and my income came to surpass my father's, he had bought Grandmother Radiyya's house at the top of al-Jabal al-Abyad in al-Zarqa, paying in what seemed like easy instalments. Grandmother Radiyya had received the house from my grandfather Imran, who had put it in her name in a vain attempt to win her back after she insisted on being divorced from him. Grandmother kept the house without, however, returning to my grandfather. When he died, Grandmother discovered that he had left her the house where they lived as a married couple, downtown in al-Zarqa; it was pleasanter and better situated, so she moved into it and sold my father the house in al-Jabal al-Abyad. My father rented out the house, and the rent covered the monthly instalments. During our summer holidays we still stayed as guests in Aunt Rahma's house in Jabal al-Taj in Amman, our favourite place to stay, or in Grandmother Radiyya's house in downtown Zarqa, our less favourite place. From time to time we might spend a few days scattered among the houses of my uncle Abu Taisir and my grandmother Fatima in the Wehdat Camp. This last was my personal favourite, as my senses were rooted in the mornings of richly flavoured olive oil, deeply green zaatar mix with abundant sesame, pickled olives with latent bitterness (a hidden delight), soft Nabulsi cheese with the saltiness removed, and loaves of bread that Aunt Najah brought back from the baker's oven, deeply exhaling the aroma of the beginning of life.

When Saddam broke into Kuwait, my mother thought it was a matter of a passing dispute over "a bit of money" between the two countries, not a state of war that could last; it would be only a few days until it was settled. Then it would be only a few weeks, even if somewhat long and disturbing, until the trouble would vanish, she assured herself, when she was pierced by doubts and anxieties. But the days passed and the money – her money – was consumed; the armies of the world descended on the region, and Jordanians for no reason busied themselves storing food, stuffing sacks with dried bread, and reinforcing the window glass in their houses with strips of tape. Then the trouble became terrible, a dark cloud, weighed down by a rainstorm that might sweep away many people who had foolishly thought that they were settled in a homeland that was not their own, just as it might carry lives from the places they knew and fling them into strange places, stripped even of their imagined homeland. My mother and my brothers and sisters were staying in my grandmother Radiyya's house. My father sent her instructions, with someone leaving Kuwait for Jordan, to register Rula, Nasir, Bella, and Rasha in state schools so they wouldn't lose an academic year while they were waiting for a return to Kuwait that seemed more difficult day by day.

Grandmother Radiyya opened the door. Before her stood a thin woman in dusty, dirty clothes, her hair fastened in a short, matted ponytail, her cheeks hollow, her jaw sharpened, her teeth protruding, and her eyes sunken. Her lips were trembling in a shiver that encompassed her whole body, which was lost in clothing too large for it. The woman's arms feebly held a child in her tenth month with a face round as a pitta loaf, filled with fresh life, and a body like a lamb's, bursting with vitality. The woman's legs were supported against the door so she wouldn't fall. Grandmother Radiyya looked at the woman and her miserable face, quivering over a withered being that wore a light cloak of flesh. She looked closely; the features did not seem completely strange to her. Then she opened her eyes on a clear, painful discovery, striking her cheek with a sharp slap:

"Who is it? *Jihad?!*"

I smiled, and my teeth protruded. Then I lifted you near my face, with all the resolve I had held in reserve during the preceding days, and brushed my lips against your dewy cheek. Without taking my eyes off you, I said to my grandmother,

"Have you ever seen anything more beautiful than Maleka?"

At that moment – because of my shocking state, not because of your radiance – Grandmother Radiyya realised that we had left Kuwait behind us, for what could be forever . . . or nearly so.

Grandmother Radiyya did not seem truly pleased by the fact we were living with her, though she had told us we could stay with her until things got better. Grandmother had always welcomed us during our holidays, delighting in the nightgowns my mother brought her from Kuwait (which did not reflect her age), as well as the moisturising creams for her skin, the bottles of perfume and shampoo and foreign hair dye, the blackhead strips for her nose and chin, and the sandals and slippers in bright colours that showed her carefully pedicured toenails. She was tolerant of our occupation of her house and of how we overlaid our life on hers, as long as we were transient guests. Grandmother Radiyya liked to keep her house and its contents to herself. Her things, arranged with great care, imposed caution on her guests as they moved among them and around them. Likewise the shine of her floor tiles, cleaned daily, required us to jump over them like barefoot birds in the summer; then when the floor was covered with carpets in the winter, we like all guests had to take off our shoes, making do with socks, our toes peeping out of the holes and shrivelling in the cold. In fact, Grandmother Radiyya had set aside one room for guests, furnished with a set of sofas and chairs in the traditional Victorian style of heavy wood and upholstered with gold jacquard, but she didn't allow anyone to enter it, not even guests. Once Bella hid in it during a game of hide-and-seek and she nearly pulled his ear off. When Grandmother finally picked up the frying pan we had left in the sink, unwashed, since dinner the day before, and threw it from the kitchen window into the street in anger and disgust, I knew that we had to speed up our departure.

Over a cup of coffee in the middle of one night, in Grandmother Radiyya's kitchen that smelled of detergent, I sat with my mother discussing how we might survive. I spread out on the table the money I had: nine hundred American dollars, one thousand Kuwaiti dinars, and a handful of Iraqi dinars. My mother put before me a bag containing the sole gold bracelet left to her, the one piece of jewellery remaining in her possession from the time of her marriage. She had kept it for a hard day – a very hard day, harder than all the past days of her life. Then she cried, not because she was going to give up the lone bracelet at last, but because the hard day – the very hard day, much harder than all the other days – had come. The bag also held earrings, rings, and light bracelets my mother had stripped off my sisters' ears, fingers, and wrists when the crisis lengthened. She sipped the last of her coffee, then pushed the money and the bag towards me. She sighed and said,

"You figure it out!"

The problem was not getting a house, as the renter had agreed to leave our house in al-Jabal al-Abyad, and Grandmother Radiyya agreed that we could delay paying the instalments. The problem was life itself within the house. We took it over in terrible condition, worn, littered, and falling apart, as if the residents had not lived their lives, or part of them, within it. I didn't like the house. When I left it in the morning, to gather our livelihood from steep roads and towering days, I did not hurry my harvest, or hasten my steps back home in the evening. The silhouette of my mother's face, glimpsed through the opening of the curtains in the window overlooking the street, as she sat on the sofa with her head in her hand, made me withdraw even as I drew near. We made the minimum of the repairs needed in the house, we painted the walls, and my mother hung some pictures of no value, though they acquired some value perforce from a life cut off from the history that was forming outside our house, without having any part in forming it. The war was going to happen. My father had preferred to remain in Kuwait, an absent witness to history, as no-one would ask him about it, nor cite him as a reference of any sort. He had realised, quite simply, that his life had ended its last chapter in Kuwait and that he could not begin anew or start a chapter in Jordan after declaring that end. For myself, I had not planned on a second life in Jordan. It was only that I approached the life that had descended on me forcibly, without my asking for it, and I walked alongside history.

The house had two bedrooms, a living room, and a formal front room. My mother agreed that I would turn the front room into a third bedroom, so I designated one of the bedrooms for the boys and the other for the girls, and the third – the largest – for you, me, and my mother. You and I slept on a single bed while my mother slept on a sofa bed. We used the living room, opening directly onto the kitchen, as a room for all purposes. I bought some necessary items from a shop selling used furniture and electrical appliances. I paid off some of the money my mother had spent, borrowing from acquaintances, and I set aside a sum not to be touched, to cover school expenses and what Rima and Jamal needed for university, including the payment for the second semester. The sum left was to last us for the month during which I would look for a job.

What kept my distaste for the house from reaching the level of absolute hatred was its surrounding garden: spontaneous, exuberant, and overflowing. Before the war my father had planned to enlarge the house by taking a piece of the garden, but the garden remained as it was for years, rescuing me from psychological suicide on the threshold of that place, which ate away pieces of my spirit. I would slip out to the garden at dawn, carrying a large cup of black coffee and a notebook and pen that had crossed the borders with me, passing over pain. I would sit at the edge of a bed of mint, rubbing the sleepy green leaves; they would yawn and exhale an aroma embellished by dew. Then I would let the pen move slowly over the cold paper, absent any thought, warming with time and becoming human with persistence, its tongue pouring forth chatter that was often meaningless and occasionally held some eloquence, as I sketched the talk on the companionable whiteness. People were created and others annihilated, with a violent, stinging stroke. Voices appeared and others were muzzled. On the steppes of imagination reality formed, my reality, living in words that wove my narrative, slowly and quickly, cautiously and with daring.

The coffee ends but not the talk. With the outpouring of the morning, thoughts surge and struggle with the voices of lives opening gradually on the street, led by the seller of sesame bread rings. His voice stands on the threshold of early manhood, though his childhood pulls him back forcefully by the shirt. "*Kaa-aak! Kaa-aak! Kaa-aak!*" he shouts, making the letter *kaaf* unduly emphatic and assertively doubling the *aain*. I call him from behind the wall, and he's at the door before me. I buy five or six sesame bread rings from him.

After a while, I began to call him by his name, Walid. He was a boy of eleven, in fifth grade, going to school after he finished selling all his bread. Then he began to come to me after school, on some days, with his English book. I explained the meanings of some of the vocabulary words to him and taught him how to pronounce them, with him repeating them for me. At first he was embarrassed to come into our house, then he made do with sitting on the steps near the door. Afterwards he would venture into the garden, and I would sit with him at the edge of one of the flower beds. I held his finger to my lips so he could distinguish the heavy sound of the *B* from the lighter *P* in English; he was fascinated by the puff of air coming from my lips, imprinting his savouring of the letter on his finger while his eyes shone with amazement. I paged through his notebook with its messy writing; I dictated to him some of the words he had memorised and helped him draw the letters more neatly. I spread my hand over his small hand, closed over the pen, revealing to him the allure of life created through letters; his hand would relax and his senses follow me, obediently. Brown, irregular lines spread over the back of his hand and his arm; I asked him about them and he told me they were marks left by a heated knife, used by his stepmother to scald him as punishment. I learned that his father worked in the market selling meat and frozen food, and that he supported a family of four children from his first wife, Walid's mother, whom he had divorced, and of two from his second wife. Walid asked me to please not go to his father – the last thing the boy wanted was to anger his father. Even my mother disapproved of the idea of complaining of the stepmother to the father, as that sort of woman, my mother said, was a "criminal by nature", and words would not deter her. In fact, "the shameless woman" (that is, the stepmother) might become more vicious, and greater harm might befall the boy. Walid was afraid that his father, at his stepmother's urging, might forbid him to come to us. My mother looked closely at his timid hand, then pressed on the marks with her fingers, asking him as she looked at me, "Does that hurt?" Walid answered "No!", moving his bewildered eyes between us. My mother stroked his hand with her ample palm and said, "When you grow up, all the marks will disappear. Your hand will be beautiful, and large, larger than your stepmother's hand!" Walid's eyes opened in a blooming laugh. He looked at me as if he wanted to reassure me: "I know!"

In the middle of the garden there were three trellises for grapes that formed a broad arbour, and we took advantage of the shaded space beneath it to sit and drink tea in the mornings or afternoons. On summer evenings, when the sun withdrew its merciless lash from the sky, and settled into the cramped rooms of the house, splattering its flame on the veined walls, the pleasant arbour would keep us in the kinder embrace of its breezes, its summer less harsh, until a late hour of the night. We put cheap plastic tables and chairs in the space, and a wooden sofa. There were nights when I preferred that we sleep, you and I, on this sofa under the arbour, waking to the eye of the sun striking my senses first thing in the morning. I would cover your plump face with my hands so the hot eye would not strike you, gaily watching your tender eyelids resisting the light harassing them. Or perhaps I would be awakened by street cats battling underneath us, while you pressed your feet into my belly.

Along the front wall of the garden on the side overlooking the main street grew two plum trees and a very tall loquat tree, which spread its arms over the wall to the street. Against the three garden walls stood lemon, apple, and fig trees, as well as a tangled mulberry tree and various unidentified bushes, distributed in no particular order. The loquat tree was my friend; I sat under it, stretching out my legs and making space for the possibilities of writing, in a notebook on my lap. I raised my eyes, encouraging the fruit of thought to fall on the paper; then you bounced towards me and struck the empty paper with your hands, your pure, clear laughter pouring down on it. You lifted your head, looking for real fruit, not the imagined fruit of thought. You pointed with sure fingers to a cluster of loquats, so I climbed the tree with its twisted trunk and cut down a bunch for you. I pulled the fruit from the branch and washed it, then I watched you chew the pulp, whose juice had grown sweet, and spit out the large pits into my hand. With the coming of the springtime fruits, which revealed their secrets to the arid mountain road outside our house, we had to confront the boys of the neighbourhood, with their pliant, lithe, adolescent bodies. They climbed the wall and descended on the shoulders of the trees like spiders, their arms and legs supported on the branches, coveting the fruit out of their reach. Bella and Nasir drove them away by throwing stones at them, and I often found myself forced to intervene, stripping the stones out of their hands so the unskilled thieves would not be harmed.

The towering loquat tree appealed to the boys of the Jabal more than the others, because it leaned towards the edge of the wall, and that made it easier for the thieves to snatch the fruit. One afternoon towards sunset, we ran from the house to the garden at the sound of a horrified shout. A boy was dangling upside down from the loquat tree, his arm and leg caught in the maze of its shattered branches, while his other hand clung to a branch that was bending and about to break at any moment and his terrified eyes measured the distance between his head and the ground. We rushed to him. My mother, Rima, Rula, and I stood directly under him, weaving our arms together in a net to catch him if he fell. I saw Bella pick up a rock from the ground, so I swore by the Lord of Heaven that I would break his head if he did what I thought he would. Nasir brought a ladder and Jamal climbed it until he reached the boy hanging from the frail branches. He took him by the shoulders and pulled him by force, bringing down many small branches before the one the boy still clung to finally broke.

He had curly coppery-blond hair, honey-coloured eyes with a touch of yellow, and skin scorched by the sun and the aridity of life. The colours of his clothes had disappeared under accumulated filth that could not be removed by washing with cheap soap. The boy's appearance told of misery appropriate to the land where we made a home, a land where a loquat tree that produces a little fruit becomes a landmark event. Nasir pulled the little thief by the hand and he moaned in pain. I drew him to me and asked everyone to leave him. The branches had left bloody scratches all over his arms and legs. I dusted off his blond head, to remove the cloud of dirt clinging to it, and asked him his name. He looked around at us, fearfully, before he answered:

"Maher."

"Maher who? Son of . . .?"

"Ibn Umm Maher." ("Son of Maher's mother.")

I laughed. He asked me, anxiously,

"Are you gonna tell my mother?"

He was eight years old, or maybe nine. He was wearing one sneaker, which must have been white originally. It was torn in every place that could be torn and had lost its shape, as well as its laces, so its tongue lolled as an unnecessary fold. I asked him about the other shoe and he pointed to the tree – there, at the top. Bella could now throw the rock he still held excitedly in his hand.

He aimed it skilfully and brought down the shoe. Then I asked Bella to pick some loquats. Maher walked with me, hesitantly, to the bathroom in the house. I stripped off his clothes and he stood before me in his underwear in the tub, where I sprayed his legs with water, making his sunburnt skin, covered with a paste of dirt, shine. I washed his arms and rubbed his neck and face, then I dried him. I wiped the obvious scratches with cotton dipped in antiseptic alcohol. He closed his eyes in pain, restraining his senses every time the cotton passed over the scratches, as his thin body contracted involuntarily. Bella gave him four loquats; he hesitated to take them, looking at me as if asking my permission, and I nodded to him. He took them quickly and put them in his trouser pockets. I made him a sandwich of labneh spread and he ate it, then I mixed a glass of juice for him from powder, which he gulped down all at once.

"Are you gonna tell my mother?"

"Look at me!" I said to him, so he lifted his eyes to me. "You could very well have broken your leg or your arm or even cracked your head open – is that what you want?" I thought that these words would frighten him more than his mother's learning about what happened.

"But you're not gonna tell my mother!"

At last he trusted that I would not tell on him to his mother. He trusted even more in the loquats in his pockets, and he took off in a hurry.

We sought the help of a neighbour in the lane, a farmer, who set about trimming the branches at the top of the tree and disarmed it by pruning those near the wall, so it was lighter, less agitated, and less haughty. Then the season of its fruit came to a quick end, and the raids of unskilled thieves on our house receded. Under the loquat tree, I continued stitching my words on paper. I sensed gazes falling from above over my shoulder, encircling my words. I lifted my head and glimpsed a face I knew on the wall, one that hid before falling into the net of my eyes. I went back to where I had left my words waiting, and the face hovered again over my head, the eyes making their way through the open spaces between the branches. Without lifting my head, I said: "What do you want? We don't have any loquats anymore." The face remained silent but did not disappear. I said to him, without my eyes leaving the paper, "Why not come in, instead of hanging on to the wall all day?" When my mother saw Maher ibn Umm Maher, as we came to call him, she looked at me with a question in her eyes – *are we going to gather in all the street urchins?* The child had on the same clothes, but he did not look dirty. He opened his hands for my mother and pointed to his thin legs; the cleanliness revealed ancient bruises and healed wounds that reflected daily naughtiness. He added, "I took a bath." My mother called to Rula, "Make a sandwich for Maher ibn Umm Maher!"

During the two months after my arrival in Jordan, I worked moving around among tutoring centres specialising in the curriculum for the *taujihi* exam at the end of high school; then I settled at a centre known as "The Centre for Excellence", which was among the best and most renowned to students in al-Zarqa. I went to it five days a week from five to seven in the evening, teaching two classes for two student groups. Both were for boys, some of whom had failed several times and were near my own age. That made the owner hold on to me, since he was incapable of attracting male students in numbers that would balance the enormous number of female students. For the girls, going to the centre was an opportunity to show how pretty they really were, away from the miserable school uniforms. They were elaborately adorned, despite the required hijab, enough to guarantee they would attract attention. The owner of the institute was also a teacher of English. In addition to the group-tutoring sessions at the centre, he gave private lessons in the homes of relatively well-off students, receiving the highest hourly rate of all the *taujihi* instructors, who had a reputation for high prices. He also prepared "model" student summaries which he forced the students to buy. I had presented my papers to the Civil Service Bureau, but I knew that I would not receive an appointment in the Ministry of Education before the beginning of the new school year, so I worked for the period of a semester as a part-time English teacher in a community college that awarded diplomas, and that was located on the outskirts of al-Zarqa.

Our money ran out in Jordan immeasurably faster than it had in Kuwait, and hands and mouths snatched food with a greater appetite for life, despite our meagre circumstances. We did not have secret hiding places to help us in our continual times of need or emerging to save us in successive periods of emergency. From week to week the very dear pennies slipped through my fingers, as well as the still dearer gold of days. We developed means of satisfying hunger that depended on quantity rather than quality. Sesame bread rings were the broad base of our daily breakfast, enriched with olive oil and zaatar thyme mix; and for our signature supper, a crowded cloth spread on the floor held plates of stewed broad beans, hummus, whole chickpeas cooked with garlic, and falafel, which Bella brought from a small restaurant just down the mountain from us: food that stuffed the belly with a brick that was not easily digested. No more to be found were the delicacies of our table in Kuwait: cold meats of various kinds and foreign cheeses. We replaced those with local luncheon meat that came in a large, disc-shaped packet that lasted us for days, and modest, locally produced processed yellow cheese, which came in an unattractive carton. My favourite Greek olives were no longer available as a choice; we made do with the green olives my aunt Rahma pickled, which I must confess were very good. We also gave up boiled eggs, which did not satisfy innate, ingrained hunger, for fried eggs. My mother would spread three or four eggs in the frying pan and move them around in a way that suggested plenty, so hands would vie to be the first to reach the plate of eggs, and it would be wiped clean in seconds.

Nonetheless, O my queen, we never went to bed hungry, and a very few times (but they were very happy) magic might descend and bring a bit of luxury to our house, which was filled with deep patience and steadfastness. After an unexpected private lesson given to a student in her home, I might return to our house with a kilo of chestnuts, which my mother would grill in the oven. We hovered around, listening to the crackling of the nuts as they expanded in their woody shells. Then when they were ready, I distributed them to everyone equally. Or my mother might make us a sumptuous meal, featuring ten boiled eggs, which we deserved, after all. We would sit cross-legged on the floor in a circle, warming each other, snatching loaves of bread. Waiting for the sign to begin. A hand might creep towards the plate of fried potatoes and be struck by another, watchful hand, intent that the race be fair and not start until all were seated. "In the name of God," my mother says; "In the name of God," we repeat, with our mouths full. I seat you on my folded leg and you explore our pleasures with a fried potato in one hand, which you munch curiously, and in the other a piece of falafel, which you chew.

I look over the eager faces, which include those of Walid and Maher, who have become a nearly constant part of our meals and our crowding. I take a boiled egg and lift it in the air, and eyes turn to me, waiting. Then I strike it on Walid's forehead and peel it for him, and you gurgle with laughter. Then other foreheads stretch towards me: Bella's, Rasha's, Maher's, and yours, the most beautiful – pure foreheads and fresh, with no lines, wrinkles, or wounds upon them.

Since we had to live, we lived.

We took shelter in our life in Jordan, insofar as the days allowed us to hold up our heads, and the nights allowed our feet to stretch out under winter blankets and summer covers, without being exposed . . . very much.

A year had crept by since we had dug ourselves into a country that didn't ask for us, a year during which the shattering American war occurred. Kuwait was liberated, as anticipated, without the Jordanians' windows being shattered, though they remained fortified by strips of tape for months before and after the war, in a foolish popular precaution that was almost universally relished. During that time we learned to liberate ourselves from our past life in Kuwait, as well as liberating ourselves from any possible future in it. With time, we resected the place and its people from our memories. It was a surgical operation that seemed necessary in order to accommodate ourselves to our new life, and surprisingly it was not very difficult, nor was it painful, as might have been expected. Perhaps that was because the place and its people remained marginal and colourless, largely disconnected and separated, in our ghetto past.

My father stayed in Kuwait, believing, deludedly, that Kuwait would make room for us after being liberated, or at the least that it would make room for him. But the Health Ministry dismissed him from his job, under the pretext of restructuring the government sector and (though this was not announced openly) of doing away with nationalities whose regimes, short-sighted with respect to their own interests, had colluded with the "tyrannical" Iraqi occupation. Thus the regimes were discredited and along with them the lives of their citizens, on the assumption that the citizen is naturally punished for the crimes of their regime. My father's partner in the electrical repair shop liquidated his life in Kuwait; my father didn't have the money to buy his share, so both he and my father sold their shares to their Kuwaiti sponsor, for pocket money. My father left our large apartment in al-Farwaniyah, where we had not been able to plant enough seedlings of our history, and moved to a small apartment. He sold most of our furniture, and he threw in my boxes of books as part of the bargain. Then the son of a neighbour of ours in the Nuqra ghetto helped my father get a job in an agency selling American cars, run by an uncle of his who was a Palestinian with Canadian citizenship, and he began to send us some money whenever he could. That helped us patch together our days, when our feet still withdrew under blankets and covers, though we knew the blankets and the covers had increased and pressed together with the days, and that the feet of all sizes, colours, ages, and markings, with traces of wounds and burns on their miserable flesh, had multiplied. For in the cold twilight, Walid might sit next to me on a thick floor cushion in front of the kerosene heater, writing his homework while I prepared my lessons for the next day or corrected exam papers. Then his thin body would subside into sleep, his eyes extinguished and his head falling on my arm, so I would stretch him out on the cushion and spread a heavy blanket over the body settled beside me. On summer nights, Maher might slip into bed next to Bella, his dignity (still not fully formed) untouched by Bella's attempts to push him out. Maher had begged his mother to allow him to stay overnight with us, and she had not objected, content for another household to take him in and offer a supper to one of the many mouths in her care. If the skirmishes between the two boys developed into a clash I intervened to separate them, putting a pad on the floor for Maher. At the end of the night Bella might roll out of bed and onto the pad next to Maher, and my mother would spread a cover over them.

In our new life, we had to free ourselves from the idea that a day could pass easily and appropriately, without drama. Our senses were always alert for bad news and events that escaped the bounds of logic, the least and lightest of which might be that our washing was stolen from the roof, the most expensive piece being a pair of Jamal's jeans, made in Turkey, which he had worn only once and that had cost me twelve dinars. Or Nasir might split open the head of one of the loquat and plum thieves, splitting it "deeply", so the family of the wounded thief would file a complaint against us with the police, claiming that Nasir injured the boy when he was playing in the street. I would go to the nearby police station, confessing that I was the one who had wounded the boy's head, contradicting the boy and his mother, who swore that Nasir was the culprit. The officer knew I was lying, but he wanted to believe me. I advanced arguments in refined language, infused with an elaborate urban dialect, different from the rocky dialect of the mountain residents. I called on legal axioms like "the right to defend oneself and one's property from attack", while the mother of the boy with the injured head felt her way in the labyrinth of my language. When the scale of justice began to tip in favour of my defence, the officer persuaded them to apologise to me, so he would not be forced to hold her son. But I waived my right to an apology, after extracting from the boy and his mother a pledge not to meddle with us. I only left the police station after the officer gave me a useful lesson about aggression concealed under the cover of self-defence.

During the give and take between the officer and me, a policeman entered, dragging with him two young men who looked like high-school students. Blood was coagulating on the nose of one while the other had a lilac halo around one eye. The policeman explained that they had been fighting at one of the stops in al-Jabal for the service taxis that ran regular routes. The officer sized up the pair and then asked, "Which of you hit the other?" Each one pointed to the other, and the officer asked the policeman to take them to detention, after they had left their bags in the office. He opened one of the bags and pulled out a notebook, which he paged through scornfully, saying, "It's the usual, a troublemaker and an ass!" Then he pulled a blank page from the notebook and spread it in front of me. He drew a horizontal line in pen, which I gathered from his explanation represented the wall of our house. On the wall he put a distorted drawing of a man, who I understood to be the alleged thief or robber. The officer asked me to listen to him well, so I gave him my attention, if only out of curiosity. He explained to me, while making straight and curved lines at the top and bottom of the paper, that if I split open the head of the intruder while his body was hanging from the wall on our side, so that he would fall on our land, then we were innocent of his blood. But if the body of the thief was hanging on the other side of the wall, so that he might fall in the street, outside of our property line, then we were in fact the aggressors. Consequently I must wait next time, and watch and hold back until the thief was hanging on our side within the lines of our property (and if I liked, I could entice him), and then crack open his head. I looked doubtfully at the officer, and he crumpled the paper with the abundant explanation and threw it in the wastebasket. He shook his head and asserted, "Yes . . . you can even kill him as long as he's on your land."

Matters did not escalate to the point of killing. I kept on picking up the boys who fell out of our trees, giving them some of the fruit that had fallen with them and leading them to the outside door, to run away quickly before Bella or Nasir could catch them. I was summoned to the police station multiple times, most of them in connection with Bella. I would attribute the accusation to myself, so that neither he nor any of my brothers would have a criminal record or a security file to obstruct the path of their study or their work in the future. For every misdemeanour, with the help of the officer Abu Faisal (for I had come to be on informal terms with him), I was able to arrive at a solution with the complainant. Bella was a hot mix of rebellion, naughtiness, and some havoc, rushing blindly to explore what no-one else would ever think of exploring. He was a pigeon breeder with the heart of a thief. He would entice pigeons belonging to other breeders like himself from the neighbours' roofs, calling to them, "*Ta-aan . . . ta-aan . . . ta-aan*". Or he might release his male pigeons so they would lure proud females from distant rooftops. One time, an Austrian pigeon dear to his heart became sulky and hopped onto our neighbours' roof, which was nearly attached to ours,

209

neighbours who had long complained of Bella's antics with his pigeons. Bella kept pleading with her, calling "*Ta-aan . . . ta-aan . . . ta-aan*", but she denied her own instinct. Bella wept over the pigeon turning away from him, and knocked on the neighbours' door, asking that they allow him to go up to their roof to bring back his pigeon. But the neighbours refused, slamming the door in his face, wishing that all his pigeons would flee from him.

"Jihad . . . Jihad . . . *Jihaaad!*"

The sound of my name woke me, the voice choked in tears. The time was a little after midnight; Bella was leaning over me. "I can't sleep," he told me. Behind him stood Maher. I got up carefully so as not to awaken you, and went out to the garden, with Bella and Maher following me. With their help I picked up the broad wooden ladder, and we went up onto the roof. The space between our wall and that of our neighbours was no more than a metre and a half. Using the ladder, which was more than two metres long, we made a bridge that connected the two roofs. I steadied the bridge with my hands, then Bella climbed up on the wall, while Maher acted as lookout in case our enemies (our neighbours) appeared. Gloom and silence enveloped everything, except for a distant barking. I had brought a small torch that created a thin corridor of light, to make it easier for Bella to find his way across the bridge. He crossed it on all fours. He was thirteen and his body was thin, with supple flesh and bones that could fold. The neighbours had tied his pigeon by the leg to a water pipe. Bella's withered soul awoke as he approached her. He embraced her lovingly, untied her leg, and kissed her head, and she threw herself on him as if she had been waiting for her knight to save her or for a lover who had been parted from her for a long time. On my side, Maher climbed up on the wall and covered half the span of the bridge while I held on to his feet, so he wouldn't slip or fall through the gaps in the ladder-bridge. He took the pigeon from Bella and passed her to me, and then crawled back towards me. Bella was in the middle of crossing the bridge back to us when a shout and a violent clamour were heard from the neighbours' house. Heads looked up at us from the window of one of the rooms, where a light had been lit, while Bella was still suspended in the middle of the bridge. Many tongues loosed a stream of abuse and threats. Then the door to the roof opened and a large young man headed for the wall on their side. I held the pigeon to my chest and shouted to Bella, urging him, "Hurry!" He hopped over the bridge like a graceful young goat and jumped onto our roof before the young man could pull back the ladder forcefully and throw it over the edge, sending it plunging violently to the ground.

Abu Faisal put four spoonfuls of sugar in his teacup, stirred it, and went on stirring. He rested his head on his hand, and then asked me to explain to him, on this lovely morning (as he said mockingly, lifting the cup in the air and contemplating the cloudy red liquid in the daylight), just how it was possible that I had set up a bridge from our house to the neighbours' house, had jumped over to their house, had taken a pigeon – which might not be ours, and which in that case I would actually have stolen – without all of that amounting to an attack on my part on the possessions of another? I had gone to the police station the next morning in the company of Bella, who the neighbours insisted was the one who had jumped onto their rooftop, with my assistance, and Maher had joined us. Abu Faisal knew Bella. He looked at Maher, whom he had not seen before, and asked him,

"Who are you, young man?"

Maher hid behind me, afraid that the policeman might recognise him as a former fruit thief, and answered him anxiously,

"Maher."

"Son of . . .?"

All three of us, Maher, Bella, and I, answered him together:

"Maher ibn Umm Maher."

But Bella could not be anything except . . . Bella. One day Abu Faisal called me, demanding that I return the billy goat that I, presumably – that is, Bella – had rented, without it seemed paying the rent, so it could cover the female goats of al-Jabal. I hung up the receiver and raced out to the garden like a madwoman. My mother had asked my permission for Bella to keep a billy goat – which he convinced her he had borrowed temporarily from a friend – in the rear area of the garden, where he would feed it and keep it company. When you went up to the goat in delight, O my queen, and you made friends with each other, and you rode on its back like a horse, I hadn't had any objection to keeping the innocent animal for some time. Now I emptied my fury on Bella's young body, and Jamal, Nasir, and my mother saved him from me only with difficulty.

But our new life, like our previous life, continued to abound with people, and our modest home continued to answer to our needs and to contend, in its own way, with what was forbidden or prohibited. More than that, it continued to be loved and wanted for itself. Whoever said that houses are not loved except for compelling reasons? Whatever those reasons were, even if people were not dropping in on us from the trees, then they were flocking to the door. Maher's mother, Umm Maher, began to come to us regularly. She sold us nightshirts, pyjamas, sheets, underwear, shanklish cheese, labneh, and other cheap Syrian products her husband traded in, bringing them from the border town of Al-Ramtha. From time to time she would give us a gift of several kilos of mouloukhiya greens, or tomatoes, or aubergines, from a farm belonging to one of their relatives, and she wouldn't leave our house until she had shared breakfast bread and morning coffee with my mother. Then we opened our door to Umm George, Umm Kamel, Umm Khidr, and many women telling tales, with sharp and bawdy tongues as the tale demanded, and with lives dangling between craving and deprivation, between small gains and larger losses.

My grandmother Radiyya began to complain of boredom after we bundled up our chaos and left her, so she would close her clean, carefully ordered house and visit us, settling in our house from morning till evening and sometimes staying overnight. During this time she rained down instructions for us, such as "get up", "take away", "put down", "bring", and "come here"; most of my sisters and brothers would scatter, leaving it to me and my mother to accommodate her. When she had dinner with us, she would count the heads and the hands that raced each other to the platters, her eyes moving to Maher and Walid before settling on me, with the comment, "Don't you have enough trouble already?" But Grandmother Radiyya could not annoy us very much. She missed us "really and truly", and came bearing bags of crisps and chocolate, careful to include enough for Maher and Walid and any others who might fall in from the trees or the windows, as she said. Then she began to open her large jars and bring out some of the treasures stored within, which she showered, in a calculated manner, on Rima and Rula, who had taken over her beauty care. Rima would set her hair, dyed wine red, and soften it for her with a curling iron, while Rula manicured her nails.

Grandmother Fatima and Aunt Najah visited us regularly, making the long trip from al-Wehdat Camp bearing pastries of fresh zaatar and of spinach. Aunt Najah no longer expected marriage, making do with many gold bracelets at her wrists, though their glow was extinguished and the metal had aged. No sooner did Aunt Najah stand at the door than you threw yourself at her and she gathered you to her chest with overflowing tenderness, raining wet kisses on your face. Then she took a doll from one of the bags she was carrying; she held it in her hand for a while, enjoying watching the excitement on your face, before you raised your little arms to her and took your doll. Aunt Najah had entered her forties but she looked much older; with time she began to look a lot like Grandmother Fatima, and people began to believe that they were sisters. They began to fight and bicker with each other like two spinster sisters, and my mother would intervene to separate them. We loved Grandmother Fatima and Aunt Najah and begged them to spend the night with us, for their talk, revealing the secrets of women we did not know in the camp, was amusing. But Grandmother Fatima was not much in agreement or in harmony with Grandmother Radiyya – her "co-wife", as we called her – nor did she hesitate to comment about Grandmother Radiyya's excessive attention to her appearance. Grandmother Fatima and Aunt Najah would wink and nod to each other when they saw Rima combing Grandmother Radiyya's hair, and Grandmother Fatima would exclaim, "May God make fast our reason and religion!"

My uncle Abu Taisir, though his visits to us were infrequent, was nonetheless careful to come to us outfitted in trousers and a jacket that had nothing to do with each other, and girded with his analyses of the political situation, which he insisted on sharing with me. His reading of events was usually witty and amusing, supported by descriptions and undisguised insults aimed at the politicians behind the events. You might find me agreeing with some of his interpretations, despite their irrationality and entanglement with conspiracy theories. Uncle Abu Taisir also made clear his disdain for those pretentious analysts who explain things to us in difficult, lumpy language – we don't need an expert or a genius, he said, to tell us that the situation is shit. After two of his sons went to work, Uncle Abu Taisir no longer looked for work in the vegetable market, or anywhere else. In fact, work itself no longer looked for him but rather avoided him, averting disaster, as his wife said of him, mockingly. Every time he asked me about my father, wondering when he was going to leave that country and come back, his wife would take it on herself to answer for me and explain: "Why would he leave that country as long as he's working? Do you want him to come back and sit at home, just getting in their way?" But Uncle Abu Taisir showed no desire or willingness to understand that his wife was referring to him. Then he would bring his face close to me and whisper, "Did your father athk about me?" I would get up and go to my room, returning with money folded small which I would slip into his hand without anyone noticing. He would say, happily, "By God, niethe, you're more of a man than any thouthand guys!"

As for my aunt Rahma, we opened wide our doors and our lives to her. She would usually come on Fridays. No sooner had she crossed the threshold with her daughters, who went ahead to the kitchen with a huge pot of stuffed marrows and aubergines or of tripe, than she would bend over towards you, lowering the opening of her shirt and inviting you to raid her chest (still firm despite the years): "Where's the *bariza*, Maleka?" You would clap your hands gaily then attack her generous breasts, searching those cushions until you found your ten-piastre coin. Your laughter would engulf us, though you didn't know what to do with the coin. Aunt Rahma would button up her dress while Bella and Maher and Walid gathered around her. She would shoo them away with her hand: "Away with you, you bastards!" But the great cheer that Aunt Rahma sprinkled in our house could not hide the bruises that appeared sometimes on her temples, sometimes around her eyes, sometimes on her arms. My mother would ask how long she was going to put up with the "shoe" (the semi-official term we used, as she did, for her husband Mundhir). Grandmother Radiyya would intervene, "Let her be, I'm done with her! I've told her a million times to kick that shoe off her foot!" But Aunt Najah had a different view: "A husband makes you whole, even if he brings coal." My mother would respond to that, "May God send fire to burn him up!" and Grandmother Radiyya would say "Amen!" to her angry curse.

You come into the room with a bicycle, racing ahead to your second birthday. Rasha catches you on a larger bicycle, a few days before her eighth birthday, and my mother scolds you both, sending you out to play in the garden. My sisters are whispering and laughing in their bedroom with Aunt Rahma's daughters, talking of things partially shameful. "Come on, girls!" calls Aunt Najah, summoning them to work with her in the kitchen. My mother asks Maher to pick some lemons for her from the lemon tree, telling him to find ones filled with juice. Walid's voice mixes with Bella's on the roof as they coo with the pigeons, "*Ta-aan . . . ta-aan . . . ta-aan*". Then the sound of a stone crashing is heard and my mother yells, "Get down off the roof, you animal!" Grandmother Fatima gets up from where she's been dozing on the sofa and asks, "Is lunch ready?"

Precious, hard-to-get money remained precious and very hard to get, but even so, we were not without some deserved luxury. At the end of some days I might return to the house with a dress for you that looked like a colourful doll's dress; with plastic bracelets set with cheap, shiny beads for Rasha; with sandals that would stand up to the rough roads of al-Jabal for my mother; with pyjamas for the girls and shirts they wanted, bearing cheerful phrases; with trainers for the boys (including Maher and Walid) bought for one or two dinars in the flea market, some showing a fake Nike trademark, stressing to them that they had to last on their fast-growing feet. I might buy three kilos of meat and four frozen chickens for half price from Walid's father, after the freezer in the shop broke down and threatened to spoil the goods. (Abu Walid would not listen to me as I talked to him about the great progress Walid had made in his English lessons, instead damning the freezer to hell.) Then I might pass by the pharmacy to buy red hair dye for Grandmother Radiyya and cream for burns to put on Walid's hands and arms.

Life insisted on knocking on the door urgently. One night Walid's hand rang the bell continuously, the sign of a catastrophe or what seemed like one. "Bella fell in the street!" Jamal was spending the night with Grandmother Fatima in the Wehdat Camp,

217

Nasir was visiting a friend, and my mother had gone to check on Grandmother Radiyya. I hurried outside. Bella was lying at the side of the street, opposite our house; his hand was on his waist and he was kicking the air and the dirt of the street with his feet, continually turning over on his back and his belly in great agitation. I asked him what was wrong and he shouted, "I'm going to die, I'm going to die!" He was crying, in the grip of pain. I managed to get him on his feet, but he could not walk. I went down on my knees and bent over and asked him to get on my back. He put his arms around my neck and I held on to his legs, holding them around my sides, and pushed myself up. He was heavier than I expected. I needed time to accustom my back, without straightening it, to the heavy load. We had to go at least a kilometre before we reached the Jabal al-Abyad roundabout, where there was a stop for service cars and taxis. I told Walid to go home, but he insisted on going with us to the hospital. I remembered that I wasn't carrying any money, so I asked Walid to fetch my purse from our house. Instead he brought out a small, old wallet from one of his jeans pockets, and from one of the swollen inner compartments he took a lot of notes, most of them one dinar, and gave them to me. There were about fifteen dinars, the money he had saved from selling sesame bread rings.

We walked, the three of us, on the downhill road washed with dim light, brushed by sounds of life and its people that came and went as we approached or left them behind. Bella's voice came anxiously in my ear:

"Jihad! I love you!"

"I love you too."

Walid looked at me, as if afraid of losing me:

"Me too, I love you!"

From under my load I reassured him, smiling:

"Of course . . . and I love you."

We went on our way, a woman whose back was bent, Naaesa of the folktale carrying her husband Job, a brother, a son, a beloved, a weight, a pain, and a life; and a boy who came to us from another story, who adhered to us and became part of our story . . . who became part of our life, and of our love.

It's love, Maleka . . . it's love. Learn that if we can live life less broken despite our burdens, then it's only because love is the evidence of life and its miraculous sign, even if it threatens us with the torture of boundless pain, even if in the end desire is not attained and aspiration finds no answer.

My father saw love, our love, and he approached it from afar, more than he had from nearby. At the end of the night the ringing of the telephone descended on the calm, and my father's voice washed over me, thirsty for our life far from him. He would ask about the days we were inscribing on crowded walls – unlike his lonely walls in Kuwait – where the paint had begun to yellow and peel, the signature of our stable presence. He would ask about the people of our house, sleeping, jostling, spreading their desires under their covers, unaware of their flesh and blood and consciousness, since they developed apart from their waking state. He would ask about our food and I would reassure him that it was plentiful, that we never went to bed hungry, that if Rula craved strawberries I would give her a handful of the expensive fruit, virtually absent from ordinary life, for her to eat far from the many watchful eyes forced to abstain from it. He would ask me about Rasha's nightmares, resting easy when he learned that she would rush to me, giving me her face and head damp with sweat, and that I would wipe them off and tuck her into her bed, staying with her until her dreams floated on the pillow. He would ask me about Bella and be reassured, since I separated his naughty pranks from people's anger at him. He would ask about you and I would stretch my neck, as if telepathy would show him my image at a distance of hundreds of kilometres of yearning and wishing, pointing to the marks of your fingers implanted in my flesh as you hung on to my neck and chest, in my waking and sleeping, your hands and whole body ceaselessly clinging to me, rooted in my spirit and unwilling to disengage from me. He would ask me about how tall we were and I would measure for him how much we had stretched out in his absence. He would ask me about our laughter and our clamour, our coming and going ... then he would fall silent. I would wait in the spaces of his laden voice and his weeping would surround me, enwrapping me, shaking my heart and pulling my spirit from my head to my feet. I would collapse on the nearest chair.

"Come, leave everything and come!" I said to him, my voice choked. But he would answer with some dismay, speaking of a possibility that was hard for him to imagine, the possibility that he would not be able to offer us anything. In time, my father would completely surrender to this possibility.

My father loved me, not as the being that inevitably took some of his genes and biological features, neither unique nor distinguished, along with his relaxed walk and his head that tilted to one side, for no reason, when he spoke. Rather he loved me, as I imagined, for the man in me, or the one he saw in me, the one he wanted to be. In my earliest adolescence he began to address me using masculine forms, first jokingly, then because of the explicit claims of the jihad in my name, then to restrain the female that was emerging timidly, unremarkably, from under my wide trousers, my checked shirts, and my unisex cotton T-shirts, which my mother kept for Jamal after me and for Nasir after him. "Come here, Jihad!" "Go, Jihad!" "Where are you, Jihad?" "Listen well, Jihad!" – all using masculine commands and pronouns. In accord with the rough, masculine form of the address, I had to come to him with my shoulders raised, my arms bent and my hands in my pants pockets, something which helped to flatten the mound of my chest, hidden at the onset. When I sat before my father I spread my legs, laced my fingers together, bent my back, and let my head hang, like boys who reach puberty before their time and make themselves rough, hurrying to claim manhood, and collaborating with their serious fathers on decisive, dangerous undertakings. My father did not so much reject the female I was as he rejected the male that he was. Since he had no other man around him that he could be, he wanted me as his man. Perhaps he wanted me to make up for his many shortcomings; in the process, I became much less. By the time that Jamal and Nasir were old enough to be the logical, or assumed, or even asserted extension of him, I had become – without any claim or completely logical explanation – the tried-and-true man.

For my part, I loved my father for all he was and all he wanted to be but failed to be. I loved the wandering father more than the model, the one who did not aspire to the ideal to start with, as he blundered in his money, his life, and his love. During the nights of the Iraqi occupation of Kuwait, we would sit, my father and I, on the balcony or in the living room, usually talking man to man. This conversational interaction between us was reinforced by the fact that there was no-one but me for him to talk to, and that he was forced both to rise and fall in his speech to that masculine level that does away with formality, and even barriers between us. To reduce the gender distance between us, after the parental distance had disappeared, he invited me to have a cigarette even though I don't smoke, suggesting that I puff but not inhale the smoke. My father talked to me about a woman he had fallen in love with ten years earlier, or a little less. I was surprised – not because my father loved someone else, since I did not assume he was in love with my mother to begin with. I was surprised because he loved passionately, and usually we don't imagine our fathers loving passionately, especially when they are married to our mothers. He did not know the name of the woman and had not spoken to her, and he did not understand, by his own admission, how he had fallen in love with her. But it was enough for him, at the time, that when he glimpsed her his heart leaped and he felt his whole body throb. Is this love? he asked me, seeking an explanation from me or from the many books I read. "I believe so," I answered. Does it make much difference if we know the name of the one we love, or hear their voice or speak with them? He asked one question after another, as if he doubted his feelings, that by then had gone their way. I smiled, and my father thought I wasn't taking seriously what might be his most beautiful love story, perhaps his only one. Then I affirmed his deep conviction when I explained that this was very possible, that it was one form of eloquence in love, and that sometimes talk is only dreary, boring rhetoric. Words do not necessarily indicate love.

"After all, Naeem, they say love at first glance, not first word!"

I spread out my theory before him, and he was convinced. His eyes lit up as he recalled his love story, through the cloud of cigarette smoke that lingered over our heads. It had happened one morning on his way to work. He was thinking about many unpleasant things, believing he had reached a point where he could say he hated life, without putting his finger on the source of the hatred, when for no particular reason he stopped at a junction. Then it was as if a spectre called out to him; he lifted his eyes, looking up through the windscreen, and saw her. She was standing on a small balcony on the third floor of an apartment building, holding a cup of coffee in one hand and a cigarette in the other. The balcony railing was not very high, so the top half of her body could be seen. He judged that she was tall, with some desirable plumpness, revealed by her bare arms. She looked to be in her late twenties or early thirties. Her complexion was very white, and her hair was very black and very long, reaching to the middle of her back or a little more. When she bent her body, resting her arms on the balcony railing, a waterfall of black hair fell over the milk-white flesh of her arms, making a dazzling picture with a rich colour composition, though it seemed austere, the shadows completed by the smoke from her cigarette. The features of her face were somewhat blurred, but her wide eyes drew him from afar. Her lips, embracing the cigarette end, were broad and full, as if they were infused with water. Naeem fell in love with the picture. From behind the windscreen of his car, he went on observing the woman with the black hair whose white complexion was unaffected by the sun, his heart fixed on her face and his eyes drinking in the scene, and he was captivated. When she finished her cigarette she flicked the butt in the air and withdrew from the balcony. At that Naeem went on his way with more energy, not for his work but for some of life's possibilities. Naeem began to go to work earlier than usual. He began to stop under the balcony of the woman with the white arms and black hair that enclosed her arms in night before night came, as her movements alternated between drinking coffee and smoking a cigarette. He chose the perfect place, one that would allow him to take in the entire picture from behind the windscreen. Then it was as if Snow White, as he came to call her secretly, in his heart and sometimes in his bed, sensed him. She began to wait for him to come every morning and stop his car under her balcony; she smoked slowly and drank her coffee even more slowly, distributing her abundant, silky night over her cloud-like arms. Then she leaned half her body over the balcony railing, allowing the waterfall of her hair to fall into the air, ignoring his eyes that devoured her form. Her eyes wandered in all directions except his until she finished the last puff of the cigarette, when she flicked the butt into the air and gave him, compassionately, that brief look that seemed to say, "Same time tomorrow." Then she went inside.

"And after that? What happened?"

Naeem was silent for a time, and then answered, "Nothing happened!" He went on meeting Snow White daily, their eyes enlacing through the windscreen glass on the last moment of the meeting, before she flicked her cigarette butt in the air, when she gave him a glance from above and he received it from below. Then they would part, tacitly agreed on their eyes meeting the following day – until a morning came when Snow White did not appear. He waited a long time for her, making himself late for work, and he waited for her a second morning, and a third; ten mornings in a row when she did not appear. Two weeks later,

Naeem passed near Snow White's apartment building and found the windows of the third-floor apartment stripped of their curtains. A month later, Naeem passed her building, his heart racing ahead to the balcony on the third floor, and found curtains covering the windows. A woman in her forties stood on the balcony; there was a prayer hijab hanging from her head over her shoulders and the upper half of her body, and she was shaking pieces of laundry in the air and then hanging them on the clothes line. Six months and fourteen days, that was the length of Naeem's relationship with Snow White. They were the most beautiful days of his life, he said. I asked him if he had thought of looking for her, or why he hadn't asked the doorman of the building, her building, about her new address. He crushed his cigarette in the ashtray.

"I was afraid."

"Of my mother?"

"Of myself."

He seemed surprised when I asked him, "Did you love my mother?" He took from me the cigarette that was burning in my hand more than between my lips and took a long drag, his eyes climbing the ladder of his life with Rauaa. He said,

"I think so."

My mother threw down the telephone receiver and hurried to the kitchen, drying her tears out of our sight. Her voice had been tense during the last few minutes of her phone call with my father. That was our second winter in Jordan without him, and the frightening thing was that our life with him missing did not seem to be missing anything essential. We were afraid that we would get used to the situation, though we did not admit our fears openly to each other. With the passing days my father had become a distant voice, at a distance greater than that between Jordan and Kuwait, sad, dispirited, and mournful, breaking at the mere sound of our voices and the noise of the people in our house. What we understood from my father was that his job, as an administrative employee of limited scope in the maintenance department of the car sales agency, was not very rewarding, but he had been promised, he assured us in each call, that his situation would improve. "Come to us!" my mother pleaded, but he did not answer her. He did not want to tell her that he would have nothing to offer us. I asked my mother,

"Do you love Naeem?"

She stopped chopping parsley on the cutting board and looked at me, disapprovingly.

"Are you crazy? What kind of question is that?"

She dried her hands on her apron, then collapsed at the kitchen table and started to cry. "You don't know your father." Her voice found its way with difficulty through ragged weeping. She dried her tears and was silent for a while, then a spark lit her eyes. Rauaa still remembered those magical days when Naeem began to get up cheerful, happy with his life in a way she had not seen before. In fact he started making coffee for her and for himself, humming off-key in a voice that was no longer very annoying. Rauaa was surprised that he brought her coffee in bed, in an act of love that was out of character for him even when she had come to him as a bride. She was not worried when he began to stand in front of the mirror for a long time, combing his thinning hair, sucking in his belly, and puffing up his chest; that was all part of a ritual of delight in himself that encompassed her and all of us. He brought home a lot of things for us, and no longer grumbled about our demands or had stomach cramps because of our spending. In fact, Rauaa woke up one morning with Indian mangoes on her mind; she had smelled their aroma even though she wasn't pregnant and experiencing cravings, something he considered to be heresy in any case. Naeem toured all the vegetable stores and co-ops in Kuwait until he found the aromatic fruit, which was out of season. "Naeem was even more handsome!" The smell of the deodorant he sprayed in the morning, which left droplets hanging in the bedroom air, pleased her and brought him back to her after he left, she said. She had not known that happiness can make a man more handsome. That happiness went on for months; they were the most beautiful days of her life, and what came before or after was no longer important. I asked her when that was. She closed her eyes and pressed her memory:

"Ten years ago . . . or more."

I don't think I ever understood the mechanisms of love, and how they turned into the mechanisms of staying in and continuing a relationship between a man and a woman. Four years after the Kuwait war Rania came to us with her children, now three, and many suitcases. We learned that she was furious and had fled her home. She and her husband Ala' had remained in Kuwait. After the war she had left her job at the bank officially and opened a beauty salon with a Kuwaiti woman and a Lebanese as her partners. Ala', who had retained his job, acted as financial manager for the salon. But his relationship with the salon went beyond money matters, as he had secretly married Zainab, Rania's Lebanese partner; the secret had come to light a year later when Zainab came into the salon visibly pregnant. Rania swore to bring down the house on Ala's head and to go to Jordan and deprive him of his children. A month after her arrival in Jordan – a month she spent sleeping, eating, watching the dubbed soap opera *Cassandra* on Syrian television, drinking a pot of coffee at a single sitting, and smoking two packs of cigarettes a day (a habit she had learned, as she confessed, from her Lebanese partner) – I suggested that she look for work in a bank, or if she liked, she could open a beauty salon. She did not like what I said, and accused me of being tired of her and of spending money on her and her children. The accusation was not entirely misplaced, especially as her children alone ate a one-kilo packet of luncheon meat in a day; but I assured her that she could stay with us her whole life without working. She went on for another month, sleeping, eating, watching television, drinking coffee, and smoking two packs of cigarettes a day. One evening I went out to the garden and saw her sitting near the bed of mint, drinking coffee and smoking. Anxiety had written words and whole lines of text on her face. I felt sorry for her and sat down next to her. I put my hand on her shoulder, and suddenly she burst into tears. I put her head on my chest and patted her back, asking her,

"You love him?"

It was as if I had struck her with a high-voltage electric wire. She sprang up, threw the cigarette on the ground, and snuffed it out with her sandal, almost screaming,

"Are you crazy? What love, what shit? The salon is my hard work . . . I made it with my money . . . do you know what my money means? It'll all be lost . . . everything will be lost!"

I didn't understand completely, but within a week Rania had packed up her many possessions and her children (who had loved going barefoot most of the day in our house) and had gone back to Kuwait. She did not get a divorce from Ala' and adjusted to sharing her man with Zainab. The two women were forced to come to an agreement after the growing family opened another salon, larger and more modern, under Rania's direction and Ala's financial management.

"Love? Are you crazy?" lashed out my mother when she heard my aunt Rahma talking about love. Her husband Mundhir might be a pair of shoes, certainly, but his being a *shoe* did not mean that Rahma could have a love affair. Besides, love could not strike women like her, devoted to their marriages, their children, their water pipes with terrible plumbing. Women's love is hellfire that burns them, consuming the chaff of their spirits, destroying them, and with them, their lives. Aunt Rahma, who was three years older than my mother, was then bordering on her forties and beautiful, still and always. She was tall, her stature thick as suited her height, with a round face, wide eyes, and a moulded ivory neck that looked like the necks of the figurines my mother loved. I was then fifteen, and we were visiting Aunt Rahma in Jabal al-Taj during a summer vacation, when Aunt Rahma threw herself at my mother's feet pleading with her for salvation. My mother rained down blows on her, slapping her repeatedly so that Aunt Rahma's taut face resounded and her nose bled. "You let him into your bedroom?" my mother kept asking, condemning her, and each time Aunt Rahma answered, "Yes," "Yes," "Yes," my mother slapped her with greater anger. Then they both fell on the floor and sobbed for a long time. I was spying on them from the crack of the door, imagining my aunt dallying with another man in bed, her yearning flesh under a hovering, heavy cloud of lust which gave no rain.

Then years later, Aunt Rahma would throw herself at my mother's feet pleading for mercy for her daughter Samah. Samah was the youngest of her four girls, the jewel she had produced from the bedevilled grind of her life, so she spared her the toil she shared with her three older daughters. They embroidered shawls and pillow covers and decorated picture frames, purses, and trays with light embroidery, selling them to artisans' shops in Amman, as well as helping their mother with her catering. Unlike her sisters, who had suffered and struggled with learning, Samah distinguished herself from an early age. Aunt Rahma would bring us her notebooks so we could see her beautiful handwriting, proud of her school certificates bearing near-perfect grades, and she decided to send her to university even if she had to sell everything she owned. Samah's sisters were late to marry. When they passed twenty-five without having begun to populate God's earth by marrying and having children they were alarmed, and they bit their fingernails as they watched and waited. Then when they drew near to thirty, and despair had begun to accumulate as fat around their waists, men who were not hoped for knocked on their doors, widowers and married men; and they considered that marrying them, despite their lack of employment, was personal jihad, a commendable act of self-sacrifice. Samah was in her third year at university when her father Mundhir woke her up one morning and asked her to go with him on an important errand, after which she could go to her lectures at the university. Mundhir stopped at a stand selling natural fruit juice and bought a juice cocktail for himself and one for her. Then he spoke about a happy surprise for her, though Samah could not imagine what it could be, or what was the secret of her father's unprecedented generosity, even when she stood on the steps of the magistrates' court. After a few minutes a man came; he was in his forties, with an unkempt beard, a face eaten by ugliness and sweat, and clothes that smelled of long wear. He examined Samah, who stared at him with a mixture of amazement and disgust at his appearance. Then he backed away a little, to see her full measure clearly, before turning to her father and saying, "Agreed." Samah does not know how she got away from her father and his companion, or whether she got back to the house running or flying. All she remembers is that she and her mother locked the door and did not give in to Mundhir's demented pounding as he threatened to drag Samah to the court by her hair, "Before your very eyes, Rahma!" When Aunt Rahma did not open the door for him, he screamed at her to pass him ten dinars under the door, or else he would break it down. She rushed to pass him the money, to buy them some time. She dressed hurriedly and told Samah to gather her books and some clothes in a suitcase, then they left their house in Jabal al-Taj for our house in al-Jabal al-Abyad.

Mundhir sought to marry off Samah to one of his card-playing companions to pay off some money he owed, after he had run through most of the electrical appliances in the house in paying off his losing bets and his accumulating gambling debts. "Let him sell me!" said Aunt Rahma to my mother, crying, and swearing that she would not go back to their house with Samah. Then without anyone asking it of him, Bella asked for Samah's hand. Bella had studied mechanical engineering and joined a big company in Amman that offered maintenance services for Korean cars. We had to buy Samah from her father, who asked for three thousand dinars in cash, aside from the dower payment we owed for her.

Bella took out a loan from the company for half the sum and I covered the second half for him. The day the marriage contract was to be signed in Aunt Rahma's house, Mundhir arrived late. When he came he was drunk, and he began shouting in front of everyone that Samah was worth more than three thousand dinars and that he did not agree to the marriage. I pulled him by his sleeve into the kitchen and put a hundred dinars into his hand, promising him another hundred after he signed the contract; he snatched the money and signed with no hesitation. Bella had not known Samah or even seen her except in passing, when she came to our house as a little girl to play with you and with Rasha. Nonetheless in some strange way, as can sometimes happen in life, Bella loved Samah greatly.

But just at the moment when we believe that life has begun to flow in its logical course, or when we depend on the principle of a smooth track as one of the minimum measures of smooth functioning, then things turn away towards their original, illogical path, and passing days cast away the certainty that we believed would remain. We had begun our third year in Jordan when I returned home to al-Jabal al-Abyad at the end of the day, shaking the chalk dust from my hands and my dishevelled body, to come across a scene that heralded a great disaster. My mother was sitting on the sofa in a position of suspended lamentation, her eyes worn out from weeping. Next to her sat Aunt Rahma, her face showing less the effects of a catastrophe than complete incomprehension; on the two chairs across from them sat Grandmother Fatima and Aunt Najah, watching the scene cautiously. "May it be good news . . . what's going on?" I asked. My mother, who was standing at the very last second before the time bomb exploded, burst out,

"Good? Congratulate us!" Her voice, thickened by the residue of weeping, combined bitter mockery with anger. I didn't understand what she meant.

"Your grandmother . . . your grandmother has got married!"

I looked at Grandmother Fatima in disbelief, but she threw her hands in the air if she were denying a crime, and said, "What? Do you think I'm simple? Or did someone tell you that I've dyed my hair red?"

Grandmother Radiyya used to go to the market once a week, then she started going three or four times a week. She was irritated when my mother cautioned her that at seventy years of age the errands might exhaust her, suggesting that she stay home and have Jamal or Nasir buy what she needed from the market. She was even more annoyed by my mother's falsification of her age, assuring her that she was "barely" sixty, sixty-one at most, and that her birth certificate had been forged, with five years added so the judge would accept her marriage. Grandmother's house lost its orderly, harmonious arrangement and began to fill up with many things – buckets and plastic water jugs; carpets that remained rolled and wrapped, left in the corners of rooms already carpeted; sandals and slippers she did not wear that were still in their bags; folding kitchen chairs that she leaned behind the kitchen door and did not open because the kitchen had no room for them; melamine plates and dozens of bowls and tea glasses and coffee cups, still in boxes on the kitchen table and on the floor; and a lot of fruit shrivelling in the refrigerator. Her bathroom was also filled with bottles of shampoo and packs of perfumed soap and red hair dye, not all of which she used. Grandmother Radiyya had met Hammad, a taxi driver in his thirties who wore gold-framed sunglasses; he began to pick her up at the door of her house and take her to the market, where she bought, in his company, her needs that she did not need at all. His car would fill with them and he would take her home, getting out to help her carry the things, lifting the heavy carpets and folding chairs on his broad shoulders. Then she would offer him a cold glass of juice. The juice turned into breakfast, then lunch, and sometimes dinner, followed by tea and coffee. Grandmother Radiyya was afraid of the backbiting of her wicked neighbours and explained her fears to Hammad, so he suggested they get married, and she married him.

"She got married? Just like that?"

I did not understand, and when I did understand, with difficulty, I could not imagine the living, animated image of my grandmother, coming to visit us with Hammad, the taxi driver. She would be riding next to him in the front seat, her delighted face and shining eyes appearing through the windscreen, while to her left a doll with unruly hair dangled from the mirror, shaking and dancing with the movement of the car. The rear window of the car would light up in blue, green, and red every time Hammad stepped on the brakes, while the rear speakers for the tape recorder would boom with cheerful songs like, "*He complained, he spoke, he cried, he accused me and made his claim, delighting those who blame, complaining twice to the court of love, do you know why? Because of my jealous eye!*"

Aunt Najah did not hide her bitterness and resentment, saying that she had ridden with every taxi driver in al-Wehdat Camp and not one had proposed to her. "Shut up!" Grandmother Fatima said, silencing her.

My mother stopped speaking to Grandmother Radiyya, as did

235

Aunt Rahma, under pressure from my mother. I went on visiting my grandmother whenever I could to check on how she was doing. She was very happy. She had me sit in the front room that no-one ever came near, and when I took you with me she was no longer irritated, as she had been, when you jumped on the armchairs with shoes on, or when you walked beside the furniture imprinting your sticky fingers on the highly polished veneers of the wooden side tables. But Hammad disappeared after three months of marriage. When I went to Grandmother Radiyya's house she was sitting on the kitchen floor, having overturned all the jars of rice, sugar, lentils, beans, chickpeas, and broad beans. There was no trace of the pouches of money in the containers. She was choking with sobs. Hammad had also stripped her of the money in the closet and dresser drawers in her bedroom, including the instalment I had paid her for our house. Grandmother Radiyya was not crying over the jars or the money, she was crying over the loss of Hammad. Five months later she received a divorce certificate from him. She was crushed.

Grandmother Radiyya returned to our life. My mother opened her arms to her, but Grandmother Radiyya did not find compensation for her loss in her embrace or in our house. Weeks later she fainted. We took her to the hospital and discovered that cancer had devoured deep tissues in her breast. They removed one breast and she submitted to sessions of chemotherapy, becoming thin and losing her red hair, and she was forced, unwillingly, to put on a short scarf to cover the scalp of her nearly bald head. We took turns keeping her company during the chemotherapy sessions; I would go with her one time, my mother another time, and Jamal another. I was with her during the last session, and the doctor told me frankly that my grandmother was no longer responding to the therapy, and that her body, racked by diarrhoea and vomiting, could no longer support the chemical doses. "In the end, it's your decision," the doctor said. In the taxi that took us home, I opened my arms so she could pillow her head on my shoulder. Exhaustion had weakened her limp, diminishing body. "Jihad!" she whispered. "That's enough treatments. I'm not going to die before my time." A tear escaped from my eye, which I was careful to wipe away before she saw it. She smiled and said that she wanted to be buried with a few hairs on her head at least. After a silence, her voice brightened:

"He loved me . . . he loved me a lot."

"Hammad?"

"Your grandfather Imran."

We tried to persuade Grandmother Radiyya to leave her house and come to live with us but she refused, so we arranged things so that we didn't leave her alone. We, you and I, would spend the night with her, then in the morning my mother would come to take care of her and of you, while I went to the school and then to the learning centre. Then Jamal or Nasir would spend time with her during the afternoon until sunset, and when I finished my classes at the centre, night brought us together again. From time to time Aunt Rahma would come to visit her and would spend the entire time weeping; I asked her to please stay in Jabal al-Taj to weep and wail, far from Grandmother. I did not feel any burden or fatigue from the arrangements. In fact, in the calm and death deferred in my grandmother's house I found an opportunity to make progress with some writing I had delayed. Grandmother Radiyya went to bed early, then you followed her, leaving the

237

night and its words to me, even though the words played tricks on me and eluded me. I took the dining table in the front room, open to the living room, as a place to write, and after that time it turned into a nocturnal ritual, filled with watchfulness and anticipation. I was going to the bathroom one night when I glimpsed Grandmother Radiyya in her bedroom, standing in front of the mirror and pulling a few locks of her hair, from the few places with hair on her head, to cover the bare areas. The next day I stopped in the market and bought a thick dark-red wig that reached the neck and had an evenly trimmed fringe. Grandmother Radiyya was delighted with her thick hair, and she began wearing one of her dresses, which she had barely worn before, each evening. She sat on the sofa in the living room watching television with you, tucking back any locks of her new hair that might fall on her face.

I had stopped writing, faltering over the last line of a story. I did not feel you pulling me by the sleeve of my pyjamas. You shouted at me, with all the rashness of your four years of age,

"Mama, Mama! Grandma's not talking to me!"

I asked you to lower your voice so you wouldn't wake Grandma, and went back to the line where I was stuck. But you pulled me again, then said, your voice almost a smothered scream,

"Grandma's not sleeping, Grandma's eyes are open!"

The pen fell from my hand. I rushed to the living room. Grandmother Radiyya was sitting on the sofa, her head relaxed and resting lightly on the back cushions. Her new dark-red hair was dislodged from its place, and a few individual locks fell loosely on her cheek and neck. I put the wig back into place, so the parting was in the middle, and used my fingers to comb the hair away from her face. Her eyes, the shifting colour of water, were open; I closed them with my hand, and she slept.

In the last line of her story, the woman in love entrusted her eyes to the kingdom of longing.

When we stumble in love then our hearts are bruised, and my heart, O my queen, is swollen with loss and bruised by disappointment, black and blue even now. In the midst of its collapse, my heart walked clutching its bleeding, wearing steadiness as a thin, transparent garment, assuming an upright stance, disguised with indifference, masked with well-being. For its pain was still fresh, and in its dark depth its wounds were cracked and open.

"I realised what a ridiculous lie my whole life has been." With these words borrowed from a stage character he stood before me, a towering reality, proud, vain, the summation of betrayal – betrayal of the self, of passing days, of winding paths, like a theme taken from Arthur Miller's *Death of a Salesman*. I knew him by name and by designation: Dr Iyas Suleiman, Professor of Drama and Modern American Theatre in the College of Arts of Kuwait University, Palestinian with British citizenship, having studied in England and lectured in universities there before coming to Kuwait. Then I knew him by love: Iyas, with the *s* moistened by my mouth floating as a whisper on his neck. Modern American Theatre was not the course I wanted, but I was forced to register in it because most of the required and elective courses open to me were full. That was during the first term of my third year at university. They described him to me with precision: mean, arrogant, puffed up with self-confidence, bad-tempered, and insolent. Then

I added to the list, without announcing it, that he was deep, very deep, captivating, able to penetrate fiercely into the soul – into my own soul.

It was his habit to come to a lecture five minutes late, his cigarette half-finished in his hand. When he came into the hall the students sat up in their places, and others hurried to enter – for when he reached the last moment of his smoke he would step outside the hall, stand at the door pulling the final remaining drag from the cigarette, and fling it away, coming into the hall and closing the door behind him with his foot. Even God couldn't come into the hall after him. His ritual came to be known and talk of it circulated among the students; I don't remember anyone who dared to try to open the door and come in after him. I sped up the stairs at a run to the second floor of the College of Arts, my bag hanging from my shoulder and banging against my sides, and my hair bound in a pygmy ponytail riding the wind, nearly arriving ahead of me. I was looking at my watch and trying to slow the seconds as they hurried by. I estimated that he was now in the hall, and that he was perhaps at the last puff or two of his cigarette before the final one. Then I estimated that he had reached the very end, and my anxiety doubled my speed. He was standing at the door, at the stage of the final puff of the cigarette before throwing it away, when I collided forcefully with him. I don't believe it was a collision so much as it was hurling myself, or (to my own amazement, when I thought about it later) something like taking refuge. Yes. It was as if I took refuge in him, as if I had run and run to reach him, throwing myself on him and resting my head on his chest. In a moment that lasted only a moment, but that was as old as an entire history (as great history should be),

I took him violently and stubbornly, before letting him go. When I tried to raise my head, which resisted rising from its peaceful place on his chest, my nose grazed the fabric of his shirt. In the space between two buttons, in the gap between the fabric and the overwhelming body, the scent of his flesh filled my lungs. For his part, he did not seem in a hurry for me to separate from him; then it was as if his long arms gathered me to him so I would be warmed, and enjoy the peace of my moment with him. Then he threw his cigarette far away over my head and pressed my arms gently, signalling that our moment was over. When I lifted my head and eyes to where he towered over me, his eyes pulled me into their sea. "Sorry!" I said in a whisper, and he did not answer.

From a paper he pulled out of his folder, he read out our names to check attendance. He marked the names of those present with a pen, relying on the voices that responded "Yes" from around the large hall, without lifting his eyes from the paper to connect the name with the face. When he reached my name, he lifted his head to the source of the "Yes". His eyes landed on me, and my classmates' laughter rose in the auditorium. They always anticipated the moment when the professors and lecturers would show their surprise at the "jihad" in my name, especially when they came to our names for the first time. Their laughter did not annoy me; I was still trying to shake off the traces of his body, breathed in by my own body during my long moment of refuge. He returned to the list of names and reread my name, joined to my father's name this time, as if he wanted to be sure: "Jihad Naeem?" I answered "Yes", again, without being happy about my name, even if I claimed to be confident in possessing it while separating myself from its bluntness. With his eyes on mine, he said that he had read a short story in the last issue of the cultural supplement of the newspaper *Al-Watan*, signed by Jihad Naeem. "Is that you?" he asked. My classmates swallowed their laughter and I answered "Yes" aloud, a "Yes" a little less miserable about the name and disavowing it less. He continued reading the names and marking them, without lifting his eyes from the paper.

Throughout the lecture his eyes did not come near me, but nonetheless they did not fall away from me. His sight kept track of me from the buttons of his shirt, from the flesh of his neck that extended during his speech, from the top of his chest, visible at his open collar, from his mouth forming expressions in elegant language, unlike that in textbooks, refusing any authority, from his voice coming from an immeasurable distance, from his hands that moved in the air in harmony with the rhythm of his explanation. When his look seeped into my troubled being, I quaked in my place. Even when he turned his back to me completely, his eyes still melted me.

Before the end of the lecture, he asked us to write a short paper on a theme from *Death of a Salesman*, or on one of the motifs that cast light on the dramatic development of the play, to be submitted to him in his office within a week. He gathered his papers and was about to leave when he was stopped by a student calling him from the middle of the hall, "*Doctoor!*" She was among the fearsomely beautiful girls in the college, their form and their look engineered, destined to study the English language and boast of it in the accent of private, foreign schools. They came to the college in their private cars, which it was difficult for us to picture with an old motor that coughed several times before starting, or that broke down in the street. They were antagonistic to the Arabic language

243

in a way that was forgiven to them alone, and they spoke about their fathers with unfeigned indulgence, calling them "Dad". We might bandy about this "Dad" among ourselves, we less fortunate classmates, modest in beauty and money, to joke about our fathers – who could not be called by anything but the coarse, rough "*Yaba*" – or to express resentment, buried within minds that were not altogether healthy. He raised his eyes towards her, and she leaned her head on her shoulder, playing with a pen in her mouth as she said that she felt lost reading the play, as she did not understand when the main character was in the present and when he had moved to the past. She extended the word "lost" as much as its limited letters would allow, rendering it in an American accent. I was eaten up with jealousy, for everything about her was beautiful: her face with its symmetrical features; her hair set and perfectly dyed blonde (neither assertively nor timidly); her melodious voice; her eyelids, half closed, coloured by eyeshadow in a way that made them clouds shading her lazy eyes; the pen lolling in her mouth. Her stupidity would certainly not make any difference, or be noticed to start with. She was an embodiment of beauty, and my feelings towards her had been neutral up until that moment. At that moment specifically, I felt that I was threatened in all that I had, however little it was, and in all that I did not have, which was a great deal. The demon I feared more than anything else was her name, evoking longing by its nature: Sally! I was afraid he would ask her about it, and then I would no longer exist. He raised his eyes towards her and answered, in an arrogant, dismissive tone, its accent borrowed from her fluid American accent,

"If you're lost, I suppose that's your problem, not mine! After all . . . do you really need to understand?"

The class erupted in laughter. Sally took the pen out of her mouth in a way that did not reflect her tender upbringing. She raised her head and threw back her hair, retreating to the firm footing of her beauty, which made her male classmates wait for her to choose her seat in the hall before racing to sit near her. At the door, Dr Iyas Suleiman turned to me, calling, "Jihad!" I looked at him, taken by my name in his mouth. He asked me to meet him in his office in an hour. I did nothing during that hour except wait for it to end. I headed for the periodicals section of the College of Arts library, as a space frequented by few students. I leafed through one of that day's papers, not reading anything all the way through. In all the headlines, my name was spoken: Jihad. For the first time I loved my name. I loved it on his tongue, as I replayed it in my head time after time: Jihad . . . Jihad . . . Jihad. I, the one who had always fought shy of situations that called for using my name or acknowledging it, who avoided occasions to say it publicly. My name, in his voice, went from my hearing to my body, producing in me a tremor I was afraid would give me away. I turned around to make sure that no-one else had heard my name.

He was absorbed in reading a book, his legs lifted to the edge of his desk, when I knocked on his half-open door and went in. He lowered his legs and sat up, scrutinising me. I stood before him like a schoolboy referred for punishment, my hands in my pants pockets. I avoided looking at him and did not know what I should say or if I should say anything at all. He did not leave me to my mixed feelings for long, but turned to my story, which he described as "harsh . . . very harsh", although, "I liked it," he added. "There's no such thing in critical reading as 'I liked it,'" I said, objecting. "Please!" he said, motioning for me to be seated.

The story was about a man everyone believed had died. Even the doctor who examined him confirmed his death, but the confirmed-dead man knew inside that he was very much alive, though he could not express the life that had broken down within him or offer any proof of it. He was lying on the bed in his bedroom so that his family could look at him for the last time. Then when his wife, who was assumed to have become a widow, closed the door on the two of them, she looked at the man who was presumed to be dead, and took leave of him with a long speech. It began, "If only you had known how much I hated you!" The wife, a woman in her fifties, goes on revealing her innermost soul, shattered by a man whose body bore the traces of all imaginable women but not the traces of her own body. Then she weeps, and we understand that she is weeping for her body that has withered, patient, restrained, chaste, and martyred, for no logical reason. For she had not loved him to begin with, had not desired him, had not expected to marry him; so why did she wait, then, and what did she wait for? She hated him so much that, while he was on the bed, her feelings penetrated to his barely functioning heart. It stopped altogether, and he died.

Dr Suleiman opened a drawer of his desk and took out the story published in the supplement, where he had marked some of the paragraphs. "Do you know what I'm thinking?" I knew that he was thinking about making it into a play, for he opened his deep eyes in admiration. But I did not wish to give him the mistaken impression that I could read thoughts, or worse yet, that I was smart, so with my eyes I indicated a draft of a one-act play on his desk that bore his name as author. He looked at the draft and shook his head, explaining that he was trying, as he said, claiming a humility that did not suit him. Then he looked at me closely.

"But frankly, I was surprised when I saw you."

I smiled. "You didn't expect 'Jihad Naeem' to be a girl."

It was as if he resented the idea that I might suppose even for a moment that his thinking was stereotypical. He said quickly,

"I didn't expect you to be young! The harshness in a story usually comes from the wisdom of age."

"Wisdom is the result of losses . . . how do you know? Maybe I've lost a lot already."

He tried to read what was behind the mask of a "young girl" that I wore. All I hoped for was that he would not see the boy inside me. When I left his office I was certain that his eyes were on me, so I took my hands out of my pockets and tried – I sincerely tried – not to walk hurriedly, with my legs spread wide.

At night I played the music of my name in my body, as he had composed it, and my body knew neither deep sleep nor real unconsciousness for many long nights after that one. *Jihad*, the *jeem* not imperious or ringing, thirsting a little; the *i* not broken; then the airy, flitting *heh*, followed by the long *a* seeking the furthest horizon without collapsing into silence at the *daal*, which did not signal a necessary descent. I loved my name when the letters redolent from his mouth touched my ear, intermeshed on my flesh.

That's how it happened. A week later I went to his office, a week which had included two lectures with him, during which he had not spoken my name, the name I longed to hear in his version, though his eyes besieged me while pretending to be swept far away. The door to his office was nearly closed. I knocked on it, then opened it a crack. He was standing behind the door, rummaging through papers from a file he had taken from a filing cabinet. In a voice I charged with the greatest possible confidence and satisfaction, I told him I had come to submit the essay he had asked for. "What essay?" he asked, with that distant, disengaged tone that betrayed a bit of arrogance, disdain, and some intrinsic malice. He did not raise his head from the file of papers. Immediately, something broke within me. I answered, striving to conceal from him the sound of my internal shattering. "The essay you told us to write, sir!" He paid no attention to the mocking lilt I intended to give my voice, overtaken by a gurgle, and asked me to put the paper on his desk. I half threw it on the desk and was about to leave quickly, when he stopped me to ask me, still turning his eyes away from me, about the theme I had discussed in the paper. "Abandonment," I answered, angry for no reason. He threw the file on the cabinet and pulled me by my arms, closing the door with his foot and blocking it, so we were standing, he and I, behind the door. He imprinted the letters of my name on my ears with the same music I had adored the first time, though the tune was slower . . . much slower, falling gradually into valleys of whispering. Then he planted a kiss on my lips and fell upon me in love. I believe my feet lifted from the floor to reach him, or perhaps the wings of his arms lifted me, encompassing me and picking me up so that his vast space could shelter my small one.

I walked with Iyas in time we stole from my empty days, as I continued to wait for him, and from his crowded, full days, where he continued to try to find a place for me, if only by forcing me in. We didn't think much about the dictates of logic, or at least not at first; we did not ask what was possible and what was not, what we could do, truly, and what we absolutely could not do, who might see us and who we must carefully guard against seeing us. In fact we avoided caution, often, when our tightly bound bodily desires became so great they could not be repelled by the appeals of prudence. His office, which had witnessed our first, sudden fusion the day the genie of a woman with ravenous desires emerged from the depths of a bottle that was masquerading as a boy, continued to receive us at the end of the day, when the feet traversing the professors' and lecturers' offices were fewer. But the office was too small and the day too short to contain the subdued cooing of our bodies behind the door, half open and half closed. I began to go to the College of Arts library after my lectures, to study and work on researching and writing papers, or I might leave home in the late afternoon, walking to the public library near our house, where I would stay, supposedly, until it closed. It was an excuse that was not entirely idle since I had been used to fleeing the house for the library when I was in school, seeking a little silence and fewer people. My absence did not raise any questions for my mother. When I got back from the college in the evening I would hurry to the kitchen, open the refrigerator, and take whatever I found before me, explaining to her, with my mouth full and my words indistinct, that I had gone with this classmate, or that one had brought me home in her car, and she did not ask for explanations. As for my father, he would never think that his plain-featured boy (myself) might be fooling around at night. When he saw me standing in front of the mirror in the evening, styling my hair in a new way and putting light lipstick on my lips, which I could not outline exactly – I who had shunned make-up for long years and later fumbled in applying it – he nearly died laughing, as if he were looking at a boy disguising himself as a girl.

As the eyelids of the sunset lowered, his car approached, at the time we had agreed on. I would sense him coming before he arrived, my soul fluttering towards him, my body fearing to reveal to all that it was inconceivably, unbearably yearning and yearned for. I would gather it up together with my bag of books and notebooks and leave the library. I would go a few steps towards where the blinking lights of his car called me, then I would get in beside him, and he would set off. When he went beyond the streets of the city, shining with lights and people, to streets on the outskirts, partially vacant, and then to the highway and on to roads resembling those of desert trips, we would undo what was closed and explore overlooked facets of the body and its unlimited gifts on the front seats of a car making its way, heedlessly, amid the whisperings of our flesh and the nakedness of our spirits, to the greatest extent possible in those moments. When at times the streets betrayed us and their eyes continued to follow us, we talked, we talked a lot, and as we talked we delved into our lives, which had met, as later they would part.

I asked him: "Do I look pretty to you?"

"No," he answered, laughing. Then I tried to appear serious and insistent on an answer, so he answered: "You look strange!" He was in his forties and handsome, more handsome than I was at the beginning of my twenties. I did not tell him that my father saw me as a boy, fearing that he would dislike the idea. After a while, he looked at me as if to say, "I've got it!" and cried, "You're a boy!" He was analysing his unexplained attraction to me as a man's natural inclination, at times, towards bisexual desires. But aside from his provoking malice he was tender. The most tender moments for me were those when I would put my head on his lap as he drove the car. Even when I fell asleep, he would continue travelling the roads gently, avoiding curves and sudden braking so that I would not wake.

Our bodies were secure in each other in the second term, and I did not enrol in any of his classes, despite the temptation of the lessons and of the eyes that remained far from me during the lecture but crept within me. Thus I was saved from the shrinking of a student before her professor in a relationship that gave signs of quickly becoming schizophrenic, as Dr Iyas Suleiman challenged my written arguments during the day, and Iyas – or "my Iyas", as I made him my own possession, temporarily – submitted to my writing upon him at night. In the fourth year I graduated with the distinction of a lover, and when I was employed, at the school and the tutoring centre in the evening, I acquired a small, used Mazda, so time and means were no longer a challenge. When I finished my classes at the Horizon Institute I went by car to the Corniche or to a public park, to a place we had agreed on, where I parked my car and got into his. We might choose to treat our desires rapidly, rushing, or we might choose caution, turning the obstacles of the road into something that doubled our arousal. Then we talked, and talked, and had no desire – or at least, I had no desire – to stop talking, as the sands of summer or the sudden rains of winter hit the car windows, or as brief spring breezes caressed our faces when we opened the windows to allow the steam of our bodies to dissipate. I began to long for his car, and the car became a spacious home that compensated me for my father's cramped house and its many inhabitants. One time, during

251

my last year at university, I had not slept for nearly two days, as I spent the first night finishing a paper and studying for an exam, and then Nasir and Bella spent the following night fighting a fever from a viral infection, so my mother and I took turns placing towels moistened with ice water on their heads. My body was drooping and debilitated, my eyes reddened and my face deathly pale. Iyas was appalled by my appearance. When I explained, he made me stretch out on the back seat, using my bag as a pillow and spreading over me the light wool cape I was wearing as a blanket. Then he began to drive, bearing me gently on a moving bed, cradled by soft sounds from the radio. When I awoke, Iyas had spent more than two hours travelling the streets.

After three years the car was still enough for Iyas, but it was not at all enough for me. Part of my body could still fill him, but part of his body could not fill me. I remained an incomplete woman satisfying him, while he was a complete man who did not satisfy me. I asked him, to the point of begging, that he make me a complete woman, but he considered that he should leave the consecration of the girl as a woman to another man, after him, more logically tailored to the measure of my life, one whose age would coincide better with mine. I told him that I wanted a house for me and for him, a large house with more bedrooms and more rooms and more space, some of it dedicated to silence, far from the clamour of my father's house and its people, who never stopped being there. He said that he hated his house, and that he fled from its silence to my talk and my noise. What he loved in his relationship with me was that it was free of the idea of a house, his house, and what I loved in my relationship with him was that I was free from my father's house for part of the night, when the house was cramped for those in it, some waking and some sleeping. But I still wanted a house for me with him. The last time we reaped love in the car, I asked him to marry me. He pulled the car over and stopped, opening the windows and lighting a cigarette. He drew several quick puffs from it, before throwing it away, unfinished. He looked at me and said,

"You know that the idea of marriage was never on the table."

I knew he was married and had two sons, in a life he never mentioned in front of me. I tried more than once to get him to speak of his wife, so that I could compare myself to her in a way that brought out my many flaws. Then I would convince myself, in spite of it all, that the result was in my favour as long as he was with me, and as long as his body – taller, larger, and more beautiful than mine – found my chest large enough to throw himself on me with overwhelming yearning. I imagined that it would be hard for him to immerse himself in any small woman other than me. But his mood changed rapidly, and his desire for me was clouded whenever I approached the subject of his wife or his sons; he would end our roaming in the car more quickly than I wanted, and with less love than we had sought. In the beginning, I was satisfied with being his other life, temporary, suspended; then I wanted him all, in his entirety – I wanted to be his life, period. He raised his voice:

"I hate my life, I hate my house! Are you happy now?"

"I want a house, a house for me."

"I won't be able to give you a house."

"There's someone else who could give me a house."

That was our last meeting. We ended it with a great deal of pain and crying, on my part, and with an exchange of accusations on

253

both sides. He looked at me with harsh eyes that reflected what became a cruel separation.

"Marry him!"

I had met him in Iyas's office in the first semester of my last year at university. I had gone into the office on the first day of term, anticipating Iyas's arrival after the summer vacation he had spent in Britain with his family. I was garbed in overwhelming delight and overflowing physical readiness, but my joy retreated and my body shrank, folding away my excitement, when I saw him. He looked at me curiously, then turned to Iyas, who rescued the situation, assuming the role of the distant professor. He introduced me to him: "Mr Ahmad Nahid, a new colleague with us in the department." The stranger extended his hand to me, correcting his title: "Dr Ahmad Nahid." He was Palestinian and had lived most of his life with his family in Egypt, studying in Cairo. He was in his thirties and pleased with himself, and with the many degrees he said he had earned at a young age. He was a specialist in linguistics, and he limited his schedule in the college to lectures related to modern techniques of English writing and advanced conversation. He had extensive information, but it was a type of passing, haphazard culture, without any deep essence. He was fastidiously dressed, his neck held in a shirt with a high collar and a tight tie that doubled the torture of Kuwait's September days, during which heat and humidity alternated with dust. Iyas's chest breathed from the open top of his shirt and it called to me, but I could not answer the invitation. Dr Ahmad Nahid continued to look back and forth from me to Iyas, without sensing our need, mine and Iyas's, for him to leave. Finally I left.

On the many occasions when I ran into Ahmad Nahid (or

Dr Ahmad Nahid, as he was always careful to remind anyone who ignored his title), he deliberately placed himself in my path, inviting me to drink coffee in his office and to talk with him. He thought that he aroused my interest by referring to a story of mine he had read in the newspaper, and in exchange he talked about an article of his, published in another newspaper; but I had not read it, so I felt awkward, as if I should have read it to return the favour, since he had read my story. I was not much attracted to his coffee or his conversation, but at times when Iyas was churlish with me, ignoring my flirting, I would go to Dr Ahmad Nahid's office and make sure that Iyas knew I was there. I would seem to be listening and interested, laughing noisily in a way that would give the impression of a woman enjoying a man's company. It was a strange game in which I became entangled unintentionally; or maybe it was the natural game of a female, even if this one was disguised as a boy in form and character, to arouse her man's fury. I succeeded in that, as Iyas would take me, after the game, like a lover who was mighty, jealous, and all-powerful.

When I graduated from university and began working at the school, I continued to go to Iyas in his office in the college after school two or three times a week. We might meet in the professors' cafeteria, having lunch and discussions together, since Iyas included me in turning my story into a play, giving me the task of writing the monologue of the woman to her husband lying before her, presumably dead. He would take on the dramatic construction and the scenographic adaptations. We would spread out our scribblings on the table, and exchange observations along with fries, wiping the blood of ketchup off the paper. Then I would return home and rest a little before heading for the Horizon Institute at sunset, to give a daily class or two, meeting Iyas, as agreed, at night. Many times I did not find Iyas in the office or the cafeteria, and he would have left an oral message with someone saying that he would not come, and Dr Ahmad Nahid would insist on having lunch with me. I found myself forced to listen to him without any real interest. With time, he seemed to me a young man who became troubled as he grew up, and then more so when he believed he had become something important. I gathered that he was a bachelor, with no family or relatives in Kuwait, and that he lived in one of the faculty apartments for the College of Arts, in the Shuwaikh neighbourhood. The apartment was very large for him and he felt lonely in it, he said, with its deadly quiet! When I learned that it had three bedrooms, I told him, ironically, that he could exchange his apartment for ours in al-Nuqra.

Dr Ahmad Nahid came to feel less lonely because of my presence with him, he confided to me once over lunch, whereas I became more despairing as I sat with him in the cafeteria, waiting for Iyas. When I met Iyas at night in his car, the mobile house of love, he talked about the family circumstances that prevented him from keeping his appointment with me in the afternoon, while I spoke of my situation and my despair, then asked him about his wife and his house, and the encounter ended with much ire and little love. One day Ahmad (who had asked me to dispense with formality between us and not call him "Doctor") enquired about my relationship with Iyas beyond the theatrical text that we were working on. He did not wait for my answer, which I did not have ready in any case, but said that he sensed that Iyas could very well be my father. "But his wife could not be your mother!" he said, laughing, trying to read my eyes, where all my feelings struggled together. She wasn't much older than I was, according to his description; she was lovely and elegant, and no-one who saw her could believe that she had had two sons. She had invited him to dinner one day and had captivated him with her charm and tact. I pretended to look at my watch and then got up quickly, wanting to leave, when Ahmad asked me to wait a little so he could speak to me about an important matter. "I love you," he said, without any preliminaries and without any attempt to find the ideal conditions to express love, to guarantee a better outcome. Then he followed that by asking me to marry him. I sank to my seat at the table, the surprise having robbed me of my senses. I tried to replay what I had just heard, trying to understand. I started to speak but he indicated to me that he did not want to know my answer now, nor tomorrow, nor the day after. I could take all the time I wanted to think.

How do we know that we love those we love? How do we distinguish between love in its true creation, and love that's contrived? Between love's creation and its contriving is a distance that's not vast . . . or not always. Between love that's made and love that's made up stretches a gloom in the heart that pulls us in deeply, and in its blackness we cannot tell love . . . from love. I could love a large, three-bedroom house, and more importantly I could love a man who was prepared to turn a blind eye to the fact that I spent most of the hours of my day outside of the house, working for the sake of a large family that had waited for its oldest son to graduate and go to work, to rescue it. I was confident that I was able to not love Iyas, and I was almost confident that I was able to try to love Ahmad. I did not take all my time to think. I married him.

I sat on the edge of the bed in the master bedroom, examining in the mirror a woman in a white wedding dress and veil, her face ghostly and wan, clothed by an overflowing river of tears. Ahmad leaned down before me, the man who had become my husband, and lifted my weeping face with his hand so it was in front of his eyes, then he asked me about Iyas. The water stopped flowing from my eyes. He had invited him to our wedding, but he had not come. "Maybe he's upset?" Ahmad wondered. I did not comment, only fixing my eyes on his, so that he would not read the answer he wanted in eyes that fled him. I gently took his hand from my face, and asked him to please leave me to sleep alone tonight. "I'm exhausted," I said. He took off his jacket and tie and threw them on the dressing-table chair, then said, "I'll give you tonight only . . . I'm not going to wait long." Tomorrow would be another story, for me and for him. But when tomorrow came, I came down with a severe infection; it was worst in my chest and throat, and paralysed my joints; I stayed in bed for days. My mother felt at the time that it was more than just a matter of a girl's fear of the first night, while my father dealt with it from his mocking viewpoint, sitting on the bed beside me, winking, and whispering in my ear, "This is what happens to a boy who denies his nature!" My brothers and sisters were happy with my large house. Bella discovered that he could run from the last room of the apartment to the corridor and then the outside door in a straight line with-out colliding with anyone. I begged them to stay with me and sleep in the empty rooms, but my mother refused to invade the privacy of our marital life at its beginning, especially as she did not find a welcome from Ahmad. During the night I got up from my sickbed, forcing myself despite my weakness, and covered the long distance from the bedroom to the kitchen to get a drink of water. The empty rooms lay in wait for me, silent, their doors open, and shadows of darkness followed me, spreading their arms on the ceiling and the walls, which bore no traces of age or of the scribblings of life being formed. I looked around and saw darkness staring side-eyed at me. I ran back to my bed, terrified.

On the sixth day, he came into my room. During the days of my illness he had been sleeping in the second bedroom, near the master bedroom. He did not seem to want to check on my health. He was loaded with rage. *Isn't it time yet?* He was neither enquiring nor asking permission, he simply wanted. I was reading; he took the book from my hand and tossed it away. I gathered myself and got up from the bed. "I'm tired. Please give me time," I said to him. He sat on the edge of the bed and took off his shoes, his jacket, his belt, and his tie, and then opened the buttons of his shirt, his hands trembling nervously. He said, his voice showing his impatience, "I don't have time." I was about to leave the room when he grabbed my arm, pushing and shoving me into a narrow space between the wall and the wardrobe. He put his hand on my head and loosened my short ponytail, spreading the hair on the sides of my cheeks. I trembled in fear as his smile besieged me: "Just between us, our marriage was a mistake, a huge mistake!" I did not understand what he meant completely, but in the midst of my fear of him I felt a strange sense of relief at this summation. With some calm and confidence, I said,

"Divorce me, then!"

He burst out in nervous laughter and banged my head into the wall, shouting,

"So you can go to him? If he had ever wanted you, he wouldn't have left you, would he?"

"What do you mean? Who're you talking about?"

"You don't know who I'm talking about? About your lover, Iyas! Did you think I didn't know what was going on between you?"

"Then why did you marry me, if you knew?"

He moved his hand over my cheek, rising and falling, then descended to my neck and put his hand around it, as if to strangle me. He pressed hard on my neck, then loosened his grip, and said,

"I wanted to break him! He thinks he's such a big deal. He's got everything, he thinks he can get anything."

I opened my eyes wide and looked at him challengingly, saying in a way that was almost a decisive order:

"Divorce me!"

He slapped me. My head rebounded between the wall and the side of the wardrobe. "Divorce you, just like that? I've paid money for you, my bride!" He threw me on the bed. I rolled away but he grabbed me by one leg, so I was suspended between the bed and the floor. He had taken off his clothes. He pulled me by the leg and my head hit the floor. He lay on top of me and I pushed his chest with my hands, sending a great power of refusal to my legs, which I held together over my belly. He tried to spread my legs with his hands and could not, so he hit my knees with the heel of one of his shoes. A wild scream poured from the depths of my being, exploding the minefield of my body. My failing legs fell as I was swept away in a violent whirlpool of dizziness and extended, unending pain. He pierced me. My spirit was in shreds.

The telephone rang. I was thrown on the floor, a human shard flowing with blood and brokenness. I gathered my scattered, swollen flesh and bones and reached the telephone, crawling, moaning in degradation. He had bathed, dressed, and gone out. At the door he had shouted, his voice elated, "Don't expect me for dinner!" I lifted the insistent receiver. It was my mother, asking me, in a voice that showed expectation and anxiety, "So! Is everything OK?"

"Everything's fine," I told her. "I'm a woman now."

THE LAST CHAPTER

*Concerning the Meaning, and
Some of the Metaphor*

Then morning came upon me, O queen, and many mornings after it . . .

From the kitchen window of my home on the eighth floor, Dubai spreads out its roads to many strangers, without reserve. Their destinies are more often parallel than intersecting, and within each is a homeland, most likely defeated, or at best, deferred.

After seven years, I bade farewell to Jordan. I did not come to Dubai chasing a dream or escaping from a nightmare. I did not come to the new country drawn to another potential land or seeking another borrowed homeland. I came to it fleeing from the many metaphors that clung to me and made me neglect the fundamental human thought concerning the value of existence, that made me neglect the clear, direct, unconcealed meaning of the principle of creation that states: *You are what you are, and nothing else.* I was weary of similes, metonymies, and allusions, and metaphor weighed on me, as it drew me to what was behind the apparent meaning, and I lost understanding of my clear, simple meaning.

The music of my mobile pulls me away from the window. The screen registers the arrival of a message from Walid, informing me of the number of his flight and time of his arrival. Walid works in Muscat as an engineer for a German company specialising in building bridges. A year ago his company took on the project of building a vital bridge in Dubai, and he began to come for a week every month or two, in order to monitor the course of the work.

The company would provide him with a place to stay for several days in an apartment hotel, but he likes to "park himself" at my place, as he says, most of the time. He invades your absence, unintentionally rooting your presence here even more deeply. He takes over your bedroom and some of your space, looking through the perplexing titles of books on your bookshelves and commenting (simply to get a rise out of me, nothing more), "The girl's mind's a wreck, like her mother's!" At the end of the night, the little boy who secretly saved what he made from selling sesame bread rings will be curled up under your quilt, not wanting to stretch his legs more than necessary. In the morning, I wake to the smell of bread burning in the toaster and I shout, "Maleka!", forgetting that you're far away. His voice rushes to me from the kitchen, mixed with the crunching of toast, calling, "The coffee's ready!" He brings the cups into the living room so we can drink our coffee together, his hands free of any trace of past burns. He has reached thirty without marrying. His father divorced his second wife and married for a third time, so Walid has found himself responsible for the offspring of three women from one man, who still struggles with freezers that fail and frozen food that goes bad in his shop. An unusual bird for the area catches Walid's eye, alighting on the sill of a closed window in the building opposite and looking for a way out of the besieging concrete. He asks me how I did what I did. "Believe me, I myself don't know how!" I smile and assure him that life finds its own solutions. Walid studied civil engineering at the Jordan University of Science and Technology. For years he had continued selling sesame bread rings in the morning, then he began to work at a melon stand in the summer, and then in a shop selling women's jilbab overdresses after school. Despite his high scores in the *taujihi* exam at the end of high school, his father announced that he could not pay to educate him; he suggested that he settle for a high-school diploma and look for a job. It was nearly a year after I came to Dubai that I learned about Walid from my mother, as part of her weekly telephone summary of news of the family and close connections. I paid the fees for his university study.

I check my email inbox. An invitation has arrived from a cultural association in Morocco, asking me to participate in a literary seminar, to include readings of stories. I reply quickly, thanking them for the invitation and asking for more time to respond, so I can check my circumstances and the possibility of accepting. The page proofs of my third short-story collection, which I received from the publisher days ago, are still on the table in the front room awaiting my review. Following a ritual I devised for reasons of psychology, not criticism, I avoid what I have written for some time. When I have enough distance from my words I approach them with a certain sternness and severity, deleting lines, cutting out paragraphs, and assassinating sentiments without great regret. Maher's name stands out in the inbox. His emails are usually either jokes, comical video clips from YouTube, or pictures of his kids, who stare with eyes full of mischief that will bring some major trouble to the world around them. Maher contented himself with a diploma in computer science from a community college; by his own admission, his rear was not of the sort that can sit at a desk for a long time. He got a job in an advertising company in Amman, and progressed in his work when he took several advanced courses in graphic design. Maher was the first boy in his family after four girls, and he was followed by many more boys and girls I never counted. His father insisted that he get married early. When Maher resisted the idea, his father was stricken by a heart attack, recovering from it only when he had wrung from Maher an agreement to marry his cousin. We laugh endlessly, Maher and I, whenever we meet during my short trips to Jordan, as Maher imitates his father, eyes glaring and lips stiff, in a false, temporary paralysis. Then he puts his hand on his chest and shouts, "My heart! My heart!", bending over in apparent pain, as he plays the role. When Maher married immediately, with no delay, his father's heart suddenly became normal, and he no longer complained – such is the power of God! – of anything at all. Maher had two boys and a girl, so his father was relieved to see the extension of his male line. I open the message. Under the words, "Does he remind you of anyone?" is a picture of Jihad, Maher's oldest boy, climbing a tree beside his grandfather's house. My eyes are on the threshold between laughter and crying as they fall on Maher's unfailing signature, at the end of the message: *Maher ibn Umm Maher*.

We have cut down most of the trees in the garden of our house. After we left, everyone to his or her own life, the house held only my mother and father. Then my aunt Najah joined them. After Grandmother Fatima died (of natural causes), Aunt Najah rented out the house in the camp, and chose to live with us, as she quarrelled less with my mother than she did with Uncle Abu Taisir's wife. My mother and father were no longer able to chase away the boys of the neighbourhood, whose catlike bodies whipped through the branches. Besides, most of the trees became thin and scrawny, their tops bent over because of poor care, as my mother told me when she called to let me know that she had asked Jamal and Nasir to cut the trees down. It saddened me, but I knew that from my distant land I could not save the thieves caught in the net of desires. In every call I ask my mother about my father, and she always tells me: "He's just the same."

My father came to Jordan about five years after the Kuwait war. When he came into the house with an absent look and a thin suitcase, we knew he had at last left Kuwait. He did not tell us what happened, how he left, or why he left. No-one really believed he had come empty-handed, as my mother assured everyone we knew; they were positive that he had returned from Kuwait bearing riches. My father withdrew from our mornings, our afternoons, and our evenings. He did not extend his hand to reach for anything, as we sat around our tablecloth on the floor, nor did he reach for our bread, our tea, our coffee, or our clamour. He withdrew into silence more often than he embraced speaking, and he committed himself to the night more than he explored the day. Reema had studied science and had become a biology teacher in a school for girls. She became engaged to the brother of one of the women who taught there, after that colleague had admired her and taken a great liking to her. I bought a gold bracelet and gave it to my father, so he could fasten it on her wrist as a gift at her wedding. But he refused and said firmly that I should present the bracelet. On the henna night on the eve of the wedding, the women and girls of the family, the neighbours, and near and distant female relatives occupied the rooms of the house, spreading out their stifled colours, usually hidden under their jilbab overdresses, and revealing what they could of their bare flesh. My father left the house and went up to the roof, so his eye would not collide with flesh not his to see. I followed him with a tray of coffee. I sat before him, my back bent, my legs spread, in the position of two important men engaged in serious talk. Then I asked him for a smoke; he gave me a cigarette and lit it absently. "Reema's really happy," I said. He did not speak. The night above us sprinkled some of the thin light of the street lamp over us, and our shadows embraced on the floor. The excitement of the girls below rose, along with the music of the Joubi *dabka* line dance. I stood up and extended my hand to him, and he got up heavily. I stamped my right foot lightly on the floor and he followed with his leg, though he missed the rhythm. I waited for the next phrase so he could catch my rhythm, and he matched me on the third or fourth. We danced with increasing speed, moving our shoulders, him leaning one of his shoulders on mine when he bent over in my direction, a little crookedly. We covered half the roof in a primitive *dabka*, then he stopped. He raised his eyes to a sky that had smothered its stars above us, then he looked at me as if he was thinking of many words he had prepared for this moment. He said, "Forgive me!" Then he went back to his place, covering himself with silence, folding away his feelings inside. I sat next to him as the loud music below was reaching its maximum volume. I lit a cigarette for him and one for me and we smoked, our heads and our spirits bent. My father was a lonely, defeated man, and I was – perhaps without his knowing it – a more defeated woman.

The day I spotted the advertisement in one of the local newspapers, I knew that the time had come for me to move from one absence to another, from one departure to another. An international school in Dubai needed female teachers who had an excellent command of English, for all subjects, and offered attractive salaries and benefits. Maryam was upset because I would leave her, a single queen in the school, provoking the teachers and making

"Ayush's" life miserable, all alone. She tried to persuade me to trudge through the rest of my years of service until retirement, then I could travel anywhere to work. Maryam knew perfectly well that it had nothing to do with work. Like her, I wanted to flee; I fled and she went on eyeing the idea. My relationship with Maryam had advanced to something like friendship. She would go with me sometimes to the market after school, and she would visit me with her children, whose number did not change from what it was when I first knew her. She had started to take oral contraceptives, keeping it a secret from her husband, amid her mother-in-law's worries about her delay in becoming pregnant, which lessened the chances of the number of males in her family equalling the females. Maryam might leave her children with her mother-in-law on the pretext of needing to go to Amman to consult a gynaecologist; then we would eat ice cream in the Shumaisani neighbourhood and go to the movies. On the way back at night I would help her make up a convincing story for her mother-in-law and her husband, to justify her late return from Amman. Maryam did not seem very concerned about looking for a lie. The road from Amman to al-Zarqa was crammed with heavy, rotting, human cares, along with at least two flaring dreams, which were ours; and the entire way Maryam was floating in the loftiness of love, infatuated with the meaning, stuffed with the metaphor, identifying with the beloved in the film *Braveheart*. But Braveheart's beloved died at the beginning of the film, I remind her. Maryam pulls her eyes away from the asphalt that she does not want to hurry by and looks at me absently, saying,

"It doesn't matter!"

Maryam believed that Ahmad, your father, loved me in some

way. As she saw it, a man does not choose a woman simply because she had loved another man before him. It would have been very possible for me to love him, she concluded; his problem was that he came at the wrong time. "Did you love my father?" you asked me once, in the middle of studying. You were approaching sixteen, fumbling and worried, bumping into many questions and concerns suspended where they had been walking on ropes of enquiry and doubt. "I tried to love him," I answered. But he didn't give me time, neither the right time nor the wrong time.

"And me? Did my father love me? Did he try to love me?"

You did not understand why your father had not tried to ask about you all these years, had not looked for something of himself, flung into a land he knew how to get to if he wanted. Did he die, you asked, as if hiding a wish that he had – because death relieves those who have abandoned us of prohibitions and much embarrassment, and makes us believe that they loved us, in a way that someone alive cannot love us. I also did not understand why he had not tried to find you, but I did not trouble myself or my heart to try to ask why. Every day he didn't look for you, I found . . . I found myself, and I found you more. What really matters is that I may not love myself much, but by God, I love you more than myself.

Some months after my marriage, Iyas left. He left Kuwait University and returned, with his family, to his university and his life in Britain. I caught news of him from a distance, the last piece from Ahmad, who informed me of his leaving in a gloating tone, tracing the effect of the news on my facial expression. Then Iyas's voice came to me. We were packing our things to leave our apartment in al-Nuqra for the one in al-Farwaniyah, when my mother answered the phone and called me: "Someone who says his name is Iyas Suleiman asking for you." That was the first time I met him, by voice, since our painful separation in the long-past encounter in the car. He was distant, more distant than the fact of his being in Britain, but the effect of his voice on me was closer than any other thing. He had heard of my divorce; I did not ask how. "Are you OK?" he asked me, between one silence and a longer one. "I'm fine!" I answered. Then I gave him the telephone number of our new apartment. "Isn't that your professor, who taught you at university?" asked my mother, curiously. I assumed a neutral voice and lied a little, explaining to her that he was surprised by the news of my divorce, since he had been a colleague of Ahmad's, and believed he could intervene to repair the situation. "That's good of him!" she said, not hiding her desire to bandage the wound of my divorce, which had become her wound, and for me to return to my husband. I did not try to explain to her that my marriage was one constant haemorrhage.

During my last days in Kuwait, he called. His voice was yet more distant, with less colour and lilt, less of the character that makes a voice live. He approved of my leaving Kuwait. He said that he had really begun work on turning my story into a play. He kept my original title, "An Objective Discussion". Then he asked about my address in Jordan and I gave him the telephone number at Grandmother Radiyya's house. More than two years later, Grandmother Radiyya tried to remember the name of the man who had called asking about me, certain that it was like "Somebody" Suleiman. She gave him the number of our house in al-Jabal al-Abyad, and he said he would call me later. I waited for him for more than a week, and when his voice reached me, I did not recognise it. It was very distant. "Are you OK?" I asked him, but he did not answer. Our play, as he called it, had been performed in London as part of a festival of Arab theatre, and would be presented on a tour in a number of cities in Britain, and three months later it would be part of Theatre Days, hosted by Amman and other Arab cities. I told him that I had read a positive critical review of it in an Arab newspaper, and he did not comment. Then he asked me for the number of my bank account, so he could transfer a sum of money as my "modest" compensation, as he said, in his own characteristic way – even though his voice had changed – as modesty did not suit him. When my mother learned that the "modest" compensation was nearly two thousand dinars, she could not believe that at last her dream would be realised. She had decided to enlarge the house by building a new, large room that would be a formal reception room for guests, instead of the original front room, which we had turned into a bedroom. It would extend from the family room, part of the area taken from the underused space in the back garden. I did not discuss these plans with my mother, as she sketched them broadly in the air with her hands. I withdrew to my bed, planting my tears on the pillow as petals already withered. I sensed that this might have been the last meeting between us, by voice, as he had ended it with "I love you."

I took Maryam with me to the play in the Royal Cultural Centre in Amman. She believed that Iyas was selfish since he had kept me for himself all these years. He had left me, but he had not freed me. In his time and geography, both far from me, he guessed I would free myself from him, so he called to leave the traces of his voice on my body, as the flesh of a true, tangible man leaves its touch and its odour clinging to the body of a woman for a period long enough to keep the males of his kind away from her. I had met Mueen at an evening of short-story readings in a cultural café in Amman. He was a researcher in an organisation concerned with documenting the intangible heritage, and a passionate story-teller. We met several times after that evening, and each time I laughed – and a man who makes a woman laugh is one who loves, and more than that, one who can be loved. Mueen could easily complete my fragmentary sentences, and I could easily find the word that betrayed him or escaped from his phrases. I was to have a different kind of meeting with Mueen over coffee that night, and perhaps that shared coffee would have sketched another path for me in life, and perhaps love. Then came Iyas's voice, spilling the coffee on my clothes and jolting my spirit; I left Mueen waiting, checking his watch. I did not go to that date nor to any other. Mueen waited days and weeks and ages without a signal from me. When Iyas's odour receded, on my flesh and my spirit, Mueen had left our table long before.

Maryam cried as she listened to the woman in front of her, under the dim lights of the room on the stage, telling her dead husband who was not dead, stretched out on the bed: "If only you had known how much I hated you!" She sighed with something like victory when she became certain that the dead husband who was not dead had learned of his wife's hatred and that it had pierced his heart and killed him, as it should. I met the director after the end of the performance; he welcomed me and expressed admiration for the work, which had drawn on all his energy, as he said, to direct it according to Iyas's vision. I asked him about Iyas and why he had not come. He looked at me strangely and said, with some hesitation,

"You know, of course . . .. Iyas isn't well."

I did not understand what he meant by "not well". "Is he sick?" I asked him. He tried to avoid answering the question, but my eyes implored him to speak. He drew close to me so the people around him would not hear and said that Iyas had been suffering from severe depression for some time, and that things had got to the point that he rarely left the house. In fact, he no longer spoke with anyone and was almost isolated from the world. The director thought I knew, since I had shared in writing the play with Iyas. But in the end he expressed optimism for the new play that Iyas was working on, hoping that he would finish it before his condition worsened. On the bus returning from Amman to al-Zarqa, Maryam and I sat wrapped in our own thoughts. Her blue eyes, turning away from mine, had not recovered from their redness, while I let my own eyes stick to the street, crushed under the feet of cars that rushed roughly over it. Minutes before we arrived, Maryam asked me to make up an excuse she could give her mother-in-law and her husband for returning late. She cried as she said goodbye. Less than a year later, the cultural pages of some newspapers dedicated space to the innovative playwright Iyas Suleiman, who had died at fifty years of age, in the prime of his contributions to the theatre.

My work at the international school was not always pleasant, but it was well paid. I bought a used Honda in good condition, and I rented an apartment with two bedrooms, one for you and one for me, and a large living room. As usual the living room was dedicated to all possible emotional and historic purposes, which I stretched by setting aside ample space for an office, with ceiling-height bookshelves, an antiqued wooden writing table, and a computer, along with a wooden screen of Chinese design that partially separated the office from the rest of the living room. You could hardly believe that you were going to sleep in a room by yourself, with no-one sharing it. But after a while you longed for the crowd we had left behind. Then you began to leave your bed for mine, on many days, throwing your arm over me, your legs, extending in length and in yearnings, flinging the covers off us both. I registered you in my school, and you asked me not to ask about you and not to try to play the role of a mother there; I heard and obeyed, Your Majesty. When I took over supervising the school's cultural club, the administration reduced my teaching burden. Then when I supervised a short-story competition among all the private schools, in which we took the top three prizes, I was promoted to chair of the English department, as well as managing the cultural club. From time to time I travel to participate in a symposium on fiction or a literary conference. The administration indulges me in this and facilitates it for me.

I did not live in great affluence, and the abundant life in al-Jabal al-Abyad, with all its demands, caught up to me with greater insistence. In the summer we had to make the pilgrimage to it, you and I, and you would soak up the crowd you had missed, as psychological provisions to satisfy, at least partially, your emotional hunger during the rest of the year. Meanwhile I would attempt to barricade myself in renewed solitude in the new land, so the human abundance would not overwhelm me again; but I did not completely succeed in that. I was compelled to assume the expenses for successive, exhausting weddings. I did not intervene in the marriages of any of my brothers or sisters, nor did I express a word or an opinion that might put a stop to their plans or encourage them. Even if their choices gave me pause metaphoric-ally, still with respect to meaning these choices were summoned as fate for my siblings, who perhaps deserved no others. I inter-vened in only one marriage, Rasha's, which I tried to thwart; but as was to be expected, I failed. The groom was the brother of Rula's husband, Abd al-Rahman. The first thing Abd al-Rahman did after his marriage to Rula was to make her leave her administrative job in a private hospital, on the grounds that it was not a single-sex workplace. Then he imposed a stricter hijab on her, and then he made her wear the niqab veiling the full face. That angered and annoyed us, especially my father, who started calling Rula "the crow" when she came to us. But it did not surprise us, as Abd al-Rahman had imposed on us an Islamist wedding, in which the live music was only from *daf* frame drums, while his sisters recited religious chants fitted to popular melodies, some of them trite, such as, "*Come on, come on, let's go to faith! We rejoice and say, how wonderful is God's work!*" Then he stopped shaking the hands that we stretched out to him, we, her sisters, since he now categorised us as too closely related for marriage but only tempo-rarily (as his wife might die). He also rejected the use of her fluid first name, insisting instead on her *kunya* of "Umm Talha", derived from the name of their oldest boy. Rasha had just graduated from a private university with a bachelor's degree in business. I suggested to her that she come and stay with me in Dubai and work there, experiencing a different life, which she might like, but she refused. I asked her to dismiss the idea of marriage from her mind for now, because she was beautiful, the most beautiful of us, and young, just turned twenty-two. A better fate would knock on the door of her blossoming youth. She presented to me a list of the girls in the family and among the neighbours who had married at younger ages, confident that men do not like older girls. Fine, then let it be from any family but that one, for the faces of all of Abd al-Rahman's family bore a mark of darkness. Rasha remained adamant. At that point I grasped her arms and shook her, saying,

"I can't believe it! Did we raise you and educate you so you would think like this?"

"Not everybody has to think like you."

"I don't want you to be like me, be like what you should be! Like what any free person should be."

"It's my decision and I'm free to make it."

"No! It's not only your decision. I refuse to agree to it!"

She wrested her arms out of my grasp and turned away, shouting, "You're not my parent!"

My mother's hand landed on Rasha's face, and at the sound of the slap Aunt Najah rushed to intervene. The rooms of the house were filled with shouting, sobbing, and weeping that was more like wailing. That night my father went up to the roof, where I had retreated, alone. He lit a cigarette for me and we smoked in silence. Then he looked at me and asked, "How're you doing, Jihad, how's my boy?" I laughed. I laughed a lot, my heart hurt from laughter. Then I cried, and my heart hurt less from the crying. We hugged for a long time.

Two days later, I gave my mother a sum of money and asked her to buy a gold bracelet so my father could give it to Rasha on her wedding day. I cut short my holiday and went back to Dubai.

We may not have any control over falling in love, Maleka, but we can control creating it. Two years ago, a few days after your first departure, I received an email that struck my heart with surprise. The sender apologised at the beginning for disturbing me, then he explained that he had got my email address from the publisher of my books. He said that he was coming to Dubai with his theatrical troupe within a month from that date, to present the last work of the late playwright Iyas Suleiman, as part of the Global Theatre Festival, and he would like me to attend the opening night. It was signed Tariq Iyas Suleiman, Iyas's son. Tariq was in his mid-thirties and bore a strong resemblance to his father, though he was not as mean. He smiled at my remark, saying, "You obviously knew him well!" Tariq directs a theatrical company he founded years ago, in order to present the works of his father together with those written by Arab playwrights in London and Europe. Iyas had composed his last work about a year before he passed away, but there had been no opportunity to perform it in the theatre because of the high costs of production, I understood from Tariq. I asked him the name of the play, and he opened a leather bag that reminded me of my university bag, and brought out a manuscript bound in a transparent cover, placing it before me. A large letter *jeem* in Iyas's handwriting, which I would recognise with my eyes closed, spread enigmatically over the manuscript cover. My fingers touched the edge of the letter and trembled. Tariq left me to my feelings for a while, then said,

"The play is dedicated to you."

"How did you know that I was Jeem?"

"I'm not very clever, but my father was very clear."

Tariq opened the cover and had me read the dedication at the top of the first page: *For Jihad Naeem, only.* At the small table in the coffee shop of the hotel where Tariq was staying, my emotions rushed over me, and some water spilled on my trousers. Tariq assured me that his father had not died sad, as many people believed. He promised that he would give me the manuscript, but after I had seen the play.

I traverse the paths of my house, my homeland woven from the aroma of repeated coffee and burnt toast crumbs, a homeland cut from land outside past lands and countries, even if it's a land suspended on the eighth floor. With the cuff of my pyjamas I wipe the glass covering your picture on the television table. I gather the papers scattered on the desk and put them in the drawer where they belong. I open the last drawer and the manuscript stares at me, trying my patience, until at last I pick it up. I pass my fingers over the longing smouldering in the rash, arrogant handwriting, mean, and deeply penetrating.

At the end of the play Jeem stands centre stage and decides to try everything in order to become beautiful. She sniffs a rose; she may hold her nose because of the smell of a cadaver. She grasps a hot coal at one time, and a jewel at another. She becomes a child in the womb again, and the audience applauds as the small, skilful actress shrinks into herself so that she is no taller than an arm's length. Then she assumes a shape somewhat like a camel walking brokenly, putting one leg in heaven and stretching the other into hell, as the floor of the stage burns with a fire that seems real and that threatens to consume her. Then a smaller floor rises upwards from the stage, a mountain on which Jeem stands, and to the accompaniment of rising music two wings appear from Jeem's back, growing and spreading over the sky of the stage. It's as if the heroine has been replaced by another, as the ordinary, very ordinary girl has been transformed into a beautiful woman, wearing a dress the colour of the sleeping night sea and with wings the colour of the air. When she flies from atop the mountain and lands on the earth, Jeem takes off her dress and folds her wings, becoming the original girl, yet happier . . . a more beautiful woman, with a more complete life. I did not rise with the audience in the theatre, who gave a long standing ovation at the end of the play. My wings were wet with tears, and had become heavy.

I return the manuscript to its safe place in the desk drawer, in my personal homeland, and I turn out the lights. I go to your bedroom and take *The Unbearable Lightness of Being*, your favourite novel, from one of your bookshelves. I turn the pages; your pen has underlined many sentences. I close the novel and put it back, for you don't like me to peek into your thoughts. I sit on the edge of your bed, burying my nose in your pillow, looking for your smell. You did not want to grow up more with me beside you. I suggested that you attend the American University in Dubai, or the American University in Sharjah, but you insisted on studying in Britain. "Why Britain?" I asked you. "Why not Britain?" you answered. "And me? Are you going to leave me alone?" I asked. "I'm going to leave you in my heart," you answered me, your eyes racing ahead to a personal homeland waiting for you, to a life you will water with your sorrow as well as your joy, to a love that may be spun with some desertion and deception on the way. It's alright.

In my room I lie on my bed, spreading my wings above me as a cover, ample and warm. I relax, surrendering to sleep.

TRANSLATOR'S ACKNOWLEDGEMENTS

I would like to thank all who contributed their time and effort to this translation, from making it possible originally to improving it significantly in progress: Sawad Hussain for introducing the work to MacLehose and to me; Elise Williams, Rachel Wright, and Allie Mayers at MacLehose, for care, insight, and patience; and Huzama Habayeb, for creating the work in Arabic and for boundless generosity in commenting on its many dimensions during the translation process.

SPECIAL THANKS

We are grateful for the enthusiasm of Sawad Hussain, who brought
Huzama Habayeb's novel to our attention.

HUZAMA HABAYEB is a Palestinian author and journalist. She was born in Kuwait, where she lived and worked as a journalist until she was forced to leave by the Gulf War. She settled in Jordan, establishing her reputation first as a short story writer, publishing her four prizewinning collections between 1992 and 2001, before publishing her first novel in 2007. Her first novel to be translated into English, *Velvet*, won the 2017 Naguib Mahfouz Medal for Literature and the 2020 Saif Ghobash Banipal Prize for Arabic Literary Translation. *Before the Queen Falls Asleep* is her second novel to be translated into English.

KAY HEIKKINEN earned a Ph.D. in French language and literature from Harvard University, specializing in the medieval period and studying the Arabic language as well. When she returned to academe after a hiatus, she taught Arabic at the University of Chicago and in several summer programs. Her translations include *In the Time of Love* (Naguib Mahfouz); *Ben Barka Lane* (Mahmoud Saeed); *Clouds over Alexandria* (Ibrahim Abdel Meguid); *The Woman from Tantoura* (Radwa Ashour); and *Velvet* (Huzama Habayeb), winner of the Saif Ghobash Banipal Prize for Arabic Literary Translation in 2020.